These Mortal Remains

Also by Milton T. Burton

The Rogues' Game
The Sweet and the Dead
Nights of the Red Moon
The Devil's Odds

These Mortal Remains

Milton T. Burton

Minotaur Books

A Thomas Dunne Book

New York

A THOMAS DUNNE BOOK FOR MINOTAUR BOOKS.
An imprint of St. Martin's Publishing Group.

THESE MORTAL REMAINS. Copyright © 2013 by Milton T. Burton. All rights reserved. Printed in the United States of America. For information, address St. Martin's Press, 175 Fifth Avenue, New York, N.Y. 10010.

www.thomasdunnebooks.com
www.minotaurbooks.com

Library of Congress Cataloging-in-Publication Data

Burton, Milton T.
    These mortal remains : a mystery / Milton T. Burton.—First edition.
        p. cm.
    "A Thomas Dunne Book."
    ISBN 978-1-250-00638-7 (hardcover)
    ISBN 978-1-250-03029-0 (e-book)
    1. Sheriffs—Texas—Fiction.   2. White supremacy movements—
Fiction.   3. Hate crimes—Fiction.   I. Title.
PS3602.U77T54 2013
813'.6—dc23
                                                        2013009823

Minotaur books may be purchased for educational, business, or promotional use. For information on bulk purchases, please contact Macmillan Corporate and Premium Sales Department at 1-800-221-7945 extension 5442 or write specialmarkets@macmillan.com.

First Edition: July 2013

10 9 8 7 6 5 4 3 2 1

PREFACE

Milton T. Burton passed away in the early morning hours of December 1, 2011. He will be missed by his family, his many lifelong friends, and by his adoring fans. It has been my honor to be counted among Milton's many friends.

Prior to Milton's death, several completed manuscripts were already in the hands of his agent and his publisher. The book you now hold was one of them.

Milton was one of those rare writers with the ability to capture the essence of a character in a few words such that a definite and colorful picture is drawn in the mind of the reader. He was a wordsmith, natively, of a caliber that has largely disappeared from the earth. What I will perhaps recall most fondly about Milton was his abrupt and genuine laughter. He saw humor in all things, great and small. His laugh was large and full and matched his frame and his facile, wizardlike, and professorial mind. Milton was, in many ways, both larger than life and yet down to earth. He was a common man, and he surrounded himself with common men and women. He took exception to pretentiousness in any form, whether it was from a politician—whom he could, with a laser-scalpal wit, divorce from any reason—or from an article writer who spoke much and said little. He was first and foremost a friend upon first meeting with everyone.

Texas has lost an honored son, and the world has lost one of its precious treasures. It is my fervent hope that Milton's legacy will continue long into the future. Courteous thanks are due to Kat Brzozowski and Thomas Dunne of Thomas Dunne Books for permitting me the distinction to assist in the editing of one of Milton's final literary efforts. My humble thanks to the Burton family for furthering Milton T. Burton's literary legacy.

—GEORGE WIER
Austin, Texas

These Mortal Remains

CHAPTER ONE

No one ever understood their reasons for picking the Royal. It had a brisk trade, but there were other places nearby that would have been more lucrative. Whatever their logic, it was a very unwise move on their part. According to witnesses, they burst through the door a little after seven-thirty that morning, wild-eyed and with their pistols already in hand.

"On the floor, assholes!" Topper Smith yelled.

Customers and staff alike stared at him without comprehension.

"Goddamn, am I going to have to kill somebody for you morons to figure it out? This is a robbery, so get moving!"

That got people's attention. Everybody quickly hit the deck except an elderly man named Dual Driggers who sat in the second booth back from the cash register.

"I said get down!" Topper bellowed.

"Piss on you, punk," Dual said. "I got arthritis, and I ain't getting on no damn floor."

Both bandits gaped at Dual in amazement. What they saw was a skinny, shriveled-up old geezer with bright eyes and a face that made people think of biting into persimmons. This was the first time they'd encountered resistance, and they were baffled by it. Things were at an impasse. Dean Bean apparently thought he could get the situation unstuck by firing into the ceiling three times. The little German-made .32 caliber pistol was loud in the confined space of the diner, but it wasn't nearly as loud as the .45 Colt automatic that materialized in Dual's right hand a moment later.

"Where the hell did that thing come from?" Bean asked, ogling the heavy gun with his speed-crazed eyes. He was never to learn the answer to his question. The autopsy would reveal that Dual's bullet hit him squarely in the heart and ripped it to shreds, thereby proving that Mean Dean Bean wasn't really so mean after all.

"Holy shit!" Topper Smith said as he stared down at his now defunct buddy. He looked up at Dual, and when he spoke his voice was full of childish petulance. "What did you do that for, you old son of a bitch?"

Instead of answering, Dual gave him a smile the waitress later said reminded her of something out of *Tales from the Crypt* and squeezed the trigger a second time.

This bullet missed its mark by a few inches, which was forgivable since Dual was eighty-four years old with fading eyesight. Instead of hitting the center of Topper's chest, it went through his right lung and severed a fair-sized artery. A moment later a very confused Topper dropped to the floor, his eyes beginning to glaze with shock.

The diner was dead quiet for a few seconds except for a mild gurgling sound coming from the hole in the robber's chest. Dual rose ponderously to his feet and hobbled over to where the young hoodlum lay. Topper looked up at the old man and raised his .38 snub-nose and tried to pull the trigger. Dual made two attempts to kick the gun out of the punk's hand and missed both times, almost falling on the second try. "Aw, screw it," he said, and put a bullet right between Topper's eyebrows.

A 230-grain Norma hollow-point at point-blank range has approximately the same effect on a human cranium that a cherry bomb has on a watermelon, which made the end of Topper's short and remarkably unproductive life an extremely messy affair. Not that Dual gave a damn.

Patrons and employees both began to slowly get to their feet. The cook peeped over the counter, then stood. Everybody except Dual looked dazed. "Call the sheriff," he said.

"Huh?" the counterman asked.

"Call the sheriff, fool!" Dual yelled impatiently.

As the man reached for the phone and began dialing, a nice-looking young college girl walked up beside Dual, peered down at the remnants of Topper's head, and clapped her hand to her mouth.

"I've seen lots worse than this," Dual said. "You ought to been at Omaha Beach."

The girl stared at him for a moment in horror and then bolted through the front door. A few seconds later retching sounds came from outside the building. Dual shrugged, then announced to no one in particular, "I think I'll finish my breakfast before the cops get here."

Slipping his pistol into the waistband of his pants, he hobbled back over to his table. The waitress stood gaping at the old man, her eyes enormous. Dual gave her another gruesome smile and said, "Honey, if you don't mind, bring me a couple more of them sausages."

My name is Beauregard "Bo" Handel, and I've been sheriff of Caddo County in central East Texas for almost three decades. Early one Friday morning last November, two Houston meth heads known on the street as Topper Smith and Mean Dean Bean tried to rob the Royal Coffee Shop, a new joint just beyond the city limit on the south side of Sequoya, our county seat. Subsequent investigation revealed that the Royal was only the latest stop in a crime spree that began two days earlier when the pair decided to knock over two liquor stores and a neighborhood grocery in the same evening. I use the word "decided" loosely because meth freaks don't really decide anything. In their world, action proceeds from impulse without any intervention by the frontal lobes, which are usually too fried to be of use, anyway.

The three jobs that inaugurated their odyssey brought them a combined take of something over five thousand dollars, a sum that was probably more money than either had ever seen at any one time in their lives. For reasons known only to themselves, they decided to abandon Houston that same night. After stocking up on crystal, they stole a car and headed northward into East Texas. Before they landed in Caddo County, they robbed seven more business establishments and killed two people. Their victims were an elderly lady buying cat food at a mom-and-pop store near Woodville and a Korean immigrant who owned a video rental business in Lufkin. Witnesses said both were murdered for no apparent reason.

Soon after each robbery the pair ditched their getaway vehicle and stole another, no doubt seeing this strategy as the key to a successful criminal career. What they didn't know was that the car they were currently driving was on a quad-state felony alert hot sheet, and that a deputy constable in the middle of a drunk driving arrest had spotted it fifteen miles back down the road and radioed the highway patrol.

It was all over long before I received word in the form of a phone call, which was picked up by my chief deputy, Toby Parsons.

Here's how it played out in the aftermath of Dual Drigger's run-in with Topper Smith and Mean Dean Bean.

CHAPTER TWO

He did what?" I asked.

"He killed both of them," Toby Parsons said as he hung up the phone. "At least that's what the manager claims."

Toby was a thirty-five-year-old café au lait African American who'd been a U.S. Army Special Forces career noncom serving in Iraq until a chunk of car bomb shrapnel cut his military career short.

"Both of them, you say?"

"That's right, Bo. According to the manager, he just whipped out a great big pistol and blew 'em right out of their damn shoes. He's got a concealed carry permit, you know."

"Who killed who?" Deputy Linda Willis asked as she entered the room still limping a little from the bullet she'd taken in her right foot during a shootout back in September. Linda was thirty, a bit plump and very pretty, with a tart mouth and a cheeky attitude. I put up with her sass and her occasional attempts to kick me in the shins when I annoyed her because, aside from being fun to work with, she was one of the best deputies I'd ever had—smart, persistent, and willing to charge hell with a bucket of water.

"Dual Driggers," Toby said. "The word is that he killed two thugs who tried to rob that new coffee shop out on Highway Nine South a few minutes ago."

"I just love that old man," Linda gushed.

"I don't," Toby said. "He doesn't like black people."

"Or white people," I said. "Or Mexicans or Chinamen or anybody else. He's just negative about the human race in general."

"I wonder why he's that way?"

"D-day," I replied. "The Normandy landing."

"I had no idea," Toby said.

"I don't get it," Linda said.

"Dual was in the second wave ashore at Omaha Beach and fought all the way through to the end of the war. Later analysis showed that there hadn't been nearly enough naval bombardment of the Germans' coastal fortifications in the Omaha sector. The landing was bloody hell. The experience left him impatient with his fellow man." I rose from behind my desk. "Let's go, kiddies. We need to get out there."

"You mean you're putting me on field duty?" Linda asked.

"I've got no choice," I said. "That place has been busy every morning since it opened, and that means there are going to be too many witnesses for me and Toby to interview by ourselves."

"Yahoo!" she yelled. "Back in the saddle again."

A highway patrol cruiser already sat in the parking lot when we arrived at the Royal. Inside the café, we found a very perplexed young trooper.

"I pulled in when I noticed that black Nissan parked right outside the front of the building," he said. "It's on the hot sheet. Right after I radioed for backup, a young lady came out and barfed into the shrubbery. I asked her what was wrong and she told me an old man had just killed two armed robbers. The manager said he'd called you, so I decided I'd better secure the scene and wait for you to sort it all out."

"You did good," I said.

He pointed at Dual. "That's the old man sitting right there, and I guess he's still got the gun. That concerns me a little."

"Don't worry," I said. "He won't shoot you unless you aggravate him."

"You know him?"

"Sure. All my life. You let me handle this. If you want to help, roll out the crime scene tape and keep anybody else from coming in until I get some more people on the ground."

His backup arrived a few minutes later in the person of Bob Thornton, the Texas Ranger who covered Caddo, Nacogdoches, and Angelina counties. I called in two more of my deputies to help take statements, but Thornton and I interviewed Dual ourselves.

"I heard on the ten o'clock news last night about that poor feller that got shot down in Lufkin," Dual explained. "The TV said there were two of them, so when they first come in the door and I seen them guns I figured they were the ones that done it. Spree killers, like that Charlie Starkweather back in the fifties. I slipped my old pistol out of my pants and held it under the table. They told everybody to get on the floor. I got contrary with them, and that's when the shooting started."

"They fired first, right?" Thornton asked. "Not that it really makes any difference."

"Yeah, but he put his shots into the ceiling. They never did actually shoot at me."

"But the second one was trying to raise his gun after you put him on the floor?" I asked.

"He'd done raised it and was trying to pull the trigger, but he didn't have enough steam left. See, he didn't have it cocked, and some them little old revolvers are pretty hard to pull through on the double-action cycle. Especially when you've got a forty-five bullet in the lung."

"And that was the reason you shot him a second time?" I asked. "He was attempting to shoot you?"

"Damn right he was. I tried to kick it out of his hand, but it looks like my kicking days are over. I'm not going to have any trouble over this, am I?"

Thornton folded up his notebook and shook his head. "I don't see why you would. According to the statute, the use of deadly force is permissible to prevent murder, rape, kidnapping, or armed robbery, and in cases of self-defense, which this situation clearly was with him pointing that damn thirty-eight at you. So you've got *all* the bases covered."

"I thought I was on solid ground," Dual said. "The instructor went over all that stuff when I got my permit."

Thornton stood and slipped his pen back into his shirt pocket. "The state mental health department has free psychological counseling for violent crime victims," he said. "You sure qualify if you want it."

Dual's eyes were bright but his smile was sad. "I've sat and eat hot chow within smelling distance of hundreds of dead Krauts and been damn glad to get it. What could some peckerwood shrink say that would make me feel any better?"

"These people are trained for this very thing," I said. "You might consider it, Dual."

The old man shook his head firmly. "I slept well enough last night, and I expect to do the same again tonight. But I do thank you both for your kind thoughts."

Two weeks later District Judge Leander MacGregor convened a hearing in which he took testimony from the investigators, the available witnesses, and from Dual. Thornton and I testified that the physical evidence at the scene was in perfect alignment with the witnesses' accounts, and Thornton confirmed that the guns Smith and Bean were carrying matched the ballistics of the bullets taken from the old woman in Livingston and the video store owner in Lufkin. Far from trying to get an indictment, it was

District Attorney Tom Waller himself who moved that the judge rule that the pair had died as a result of justifiable homicide. MacGregor didn't even leave the bench to review his notes before granting Tom's motion. I thought that was the end of the incident, but I was wrong. As things turned out, it was just the beginning.

CHAPTER THREE

Time marched on, as the old newsreels used to say. Thanksgiving came and went, and November gave way to December. Christmas loomed on the horizon with the New Year not far behind. It was a gray, overcast morning toward the end of the first week of the month.

"Bo's got a birthday coming up in February," Linda Willis said as she dropped a thick stack of papers into the in-box on my desk.

"I know," said my niece, Sheila Warbeck. "He's getting positively ancient." Auburn haired, slim, and very pretty, Sheila was a thirty-three-year-old reporter for the *Daily Sentinel* in nearby Nacogdoches whose occasional feature articles had appeared in a number of major magazines including *Texas Monthly*. Sheila's dad had died when she was ten, and I'd helped my sister raise her—which meant that I was the subject of all the manipulations a man would expect from a mischievous daughter. I allowed her free run of my office and access to the daily crime reports, but that morning, "ray-por-tage," as Truman Capote always called it, seemed to be the furthest thing from her mind. As far as I could see, she had nothing on her agenda beyond teaming up with Linda to see how much the two of them could pester me.

"Give us some wisdom, boss," Linda said. "Tell us all the groovy insights about life you've learned in those years."

I eyed her skeptically over the tops of my reading glasses. "If you want wisdom, you need to talk to a preacher or a professor. I'm just a country lawman."

"Yeah, right," Linda said. "A country lawman with a Phi Beta Kappa key from Rice University. Lots of those running around East Texas."

"I studied music, not philosophy. Besides, I never even finished my degree."

"Why not?" Linda asked.

"My dad died in the middle of my senior year and I had to come home and take over the family's timber business to support my mother. She had MS."

"Okay," Linda said. "That gives you academic experience plus immersion in the real world. A combination that should have caused you to do a little reflecting on the nature of things in such a long, turbulent life."

"Who says my life's been turbulent? And I don't know that being sixty-three puts me in the antique bin."

"Don't change the subject, Bo," Sheila said. "We want wisdom. Pontificate for us. Give us something profound we can tell our grandkids when you're long gone."

"Would you two please vanish? I've got work to do."

"Wisdom. Wisdom. Wisdom," Linda chanted. "Let's hear wisdom."

"Okay, okay," I said with a defeated sigh. I leaned back in my big leather chair and composed myself in order to sound suitably magisterial. "This is the personal philosophy of Beauregard Handel: I believe in common prudence, common sense, and common decency, even though all three seem to be in short supply these days. I believe in close families, loyal friends, and small communities like ours. I believe in good country cooking, sexy women, fine-blooded quarter horses, and slow rains after long droughts. I believe an occasional dram of aged whiskey is a healing balm for the troubled soul. I believe—"

"That's all pretty prosaic," Sheila said. "Mundane, even. Where are your grand, sweeping visions?"

I peered bleakly at her over the tops of my reading glasses. "Caesar had those grand visions you're talking about. So did Napoleon and Hitler and Stalin. I believe I'll stick to the mundane and be proud of it."

Just then Maylene Chambers, my longtime secretary, buzzed me on the intercom and saved me from any more depredations by the Dynamic Duo. "You better take this one, Bo," she said. "Line two."

I picked up the phone and listened for about a minute. Then I said, "Thank you, Thelma. We'll look into it."

"What?" Linda said after I hung up.

"That was Thelma Crowder, Dual Driggers's next door neighbor. She said his kitchen light didn't come on this morning at the usual time. She kept waiting to see if maybe he'd slept late, which she claims he never does. Then she called him on the phone and got no answer, but his pickup is still in the carport."

"Did she try the door?" Linda asked.

"It's standing about three inches open, and she's afraid to go in. We need to check this out."

"I want to go."

"Me too," Sheila said.

I nodded. "Okay. Linda, you need to take a cruiser in case we get a call. Sheila can ride with me in my pickup. I don't want the two of you getting your heads together to plot any more misery for me."

Dual had been a contractor who built modern, ranch-style suburban houses. But he himself chose to live in the home where he'd been born and raised, a sprawling late Victorian hodgepodge constructed a few years after the turn of the twentieth century, sans the gingerbread of earlier decades but with the high ceilings and wide porches that had marked its predecessors. I drove past the front and parked a little ways down the street. Linda pulled the cruiser up behind my pickup, and the three of us climbed from our vehicles.

Hearing Thelma tell me that the door was open a few inches didn't have the emotional impact of actually seeing it. As I told the young highway patrolman the day of the Royal Coffee Shop shootings, I'd known Dual Driggers all my life, and he was definitely *not* the sort of man to carelessly leave his front door standing ajar on a cold, damp day in late fall. Or any other time, for that matter. As I stared at the soundless and seemingly lifeless house, I felt a knot grow in the pit of my stomach. "Sheila, you stay here with the truck," I said. "And Linda, you go around back. Sidearm out and very alert."

Linda scampered off down the drive beside the house, still limping a little from the wound in her foot. Sheila looked at me, her face grave. "Bo, do you think—" she began.

"There's something wrong. You stay put."

I slipped my Colt from its holster and eased up the walkway and across the porch, staying to the side of the doorway. The house was grimly silent. I pushed on the door with the toe of my boot, and it swung open on well-oiled hinges. I remembered from previous visits that just inside the doorway stood a lazy Susan hall tree. I could see now that it had been overturned, its contents scattered all over the entryway.

I took a deep breath and slipped quietly through the doorway and down the hall. The first door on the right was the living room. I carefully thumbed the safety off my .45 and peered around the door facing.

The old man lay sprawled facedown on the shattered remains of the coffee table, a heavy cord wrapped tightly around his neck. I crossed the room, knelt, and put the back of my fingers to his throat. The body was cold, which meant that the killer was long gone. Nevertheless, I carefully checked the whole house before I let Linda in the back door. "Go get Sheila," I told her. "Tell her to be sure not to touch anything. I know she's got her little digital camera in her purse, and I want her to get me a bunch of shots of everything. We'll get official crime scene photos later, but I want some to examine as soon as possible."

A few moments later the two of them were back. Sheila is a kindhearted young woman, but just out of college she'd put in three years on the *Dallas Morning News* police beat that hardened her to this sort of carnage. Her face was impassive as she started snapping away, the flash lighting up the room each time she pressed the shutter button. After she had gotten a couple of dozen shots from different angles, I knelt once again beside the body and pointed at the rope. "Sisal," I said.

"What?" Linda asked.

"It's a kind of rope made from a variety of the yucca plant. People around here call it bear grass. They grow a lot of it in South America and Africa. It's dirt cheap and known for its knot-holding ability."

"Yeah?"

I nodded. "Look here. That's a one-way slipknot. My guess is that the killer threw the loop over the old man's head, jerked it tight and then stood back to watch the fun."

"Which means?"

"Which means we're looking for one sadistic son of a bitch." I stood up. "Linda . . ."

"Yo, boss."

"Call the Rangers."

"Bob Thornton?"

"Right. Tell him we need a DPS forensics team. And call the city police. Chief Ogilvie if you can get him. This is inside the city limit, so they need to know."

I turned to Sheila. "Hon, please go next door and see if Thelma has Dual's son's phone number down there at Vidor where he works. If not, call information and get it for me. He's the high school principal."

"Sure, Bo."

There was no need to tell her to break it to Thelma gently. My sister had raised her right, and she would know without being told. She would also know not to be too descriptive about the way Dual had died.

Without meaning to, I glanced across the room and back out into the hallway where a full-length mirror hung on the wall. I saw a grim, weather-darkened face beneath my cream-colored western hat. I saw a white dress shirt, herringbone tweed sport coat, dark dress Wranglers, oxblood Lucchese cowboy boots. My badge, my engraved and ivory-handled .45 Colt automatic in its hand-tooled holster—it was all there. The same old same old. A similar image had once appeared in *Texas Monthly* magazine captioned "Legendary East Texas Sheriff Bo Handel." I suppose I looked imposing enough. But I didn't *feel* very imposing at that particular moment. Or at all legendary. Instead, I felt helpless.

I gazed down at the limp, lifeless body once again. I hadn't told Toby the whole story on the old man. Dual had been one of the most decorated Texans of World War II, not too many rungs behind Audie Murphy in his ability to stay alive while killing hostiles in wholesale lots. He won a chest full of medals, came home, tucked them away, and refused to talk about them. He started up a small construction company that specialized in residential work, and in lean times when the housing market was off he made good money running a bulldozer and a dragline. He could be vinegary and snappish when pushed too hard, and over the years he had grown increasingly impatient with his fellow man. Yet he was still a soft touch for local kids trying to raise money for their organizations by selling something—Girl Scouts, Boy Scouts, FHA, FFA, Camp Fire—it made no difference to

Dual. His house was always one of the first stops when the youngsters set out into the streets to peddle their wares. In years past he'd served two terms on the city council during which he presided over an audit that sent a city manager to prison for embezzlement, and most unlikely of all since he wasn't much of a reader, he'd spent twenty years on the town library board where he'd hammered the city fathers mercilessly for increased funding. He served his country, contributed to his community, raised two good children, and buried his wife. And he deserved a better end than being throttled to death like a cur dog caught in a clothesline.

I glanced back at the mirror. My face was still grim. I suspected that if I didn't get this mess unraveled pretty quickly it would get progressively harder to look at in my bathroom mirror as each morning dawned.

CHAPTER FOUR

The immediate aftermath of the old man's death took the rest of the morning and half the afternoon. I had plenty of help. Bob Thornton had a Department of Public Safety team on the ground in less than an hour. Thornton was a tall, slim, droll man in his midfifties who had been a Ranger for fifteen years. Then there was Sequoya Police Chief Leon Ogilvie, himself a former Ranger. Leon was a couple of years my senior, and about four inches taller, with broad shoulders and a round, bland, happy face that displayed deep laugh wrinkles around a pair of dark eyes that took in everything and gave back nothing. The three of us had an excellent working relationship since we were all too old and seasoned to indulge in turf wars or one-upmanship.

Dual's gun cabinet was undisturbed despite holding several fine rifles and shotguns, and his .45 Colt pistol was on the nightstand beside his bed. There were no signs the house had been searched for valuables, and nothing seemed to be missing, thus ruling out robbery as even a secondary motive. Other than the rope and possible traces of DNA, the killer had left nothing in the house. The techs fingerprinted everything in sight, but we all suspected that most of what they lifted would belong to Dual. The body was sent to the state lab in Houston for the mandatory autopsy, but I expected it to reveal nothing new. They also took scrapings from under the old man's fingernails on the outside chance that he might have managed to scratch his attacker. It was a thin reed on which to pin a hope, but we had nothing else.

After the body was hauled away, Thornton, Ogilvie, and I stood in the hallway staring at the violated front door. "What do you make of this?" Thornton asked.

I pointed at the door. "The safety chain is ripped loose, but the lock isn't broken. That tells me he probably didn't know his attacker, but that the guy looked respectable enough that he was willing to open the door a few inches to talk to him."

"Right," Ogilvie said. "And as soon as he opened the door a little ways, the perp or perps swarmed him, and this hall tree got knocked over in the scuffle."

Thornton nodded. "I imagine whoever it was got the noose over his head here in the hallway, then shoved him into the living room where it was a little more private."

"That's about the size of it," I said.

"You found the body so you take the lead, Bo," Ogilvie said.

I nodded. "I'm going to have Linda canvass the neighborhood to see if anybody saw or heard anything. Somebody needs to talk to Dual's cronies and see if he'd had any trouble with anybody lately. Maybe if one of your people could do that. I'm still a deputy short since Carla left the department."

Ogilvie nodded. "I'll get Bobo Stovall on it this afternoon. He's good with old folks."

"I'm thinking this has to be some kind of blowback from that Royal Coffee Shop business," Thornton said.

Ogilvie and I both nodded. "I'm hiring a young lady tomorrow to replace Carla who will probably be able to help us on that front," I said. "Or at least she applied for the job, and I'm assuming she'll take my offer. She sounded pretty eager when I called her to set up the interview."

"Really?" Thornton asked. "Who is she?"

"Name's Eva Mendoza. She's got in ten years with the Houston PD. Was a detective sergeant. Great record."

"I wonder what she's doing in Sequoya," Ogilvie said.

"I don't know, but I suspect it's family related. If you recall, Smith and Bean both came from Houston. Maybe she can use some of her contacts down there on our behalf."

The three of us looked back into the living room. Bob Thornton gave a defeated sigh. "You know," he said, "we've got nothing to go on. Absolutely nothing. Unless something shakes loose from the victim's associates, or unless a snitch comes forward, we may never clear this one."

Ogilvie and I both nodded. Thornton had only voiced what we had all been thinking.

CHAPTER FIVE

I slept poorly that night and awoke at three the next morning. Finally at five I gave up trying to get back to sleep and was waiting at the Caravan Restaurant when it opened an hour later. After a half dozen cups of coffee and a plateful of bacon and eggs, I felt energized enough to face another day. I made my way to my office in the basement of the courthouse. The previous year the county had built a new jail on the north side of town, one that was designed to meet federal jail standards until well into the twenty-first century. In theory, I was supposed to move my office out there, but since the sheriff's department had to provide security for the district court, and since the county didn't really need the space, the decision had been made to leave the century-old office intact for the use of my department so whatever deputy was covering the court would have a place to roost. At that point I announced that I would stay put. With phones, fax, and computers, there was no reason the sheriff had to be housed in the jail. My longtime abode was a cozy old three-room suite, paneled in knotty pine that had been cut and milled from nearby forests. The walls were resplendent with gun racks, framed photos of long-dead Caddo County lawmen, and Winchester, Remington, and Colt calendars from years gone by. It gratified me that things worked out the way they had. I am a creature of habit, and the old office was as much home to me as the two-story Queen Anne Victorian five blocks down Main Street where I had been born and raised and where I still lived, alone now these five years since my wife died of cancer.

I was just beginning to organize my day when, a little after seven, Linda Willis clocked in and stuck her head through the doorway.

"How about your canvass of Dual's neighborhood yesterday?" I asked. "Learn anything helpful?"

"Maybe. Do you know Tommy Treen, the young CPA who lives across the street from Dual?"

"Sure. Nice kid."

"Well, when Tommy got up about six and went in the kitchen to put on the coffeepot he noticed a gray minivan parked in front of Dual's house. While the coffee was perking, he made his morning pilgrimage to the bathroom. When he got back the van was gone."

"I don't guess he caught the make of the vehicle, did he?"

She shook her head. "He did say it looked reasonably new. No more than a couple of years old at most."

"Okay, let's try something off the wall. Contact each deputy and have them get the tag number of every gray minivan they see in and around town. Call the city PD and ask them to do the same thing. As the numbers come in, run them with the DPS and we'll see if any known criminals or other likely suspects shake loose. Keep a log on the whole project."

"Will do."

The afternoon before I had downloaded Sheila's photos to my computer. Now I spent half an hour examining them carefully and learned nothing. Finally I gave up and dug into my paperwork, the curse of my job. Thirty minutes later Maylene buzzed to tell me I had a visitor.

———

I had already decided that Ms. Eva Mendoza was just what I needed, and that is exactly what I told her as soon as I got her seated in front of my desk and my own aging carcass installed back in my high-backed executive chair.

"The job is yours if you can go to work today," I said. "Actually, it's yours even if you can't, but I really hope you can put in a few hours this afternoon."

Dark eyes widened in a sweet, oval face. Ms. Mendoza was about five-six and slim with graceful movements and a brisk handshake. Thirty-three years old and divorced, she'd put in a decade with the Houston PD where she'd risen to detective sergeant. She'd also held her own in two shooting scrapes and a half dozen physical encounters. In the latter she had no doubt been helped by the fact that she was black belt–rated in two martial arts disciplines, activities that had been her hobby since her junior high years.

She said nothing for a few seconds.

"Cat got your tongue?" I asked.

"You've thrown me a little off balance."

I laughed. "And here you were thinking things moved so fast in the big city and so slow up here in the deep woods."

"No, I was just under the impression that this was going to be a preliminary interview."

"You've heard of a twofer? Well, with you I'm getting a three-fer. You're the best qualified applicant, and your last captain speaks highly of you. That's number one. Number two is that I'm losing a female deputy and need to hire another one to forestall any static from the Feds—"

"What happened to her?"

"She bought a security company and went PI. Also she and I are romantically involved, so this arrangement works out better for all concerned."

Those dark eyes got even wider. I suppose she was surprised

such an old fossil could still have an interest in women. I didn't blame her. It had come as something of a shock to me as well.

"The third point in your favor is that you are Hispanic, and the federal fair employment nannies have noted a couple of times that I didn't have a Hispanic deputy. But rest assured that your very impressive record is what nailed the job for you. The rest is just a bonus. You already know what the salary and benefits are, so what do you say?"

Her eyes were still wide but her face was happy. "Sure. And I'll go to work today if you need me."

"I would appreciate it. I have just a couple of questions that are more a matter of curiosity than anything else. What in thunder is a woman with your experience doing looking for a job in Caddo County?"

She sighed. "My dad worked for Southern Pacific Railroad in San Antonio for forty years. He originally came from down on the border southwest of town. A hot, dusty land. When he was just a kid he came up here to East Texas and fell in love with the country. Greenness. Real trees. Soft landscapes. He decided way back then that he would move up here when he retired. So when the time came he bought himself fifteen acres between Sequoya and Nacogdoches where he could pretend to be a peon and grow his own frijoles. Then as he and Mama got older—"

"Their health got fragile," I said, interrupting her. "So it fell to the unmarried daughter to give up her career and come take care of them."

"How did you know?"

"Because I have a little insight into family dynamics. And because I had to quit college my senior year to come home to take care of my mother and my dad's business when he died."

"What were you majoring in?"

"Music."

"Really? I would never have pegged you as a musician."

I regarded her bleakly. "Thanks. I appreciate that. I also notice that you had paramedic training and that you were a medic with the Kemah Fire Department for a year before you went to the police academy. What happened there? Did you decide you'd rather shoot 'em than patch 'em up?"

She giggled, and her giggle was a tinkling silver bell. "I just got bored with it. Too much waiting around, too little action."

"Good enough. And if you're already laughing at the boss, then you can expect to do fine on this force. Just don't try to kick me in the shins."

"Huh?"

"Linda Willis, my other female deputy. She tries to kick my shins when I exasperate her. You'll have to come up with some other ploy to aggravate me because she's got a patent on that one."

"What will you do that will exasperate me?"

"Every so often a story will come up that's just too much for your young and tender ears. And since you are female, I assume you have an ample supply of curiosity, so . . ."

She stuck out her tongue at me.

"Excellent," I said with a laugh. "Now to some rules and regulations and maybe even a couple of departmental customs. Number one. You are free to call me by my first name, which is Bo. If you aren't comfortable with that kind of quick familiarity—"

"Okay . . . Bo."

I nodded. "Good girl. Secondly, we are peace officers, and I take the 'peace' part of that very seriously. Sure we solve crimes, but a good portion of our job is mediating between what I call 'competing viewpoints' so that people can live out their lives with a minimum of fuss and bother. Which means we generally try diplomacy first. And that brings me to point three. We occasionally have to arrest some of my strongest supporters. On top of that, most of the people we will be dealing with are voters . . ." I let my voice taper off to see what she would say.

"All the tact that the situation will accommodate."

"That's what I'm asking for," I said. "The badge-heavy old beat cop act won't work on this force."

"I'm not like that, anyway. But I promise you I can take care of business when I have to."

"So your record shows. Now for one hard and fast rule. When you are on duty you will always be armed, even when pulling desk duty. You would think that wouldn't have to be spelled out, but it does. Off duty, I advise you to be, but that's your call. But I do expect you to have your badge and ID with you when you're outside your home and in public. That too is an ironclad rule. You would be surprised at the number of times an off-duty cop merely flashing a badge forestalls real problems, and that's what we're always after. Stopping trouble before it starts."

"My sentiments exactly."

"Any questions?"

She shook her head.

"Good. Now you need to go up to the county clerk's office on the second floor and get yourself sworn in and have your picture taken and your ID made. When you come back, see Maylene. She's the lady in the outer office, and she'll get all your vital data for the county records and our group insurance. She'll also give you a copy of all the specific department policies and procedures beyond what I have just told you. They are mostly common sense stuff like don't appear drunk in public, don't do anything to disgrace the department—"

"Don't barf on the mayor."

I shook my head. "That's not in there. Feel free to barf on that silly old fart any time you take the notion."

She giggled again. "I think this is going to be a fun place to work."

"Most of us like it. I've been on the job for nearly three decades. Now get going, and get back down here so I can put you to work."

———————

She was gone thirty minutes during which time I drank a cup of coffee and nibbled my way through several of Maylene's cookies. When she returned with her Caddo County deputy's badge prominently displayed on the lapel of her blazer, I got her situated at one of the desks in the outer office, then handed her the whole file on the Royal Coffee Shop shootout and gave her a quick rundown on the participants and on Dual's murder.

"So what do you want me to do?" she asked.

"What I want is a complete background on Dean Bean and Topper Smith, preferably by phone. Friends, family, fellow dopers, the whole shebang."

"Do you make one of their associates for Dual's killer?"

"At this point, I have no other motive except possible revenge for Bean and Smith's deaths. We've got a smart young city cop talking to what few of Dual's buddies are still living to see if he'd had any trouble with anyone lately. I should hear from him some time today.

"Call your buddies on the Houston PD, call in all your markers, make a nuisance of yourself if you need to. I may want you to go down there and do a little rooting around in a few days, but let's see what you can turn up by phone first."

"I know a guy in narcotics who's worked the meth trade heavily in the last couple of years. I'll start with him."

"Good show. By the way, you're on duty, so are you armed?"

"Uh . . . Actually, yes. I have my nine-mill in my purse. I know that technically I shouldn't be carrying, but—"

I held up my hand to silence her. "Spare me the explanations. I'm fine with it. This is why I have the rule about being armed while on duty, even on office duty. You and Maylene will be alone here from time to time this afternoon, and she won't touch a gun. We both know that cops' offices attract all kinds of nuts, so you're it if anything happens. By the way, my chief deputy may come by. Name's Toby Parsons. Introduce yourself. If a pretty redheaded young lady shows up, she's Sheila Warbeck, my niece, and she has the run of the place. She's also a reporter, but she *will not* violate your confidence if you tell her something. One last thing: If you get hungry around lunchtime the Texan Café across the street delivers to the courthouse. If you're short of money, they'll let any of my deputies run a tab between pay-days. Any questions?"

"Nothing that comes to mind."

"Good. Now I've got some things to do away from the office."

"Sheriff, thanks for betting on me," she said, a note of real gratitude in her voice. "I needed the job."

I gave her what I hoped was a kind smile. "You're more than welcome, but you do look a little shell-shocked."

"Well, you move awfully fast."

"The Caddo County Sheriff's Department is a lean, mean machine. No bureaucratic bottlenecks here. I'm sure you'll make us all proud."

"I'll give it my best," she said and hauled a little black address book out of her purse and began flipping through it.

When I returned to the courthouse three hours later Eva looked up and called out to me as I was passing through the outer office. "I may have something for you."

"Let's hear it."

"I reached my narco friend, and he says that Smith and Bean's buddies and associates are not the sort to wreak revenge on anybody for anything. According to him, they don't give a damn about who lives or dies as long as they have enough crank to feed their own habits."

"That's about what I expected."

"But I did come up with one possibility. I talked to one of the older felony investigators, a guy who was my mentor when I made detective. He happened to remember handling Dean Bean's maternal uncle in a felony assault beef several years ago. It stuck in his mind because when he arrested Dean on a minor drug charge he ran into the uncle who came down to see about posting bond to get the boy out."

"Any particulars on him?"

"He's faxing me the case file, but here's what it says. The man's name is Lamar DeLoach, and he's a former Navy SEAL. Came out of the service and was managing a boat rental place down at Kemah. Had a girlfriend in Houston, one he must have been really sweet on. Or maybe it was just machismo. At any rate, he caught her in the sack with some other dude and beat the guy half to death with a golf club. Aggravated battery, for which he drew five years and served two. As soon as he finished his parole, he vanished. Or at least he vanished as far as the state of Texas is concerned. No current driver's license, no forwarding address, no nothing."

"Let's see if the Feds can find this bird for us," I said and quickly jotted a cell phone number on her notepad. "Call this young man and tell him that Bo says it's time to start paying."

"Who is he and what's he paying for?"

"Special Agent Don Hotchkiss of the FBI. This department worked a major case with him last September, and he owes me in more ways than one. In fact, it's time for him to start ponying up for stealing one of my deputies. But don't mention that. Just say what I told you to say."

"Stealing one of . . . I don't understand."

"You will in a few days. You have DeLoach's Social Security number and his last license number, don't you?"

"I will as soon as the fax gets here."

"Just give it all to Hotch. Surely this guy has a driver's license somewhere."

"Okay. You're the boss."

"Dear lady, you are going to go far with an attitude like that." I rose to my feet. "After you talk to Hotchkiss, feel free to go on home. Check in at seven in the morning. I want you to start out on the day shift so either Toby or I can give you the grand orientation tour."

"I've still got a few more calls I want to make."

"Suit yourself, but you've already impressed me and got yourself good marks for the day."

I finished some paperwork and then went by my pasture to feed the three saddle horses I keep. I had just got home and stretched out on the sofa with a glass of Canadian Club when my cell phone beeped and Eva Mendoza's name appeared on the caller ID. "Why are you still at work?" I asked.

"I'm not. I'm at the Caravan about to have dinner with Officer Stovall. He came by the office to tell you that none of Mr. Driggers's friends knew anything about him having trouble with anybody lately."

"How did that lead to dinner?"

"Well . . . ," she began hesitantly.

"Bobo Stovall is a fine guy. You could do a lot worse."

"Well, this is just a first date, you know. Besides, who are you to complain? After all, you told me today that you are involved with someone, so . . ."

"I am, but I expect my deputies to be monklike in their dedication to the citizens of Caddo County."

That silver giggle again. "There's usually a big gap between what we want and what we get, Bo. Didn't you ever notice?"

I was beginning to really like this girl. "How about DeLoach?" I asked.

"I called Agent Hotchkiss right after you left and got the particulars . . ."

"Yes?"

"Bad news, I suppose. Lamar DeLoach was killed in a shoot-out with West Virginia state police two years ago."

"That *is* bad news," I said. "What was the fracas over?"

"The murder of a West Virginia state trooper."

"I hate to hear it. He's the nearest thing to a suspect I had."

"Sorry about that."

I sighed. "It's not your fault. See you in the morning."

I switched off the phone, more than a little deflated. In almost thirty years on the job I had only one other uncleared murder on the books. Yet in all my other cases I'd had more to go on than I had now. I planned to roust every snitch in the county, but a sinking feeling in my heart told me it would be a fruitless task. I sipped my drink and tried to concentrate on the news, but my mind kept creeping back to the old man as he lay dead and cold on the floor of his own violated living room.

CHAPTER SIX

Two days later, Dual Driggers was buried in a graveside service in Sycamore Ridge Cemetery, a long, narrow strip of land that lay on a low bluff about a mile east of town. Shaded by ancient cedars and magnolias and framed by the two long rows of sycamores that gave it its name, the old graveyard dated back to the earliest days of frontier settlement. Like me, Dual was descended from pioneer stock, and generations of our ancestors lay buried there. A large crowd was on hand to see the old soldier laid to rest, something that pleased me no end. I watched the crowd carefully since there is a common belief among lawmen that a murderer will often attend his victim's funeral. Although there were a few people present whom I didn't know, no one looked suspicious. As I had done several times before, I asked Leonard Ott, the funeral director, to photocopy the visitors' register before he gave it to the family. My request was habit as much as anything else. I didn't really expect it to reveal anything.

I was almost back to my pickup when I heard someone hail me. I turned to see District Attorney Tom Waller making his way slowly toward me. Tom was about forty and a hometown boy who had given up a lucrative civil practice in Houston to come home and run for the office he now held. He was in the middle of his second term, and had proven to be the best DA that I'd ever worked with.

"Hello, Tom," I said. "What's on your mind?"

"I'm sick, Bo. I mean something really bad."

"I hate to hear it, but I'll admit that you don't look too good."

"Dr. Dotty Fletcher sent me to Nacogdoches, and they're sending me to MD Anderson. I'm going down tonight so I can be there early tomorrow for a bunch of tests."

I grimaced in spite of myself. MD Anderson was world famous as a cancer research hospital.

"I'm taking a leave of absence," he said.

"Who's going to fill in for you?"

"Liddy Snow."

I nodded. "She's good."

"Yes, she is, but she likes publicity too much. I've kept her on a short rein. If she tries to run your business you may have to put her in her place. Don't hesitate if you think you need to."

"Okay, I won't. Can I do anything to help you?"

He nodded. "Tell Sheila, if you will. Discreetly, of course. She teaches my daughter Sandy's Sunday school class, and Sandy thinks the world of her. If this gets any worse I'd like for Sheila to be mindful of the situation."

"I'll do it, Tom. Please let me know something as quickly as you can."

"I will," he said. We shook hands and he walked away with the hangdog air of a defeated man. I shivered for a second even though the day wasn't particularly cold. I'd seen that same demeanor in my wife five years earlier.

Two weeks passed during which I spent my days in the routine duties of my job. Eva made a trip to Houston where she and her detective mentor rousted any number of Smith and Bean's druggy associates. They learned nothing. She also visited the families of both thugs, such as they were. Their respective fathers had long ago abandoned them, and the boys' mothers were hard-used blue collar women who had neither the energy, the disposition, nor the brains to plan and carry out a successful murder.

Christmas came. Christmas Eve afternoon Sheila and her mother and her daughter, Mindy, came over to help decorate the tree. My girlfriend, Carla Wallace, was there as well. Carla was five-eight with short dark hair and dark eyes and a svelte, graceful body. Up until a few months earlier she had been one of my deputies, but she bought a local security company and hung out her shingle as a PI, so we'd been able to come out of the closet as a couple. She was also, at age forty-two, too young for me, as I had once pointed out to her, only to be told to hush. So I hushed. I figured saying it once was an ethical obligation, but to persist would have been shaking my fist in the face of the angel of good fortune.

After we trimmed the tree and had a light supper, we all went to Christmas services at Sequoya Presbyterian, which had been my family church for five generations. Afterward, Sheila and company went home to get Mindy in bed, leaving Carla and myself to snuggle up on the sofa with a bottle of fine old Napoleon brandy. First one thing led to another, as it often does in such circumstances, and Carla didn't leave for home until almost midnight. The next day she would drive some twenty-five miles southeast to the little town of Center to spend the holiday with her own family.

I'd only been up about a half hour the next morning when my son Keith, who was a surgeon in Dallas, arrived with his wife Kristen and my two hellion grandkids, five-year-old Angie and four-year-old Martin, both thoroughly evil but a lot of fun. Soon Sheila and Mindy showed up with my sister Loretta in tow, and we all gathered around the tree and opened presents. Everyone agreed that we had all spent too much on the three kids, just as we always did and no doubt would do again next year.

We ate at one in the afternoon—smoked turkey and baked ham and Southern cornbread dressing and a half dozen side dishes along with too many pies and a rum cake that had to have been baked by Satan himself. We all ate too much and passed the rest of the day in the splendid, overfed indolence of the fully sated. It was a good day. One of the last I was to have for some time to come.

CHAPTER SEVEN

The New Year's festivities brought the usual domestic squabbles and drunk driving arrests, but the holiday proved no more bellicose than previous ones had been. Eva Mendoza hit the ground running and was rapidly proving herself to be an able replacement for Carla. The search for the gray minivan turned up nothing. Three were spotted and checked out by my deputies, and all three were registered to respectable citizens, one of whom was a retired highway patrol captain.

The Driggers murder case was dead in the water and likely to stay there unless some time in the future a confession emerged as the serendipitous effect of some criminal clearing his slate. I checked with all my snitches and my deputies did the same. Every possible lead was followed, but nothing took us anywhere.

The new year began with a bang in the form of a blue norther that plunged nighttime temperatures into the lower teens and kept them there for the better part of a week. A few minutes before noon on the fifth day of January my longtime secretary, Maylene Chambers, buzzed to tell me that a retired Munich police superintendent named Heinrich Biermann was in the outer office and wanted to see me.

"Munich?" I asked, puzzled.

"That's what he says, Bo."

The man was my age or maybe a couple of years younger, about my height and broad chested with a round, bland face, a balding head, and intelligent eyes. He wore black pleated slacks, and a tightly knit sweater of fine tan wool under a black poplin Ike jacket. His movements were lithe and agile and his handshake firm as befitted a man who had probably been an athlete at one time and who still kept in reasonably good shape.

I motioned for him to take one of the two armchairs that faced my desk and said, "You must be descended from a family of brewers to have a name like 'beer man.'"

His eyes widened in surprise. "You speak German?" he asked, pronouncing the word "T-scherman." His English was heavily accented like he didn't use it very often, but it was better than my German ever had been. His grammar was near perfect, and only occasionally as we talked did a bit of Germanic word order creep into his speech. With a frank, open manner and a face that was void of guile, he was an easy man to like.

"I took three years in college," I said. "But I've lost most of it. Nowadays I speak just enough to have made a fool of myself both times I was there. But I do recognize regional accents, and I'm pretty much convinced that you're not only from Munich, but you're a native Bavarian as well."

His face broke into a broad smile. "*Ja.* Please do not mistake me for one of those *verdammte nördlich Deutsch.*"

I laughed. "Damned north Germans, huh? Sometimes I feel the same way about our Yankees. So what can I do for you, Herr Biermann?"

"First let me give you some identification and prove to you that I am who I say I am."

He reached into an inner pocket of his jacket and pulled out a black wallet, flipped it open, and pushed it across my desk. I gave it a quick inspection and saw that it identified my caller as, indeed, one Heinrich Biermann, retired, of the Polizeipräsidium München, which I knew was a branch of the Bavarian State Police. I snapped the wallet closed and regarded him for a few moments. "I didn't really doubt you," I said.

"I appreciate that."

"So how can I help you?"

"You have an unsolved murder on your books, I believe."

I grimaced. "Actually, I have two. The last one was just a few weeks ago."

"Do you have many murders in your district?"

"My county. We call our state administrative units 'counties,' and killings have averaged one a year for the nearly thirty years I've been sheriff. Most of them have been passion murders."

"By which you mean?"

"Rage killings. Spur of the moment things. Friday night tavern fights that get out of hand. Or some fellow who comes home and catches his wife in bed with another man and then shoots both of them. Or a woman who finds a husband in a similar position."

He nodded. "That is what I thought. Those account for most of the killings in my country as well. However, I was referring to an obvious premeditated murder that took place two years ago. A man named Aaron Webern. Do you remember him?"

"Of course I do," I said, the hackles on the back of my neck rising because I recalled something I should have thought of when Dual Driggers died. Like Dual, Webern had been strangled to death, but in his case the murder weapon had been a leather strap.

The leather wallet came back out from his jacket and he extracted a color photo and slid it across the desk. It was a small studio portrait of a man who appeared to be in his midthirties. Not a particularly memorable face, but not an unpleasant one, either—a man with brown hair that was showing a little gray at the temples, blue eyes and high, broad cheekbones. He was smiling a sad sort of smile and his eyes were sad too. When I last saw him there had been more silver in his hair and more lines on his face. But that was probably five or more years down the road from the day this photo had been taken. Maybe he was sad in the picture because he had a premonition of his fate. Or maybe he was simply what the medievalists called a man of melancholic temperament. I wasn't sure. One thing I was sure about, though: he was my murder victim. I nodded. "That's him," I said.

"I felt certain that he would prove to be. How much do you remember about this man?"

I sighed and shook my head. "We never had much information on him, and most of what we did know came from the Immigration and Naturalization Service. I'd never met him because this department never had any business with him. According to what they told us, he was an ethnic German and a legal immigrant from the Czech Republic, working on his citizenship and running a video rental business. He rented a small house just outside the city limit over on the north side of town, which is why we drew the case instead of the local police. He seems to have pretty much kept to himself. His whole social life amounted to drinking a little beer at one of the clubs on weekends and a half dozen dates with a local waitress. She said he was a decent guy and thought they might have been heading toward something nice until he got killed. When it happened she was out of town with a tight alibi, so she was never a suspect. The girl has since moved on to somewhere else."

"The body?"

I shrugged. "Autopsy at the Harris County Medical Examiner's office in Houston, and then embalmed and kept in cold storage at county expense for a week. An attorney from Tyler showed up with all the paperwork to claim the remains for the family. He purchased a medium-priced casket at Ott's Funeral Home, and hired a local cemetery service to transport the body to Dallas for him."

He shook his head. "The family did not claim the body. Nor was he a Czech citizen. He was a German national. East German, in fact, and my wife was his only living relative. His real name was Alaric von Greim."

"Then who got the body?"

"Someone from your government, no doubt. Your national government, I mean."

"Why do you say that?"

"Because Alaric was in your Federal Witness Protection Program."

CHAPTER EIGHT

I offered to buy Biermann lunch at the Caravan Restaurant.

"What is good here?" he asked as soon as we were seated in a booth at the rear near the door to the kitchen.

"Everything, but I think I'll have a chicken fried steak dinner."

"Which is?"

"A breaded beef schnitzel in a peppery cream sauce with a big pile of French fries. And a salad on the side."

"I will have the same."

I had expected he would. You can rarely go wrong offering a German meat and potatoes. After the waitress had left with our orders, he leaned forward with an ironic smile on his face. "I married above my station."

I laughed. "So did I. Most of us do if we happen to get a good woman."

He returned my laugh. "*Ja,* but in this case I meant socially rather than in terms of character. She is my second wife, and *sie ist eine Gräfin.* A countess. Of course such titles convey no privilege in modern Germany, but to most of us they are a way of honoring and respecting our past. And she is also twenty years my junior, which may make me look foolish, but . . ."

"Then I will have to look foolish right along with you. My lady friend is also two decades younger than I am."

The wallet came once more out of the jacket and he extracted another photo. The woman appeared to be about forty or so. She was slim and fine boned with short ash-blond hair and high, aristocratic cheekbones. The family resemblance to Webern/von Greim was obvious except that she looked far more intelligent. "A beautiful lady," I said.

"*Danke.* We met at a charity function, one of those things that a highly placed police official is sometimes compelled to attend. While she is active in charities, she prefers the actual work to the socializing, and she was as bored as I was. The two of us passed a pleasant hour on the terrace of the home where the affair was being held. In the course of our conversation I told her that I was a widower with two grown sons. In turn I learned that she was a young widow whose husband had preferred men to women and who had only married her because of his father's insistence that he produce an heir. Of course, she knew none of this before they were married, so the union was not a happy one. Fortunately, this scoundrel had the decency to remove himself from her life by fatally crashing his Ferrari in an amateur auto race. As I say, our conversation was a pleasant interlude, but that is as far as things went that evening.

"Then some weeks later she contacted me and wanted me to speak to her cousin. She said that he had some very valuable information for me, but that it would be unsafe for him to visit my office. She asked me to come to dinner that evening at her estate about forty kilometers south of Munich in the Alpine foothills. She was a respectable person, one who was well known locally, so I saw no reason to refuse. It was there that I met this pathetic young fool, this Alaric von Greim.

"The essence of the matter was that he had become involved with a syndicate of international drug traffickers, a crew of East German and American thugs who smuggled Turkish and Afghan opiates into Europe and the United States. He knew of two murders in your country, and offered to implicate a fairly well-known

American gangster in the business. He also offered to testify against him in return for amnesty and a chance at American citizenship."

"And he was telling the truth?" I asked.

He nodded. "*Ja.* At first I was skeptical. Narcotics was not my specialty, but I knew enough that by questioning him I was able to satisfy myself that he was on the up-and-up, as you say. He knew some things that had appeared only in classified police intelligence reports, and he was also obviously frightened half out of his mind. The truth was that he had gotten in over his head and was willing to do almost anything to get out.

"Your FBI maintains offices all over the world. One is in Berlin with a substation in Frankfurt, where I knew one of the agents rather well from having worked with him in the past. The next day I took Alaric to Frankfurt. His knowledge was very convincing, and with the permission of our government your Federal Bureau of Investigation took him into protective custody. Ultimately, a major drug-smuggling ring was broken, and an American hoodlum went to prison for life. In return, your government brought him here and placed him in the Witness Protection Program. Then some days after our trip to Frankfurt, Elke—that is my wife's name—invited me once again to dinner to show her appreciation. And—"

"And one thing led to another."

He smiled. "That is a good way of putting it. What it all led to was five years of marriage and our daughter, who is now three."

"A little girl," I said. "That's wonderful.

"*Ja,* I am a happy man. Sometimes I cannot believe my good fortune. But back to Alaric. He was in protective custody for almost three years while considerable legal wrangling took place. At last the hoodlum was tried and convicted. All during this time Elke received letters from him. Then after he went into the program, she received one letter each month sent through a mailing service in Philadelphia. She could not write him back, of course, but it comforted her to know that he was doing well. Then the letters stopped. After a few months I made inquires with my friend in the FBI. At the time he could tell me nothing. But six weeks ago I got a clipping from your local newspaper about the murder. As might be expected, the letter had no return address. This was shortly after my friend in the Bureau had retired, so it was not hard to deduce that he had sent it."

"Strange that a man from such an illustrious family would have gotten into organized crime," I said.

"Elke and Alaric were the only children of two brothers who were separated by the war, one in the eastern zone, one in the western. And truthfully, Alaric's father had been a communist sympathizer. One of these privileged young men who get caught up in romantic ideas of taking to the street under the red banner on behalf of the proletariat. What you Americans call a 'limousine leftist.' The boy's mother was a one-time prostitute he married to show his solidarity with the underprivileged classes. She still occasionally had to ply her trade to feed the family, which meant that his home life was very unstable. Then, add to that forty-five years of Marxist morality, which is no morality at all. Forty-five years of Stasi brutality. Forty-five years of paranoia generated by a third of the people being secret police informants on the other two-thirds. Two whole generations raised in a savage totalitarian society that tried to extinguish every vestige of humanity and community life and our native German culture. And all this coming on the end of the Nazi period. Is it any wonder he made such foolish decisions?"

I shook my head. "I suppose not."

"But you have made my trip worthwhile, Sheriff, and I thank you for it. I came over here hoping to set my wife's mind at rest. She and Alaric were never close, but since he was her only living blood relative other than our daughter, you can see why she felt a great need to find out what had happened to him."

"Sure," I said. "I wish I could hold out some hope of catching the killer, but we had absolutely nothing to go on. And we did a whole forensic workup of the crime scene. The Texas Rangers and state crime lab technicians . . . We all gave it our best shot, but nothing emerged in the way of leads, either on the scene or in his social circle. It was as though he had lived and died in a vacuum."

"I believe you."

"But you are a seasoned policeman yourself, Herr Biermann. You know what his killing probably means."

"*Ja,*" he said, his face serious. "Either one of his former associates happened to be in your charming little town and recognized him, which seems very unlikely. Or . . ."

He left it to me to finish his sentence. "Or we have an informant somewhere in our government who sold him out."

CHAPTER NINE

Inspector Biermann and I shook hands and said good-bye in front of the courthouse. We also exchanged phone numbers and addresses, and I promised to contact him in the unlikely event that we got a break in the case.

My next move was to call Agent Hotchkiss on his cell phone.

"What can I do for you, Bo?" he asked after we swapped greetings.

"Does the name Aaron Webern ring any bells with you?"

"Sounds familiar, but that's all."

"He was murdered here in Sequoya two years ago."

"Oh yeah, that guy."

"So what do you know about him?" I asked.

"Well, I heard a few rumbles here and there."

"By any chance did you happen to hear that his real name was Alaric von Greim and that he was a German national in our Witness Protection Program?"

"Dammit, Bo! How do you find out all this shit?"

I couldn't help but laugh. "The good Lord rewards virtue and clean living, son, so let that be a lesson to you. I also suspect that somebody ratted him out, which is the reason he got killed."

"That was the rumble I mentioned."

"Well?" I demanded.

"The Witness Protection Program is run by the U.S. Marshals Service, Bo. Not the Bureau."

"I'm aware of that, Hotch."

"Well, we're generally not privy to their inside info. Is this a front-burner project?"

"I don't know. It was a strangulation killing, and now I have another similar one unsolved."

"Right. The old guy who got killed right before Christmas."

"Can you check this for me?"

"Sure, but it's going to take more than fifteen minutes. I'll try to have it in a couple of days."

"Good enough."

Despite his own prediction, he called me just before noon the next day. "Aaron Webern was definitely in the program," he said. "And there was an extensive in-house investigation done when he was killed. Nothing turned up, so the logical conclusion was that somebody who knew him just happened to run into him, and that was that."

"Maybe so," I said dubiously.

"Things like that have happened, Bo. What brought him to your attention?"

"A relative of his was here, a retired Munich police inspector, as a matter of fact."

"But how did he know about the guy being in witness protection?"

I sighed. "This has got to be between you and me, Hotch," I said.

"Sure."

"He had a friend in the Frankfurt office of the FBI who worked the Webern case. The friend retired, and a couple of weeks later the Munich guy got a clipping in the mail about Webern's murder from our local newspaper. There was no return address on the envelope, but he doesn't have any doubt where it came from."

"Sorry I couldn't do any better."

"It's not your fault. This may be one of those cases that never gets cleared." I didn't say what else was on my mind. In fact, I barely let myself think it, but I was afraid the Driggers case belonged in the same category.

About midafternoon I went into the outer office to get a cup of coffee and found Toby and Eva looking over some files at his desk. "Anything there I need to know about?" I asked.

Toby shook his head. "Just briefing her on a few current cases."

I nodded and left them to it. Once back in my own inner sanctum, I took a couple of phone calls. I had no more than hung up when Toby stuck his head in the door.

"What's up?" I asked.

"Remember that cattle theft out at Chet Morrisons's place about a month ago? The five registered Hereford heifers?"

"Sure."

"Well, the Texas and Southwestern Cattle Raisers Association detective just caught the guy who stole them."

"I don't suppose they got the cattle back, did they?"

"Oh, no. The thief sold them at the Lufkin auction barn and told them to just weigh 'em out."

I shook my head in disgust. "Prime registered breeding stock into the grinder. What a waste."

"Right. I feel like I should tell Mr. Morrison myself. Besides, I've got some papers for him to sign. But I need to be free of routine calls for a couple of hours."

"You know you don't have to check that with me. Just tell the dispatcher."

Just as I was about to leave for the day, Linda stuck her head in the doorway.

"I thought this was your day off," I said.

"It is. See?" She stepped into the room dressed in jeans and an SFA sweatshirt and a Houston Astros baseball cap. "Got a minute?" she asked.

"I've always got a little time for you. What's on your mind?"

She came over and took one of the chairs in front of my desk, uneasily perching herself on its edge. "Bo, I got to talk to you, and I feel like such a jerk."

"You're not a jerk, Linda. A twerp, certainly. But never a jerk."

She stuck out her tongue and flopped back in her chair. "This is so hard to say—"

"So I'll say it for you," I said, interrupting her. "Hotch proposed, you said yes, and you are moving to Houston because his career takes precedence."

Her mouth fell open. "Bo, how on earth did you—"

"Well, for one thing, Hotch has been in town several times since the two of you met last September and he hasn't been by the office here to see me but once."

"But how did you find that out?"

"Concerned citizens. Informants, if you want to call them that. Look, he's been on local TV. People know that he's FBI. They also know that I like to be told when the Feds are in town. Then add to that the fact that when I came to see you in the hospital after you were shot in the foot he was there, hanging over you, all dewy eyed. I also know that you've been to Houston at least three times since then. Put it all together and . . ." I shrugged and smiled at her.

She nodded. "I'm scared, Bo."

"Why?"

"I've tried marriage before, and it didn't work out for me."

I shook my head. "The first two were boys. Hotch is a real

grown-up man even if he does look like Beaver Cleaver. Meet him halfway. Try to be reasonable."

"Yeah?"

"And one last thing," I said with a laugh. "Don't wear your sidearm around the house. You'll do okay."

"Suppose we don't? I love my job, and hate giving it up, and I feel like I'm abandoning you and all the rest of the department. But I want—"

"A husband and kids and all that goes with it."

She nodded morosely.

"Linda, the commissioner's court has approved two new deputies for the department. The announcement hasn't been made yet, so you need to keep it under your hat. With you leaving this means I have three openings. I'll start interviewing in February to fill two of them. The third one I can fill with part-timers for a few months. Carla can come back some to help out, and there's a retired highway patrolman who has asked me about some part-time work. That should give you some time to see if things are going to work out or not. Besides, I can find some way to shoehorn you in at least part time if things crater out on you. There will always be a place for you in this department as long as I'm sheriff."

She looked relieved. "Thanks, Bo."

"No thanks necessary. You're one of the best deputies I've ever had. When are you leaving?"

"Is a month enough notice?"

I nodded. "Sure. When's the wedding?"

"We haven't set a date, and we're not really having a wedding. We're just going to get Judge MacGregor to marry us right here in the courthouse with my parents and a few friends and any of the courthouse people who want to come."

"I think that's a great idea. I'll be there."

We both rose, and I came around the desk and hugged her. "I'm going to miss you," I said. "So will the rest of the crew."

"I'll miss ya'll too. But do you ever wonder if you're doing the right thing?"

"All the time. But in this case I don't have any doubts that you're doing what you should do."

"You really think so?"

"I certainly do. Just try to be reasonable. And don't kick him in the shins too often."

I had just cranked my truck when Tom Waller called with the worst possible news. "What can I do, Tom?" I asked.

"Tell Sheila. Ask her to keep an eye on Sandy and maybe talk to her if she'll talk."

"Sure, Tom. And I'm so damned sorry about this."

I heard a long heaving sigh. "I've had more than those poor kids who've gotten killed over there in the Mideast. And I've been really content these last few years. I thank God I moved back home. It's great to be in a place where folks know where you live and care when you die."

"There'll be plenty who care, Tom. Don't ever think otherwise. And I'll watch after your family as best I can."

"Thanks, Bo. See you."

CHAPTER TEN

Already with a good case of the blues coming on, I got home a few minutes later to find my son's car parked in front of the house, something that had never happened before in the middle of the week. He was a surgeon in Dallas with a busy practice, and unannounced visits weren't his style, anyway. I sensed that something was wrong.

I parked in the old carriage house and entered through the back door to find him sitting at the table shuffling through some papers. "Hi, Dad," he said.

He was slimmer and finer boned than I, and he had much of his mother in him. Named Keith after his maternal grandfather, he was our only child. Back when he was about thirteen he took me to task about his name, which he said he had never liked. I have since learned that this is a frequent complaint heard from boys of that age. I replied that it was his mother's idea and that he should be grateful that I didn't get to name him what I had wanted to.

"Which was?" he had asked.

"Jack."

The idea of going through junior high and high school as Jack Handel seemed to reconcile him to Keith. It was all moonshine, of course. There had never been any doubt what we would name him, but parents sometimes resort to such creativity.

"Hi, son," I said. "To what do I owe this visit? Not that I mind."

He looked at me morosely. "We're coming home."

I nodded and tried to stay calm. "Well, I can't say that disappoints me," I said. "I'd love having you and the family close by."

"I don't have much choice. I'm broke."

I took a bottle of Canadian Club out of the cabinet and poured a good dram over ice, my hands shaking a little. "Tell me about it."

"Not much to tell. It's Kristen. She's almost spent me into the poorhouse."

"Why haven't you said something to me before now?"

He shrugged. "It's not your problem."

He was wrong. Your kids' problems are always your problems, even if they're eighty and you're a hundred. But I didn't say so since this wasn't a good time for a fatherly lecture on the longevity of parental worry. Instead I asked, "Are the two of you staying together?"

"Yeah. After all, she's the mother of my children. Besides, I'm not perfect myself, and I still . . ." His voice tapered off.

"You still love her."

"Yeah, I do."

"Good. People these days bail out of marriage too easily."

"Compulsive spending is now a recognized psychiatric disorder, Dad. Like sexual addiction. She's going into a treatment program."

I nodded thoughtfully and sipped my drink. "So what does she buy?"

"Anything and everything. Maxed out credit cards and tons of crap off the Home Shopping Network that we have no conceivable use for."

"What are you going to do profession wise?"

"I'm throwing in with a surgical clinic in Nacogdoches. And I've been accepted on the staff of the hospital."

"Of course you have," I said. "They're damned lucky to get you."

He blushed. Compliments always did embarrass him. "Well, they needed a thoracic surgeon," he said.

"Now they've got a good one. Where are you planning to live?"

"We'll have to rent a house. That's the best I can do right now. We're selling our place in Dallas, and the equity will just about bail us out."

"Do you have a buyer?"

He nodded. "Their loan is approved and the papers have been drawn up. We close day after tomorrow."

"I don't want to meddle in your business, but . . ."

He grinned at me, and I saw a little flash of the kid he'd once been. "But you will anyway, right?"

I nodded and finished my drink and poured another inch into the glass. "Last week, Bud Sample came to me with a deal. You remember Bud, don't you? A home builder, been around forever."

"Sure."

"Well, he did a custom home for a guy who declared bankruptcy just as he was getting the damned thing finished. Now Bud's butt is hanging out in the wind with the interest meters ticking away down at the bank and the housing market shot to hell. He offered it to me for what he has in it, less about half his labor costs. He thought I might like to buy it as an investment and lease it out to some young lawyer or whatever. I've considered doing that, but I hate to fool around with rental property."

"Where is it?"

"It's in a new, upscale subdivision in Nacogdoches not too far from the hospital. A very nice place. About the size of your house in Dallas. Why don't I buy it, then finance it for you and put the note in the grandchildren's trust? We could set the sale up without a down payment and fix it so you don't have to make a payment for three or four months or however long it takes you to get on your feet. How does that sound?"

He looked relieved. "I wasn't going to ask for help, but—"

"There's no sense in the interest you pay going to a bank or a savings and loan when it can go into trust for your own children. Besides, you're my only kid, and everything I have will be yours someday. Why not enjoy a little of it now, especially if it makes a hard situation a little easier?"

"That sounds too good to be true, Dad. You know, I didn't come to . . ."

"Borrow money. I know. Don't worry about it. You're lucky your father loves you and your family." A long moment began its passage on by, so I decided to fill it. "But what about Kristen? Shouldn't you show her the house before you commit yourself?"

"At the moment she's willing to do whatever we need to do, and she'll see this as a godsend."

"It's done, then," I said. "I'll call Bud before I go to bed tonight."

"Thanks, Dad."

I nodded and finished off my drink and blurted out, "Son, I'm seeing a woman."

He laughed. "That's fine. Do I know her?"

"Carla Wallace. She used to be one of my deputies."

"Sure I remember her. Very pretty. Good for you."

"I didn't know how you would take it, Keith. I mean after all, I'm almost sixty-three."

He shook his head in amusement. "So? I think it's great that you've got a girlfriend, but even if I didn't, it would be none of my business."

Just then the house phone rang. I picked up the receiver to find myself talking to the local highway patrol captain. I listened for a few moments, stunned. When I put the phone down I stared off into nowhere.

"What is it, Dad?" Keith asked. "You've gone pale as a sheet."

"Toby's been shot," I said, my voice sounding unnatural in

my own ears. "They don't know if he's going to make it. They took him to Nacogdoches."

"Shot? Where?"

"Out on the New Hope Road north of town," I said. "A passing motorist found him."

"No, I meant what part of his body?"

"His chest."

He got to his feet. "That's me. Let's go."

"Huh?" I asked stupidly.

"Pull your head out, Dad. We've got to go to the hospital."

I came to my senses. "My truck," I said. "It's got lights and a siren."

I switched on the flashers but left the siren off. Just as we were pulling out of the drive I called Walter Durbin on my cell phone. Walter was my own personal attorney in addition to being one of the best lawyers in the area. He was also close to Toby's family since Toby's older sister, Nelda Minton, was his office manager and paralegal. She was a widow, he was long divorced, and it was generally assumed around town that she was his girlfriend as well, not that such a thing would have been the only discreet black-white romance in Sequoya. Whatever their relationship— and it was certainly none of my business—they were extremely close and intensely loyal to each other.

He answered on the third ring, and I quickly explained the problem. "I'm on my way to the hospital," I said. "Can you notify the family?"

"Sure. Any idea who might have done it?"

"Not a clue, but that's what I need to get working on right now."

When I switched off, I became aware that Keith was talking on his cell phone, giving some kind of detailed medical instructions to what I assumed was someone at the hospital. I left him to his business and called the dispatcher at work and instructed her to get the night deputies in touch with the Highway Patrol to get me a full report. Then I called Texas Ranger Bob Thornton to ask for a forensics team to work the area.

"You coming out there, Bo?" he asked.

"Maybe later. Right now I feel like I need to be with the family."

"That's fine," he said. "I'll go myself. Somebody ought to do a door-to-door in the morning to find out if anybody saw or heard anything."

"I'll see to it, Bob. And thanks a million."

We pulled up in front of the emergency entrance and Keith vaulted out of the truck. "Get parked and come to the surgery waiting room," he said as he bolted off into the building.

Five minutes later I found myself alone in the waiting room. Almost a half hour passed before Walter, my attorney, arrived with Toby's wife, Latoya, and his father, Parson Parsons, longtime pastor of the Rising Star CME Church, Sequoya's largest black congregation. Latoya, petite and alluring, was head of data processing at the university in Nacogdoches. Reverend Parsons was a bit portly, with gray hair and an unassuming dignity that seemed to be, in the contemporary world at least, the exclusive property of elderly ministers.

"Have you heard anything?" Latoya asked.

I shook my head. "I suppose no news is good news," I said. "I think Keith is doing the surgery. He disappeared inside as soon as we arrived."

"Keith's working here?" Walter asked. He was fifty, six feet two, bald and broad shouldered with an angular face and hard eyes. A former National Guard colonel, he'd been called to active duty and seen combat in Desert Storm. Aside from his law practice, he owned a half interest in the local livestock commission company and had over seven hundred head of crossbred cattle in rental pastures scattered over two counties.

"Yeah," I said with a nod. "He's moving his family back home. He's been admitted to the staff."

I filled them in on what little I knew of the assault. "The local Ranger has a Department of Public Safety team out there now," I said. "And in the morning I'm going to canvass the area and see if anyone saw anything. By the way, where's Nelda?"

"She's keeping all the kids," Latoya said. "Mine and hers."

"Maybe we'll know something soon," I said.

As if on cue, a nurse swept into the room, looked directly at me, and asked, "Are you Sheriff Handel?"

"Yes, but these folks are members of Mr. Parsons's family. His wife and his father, to be exact. If you have something to report about his condition, perhaps you should speak to them."

She gave us all a very pleasant smile. "Dr. Handel wanted me to tell you that they're transfusing the patient now and preparing him for surgery. His vital signs are stabilizing. I'll let you know more when I know more myself."

And she was gone as quickly as she had come. We waited. The minutes passed with a molasseslike slowness as only hospital minutes can. Finally my cell phone buzzed. I looked at the caller ID to learn that it was the office. "Who have I got?" I asked.

"It's Linda, Bo."

"What in hell are you doing at work?"

"The dispatcher called and asked me to come in and help. They're one hand short tonight. I would have anyhow when I heard about Toby."

I sighed, both gratified and annoyed. Gratified that my deputies had such strong sense of commitment to one another, but annoyed because I hated for them to come in on their days off, though it was sometimes necessary. "So be it," I said.

"Any word yet?" she asked.

"Not yet. He's in surgery. What do you have for me?"

"He called in the tag number of a car he stopped and gave his location as the New Hope Road where he was found. It was on the recorder, and it's the last communication we have from him. That has to be the perp."

"You ran it, I suppose?"

"Of course. And you're going to love this. The vehicle is registered to one 'Bart Simpson.'"

"Like the cartoon character?"

"Right. A real smart-ass."

"What about an address for this guy?"

"The registration and title were sent to twelve twenty-three Bissonnet Street, apartment forty-seven, Houston. I also called Bob Thornton on his cell phone and asked him to have one of the Houston Rangers check the address out. I thought that's what you would want me to do."

"Good girl. Call him back and tell him that in the unlikely event that somebody claiming to be Bart Simpson opens the door they need to hold him and I'll fax them a warrant in the morning."

"Will do."

"Anything else?"

"Yeah. The tag number is for a van, Bo. A silver-gray minivan."

CHAPTER ELEVEN

Two and a half hours later, Keith came out dressed in his scrubs, his surgery cap still on his head. After greeting everyone, he said, "He lost a lot of blood. We've given him three pints and I had to remove the lower lobe of his right lung. He's stable and his vital signs are good, but now we've got another worry. When he fell, he hit his head awfully hard on the road. We X-rayed his skull, and there's no fracture. Still I'm calling in the neurosurgeon because he's simply not responding as he should. I think he's slipped into a coma state."

"Oh, God!" Latoya said, turning pale.

Keith shook his head. "Don't assume the worst. Oftentimes a coma is nothing more than the mind's way of going on vacation while the body repairs itself from some terrible trauma. If the neurosurgeon concurs, we'll have him airlifted to Mother Frances Hospital over in Tyler. They have a coma unit there."

"When will you know?" Reverend Parsons asked.

"Another hour or so should tell us something. As far as the bullet wound goes, it looks good for a complete recovery. He's in excellent physical condition with a strong constitution."

An older surgeon, a man I knew well named Dayton Andrews, stepped into the room. "You folks must be the Parsons family," he said as he put his hand on Keith's shoulder. "I want you to know that the patient's chances were improved greatly by this young man being here tonight."

My son reddened once again. "You've done pulmonary resections before, Dayton. I didn't save the day."

"Yes, I have but you've done a lot more of them than I have, and you've done them more recently. I'm mighty glad you showed up."

"What about the coma?" Reverend Parsons asked.

"That question is for the neurologists to answer," Andrews said. "But I can tell you the patient has the constitution of an ox. If he didn't, that stomach wound would have killed him. Didn't somebody tell me he got it in Iraq?"

"That's right," I said. "A car bomb. He was Special Forces before that."

Andrews nodded and looked at Toby's father. "I see by your collar that you're a minister. Don't forget your part in his recovery."

"Beg your pardon?" Reverend Parsons said.

"Pray, sir. Pray."

It took another hour. During that time I talked to Bob Thornton by phone and found out that the total recovered evidence from the site consisted of one 9mm shell casing, which was going to the Department of Public Safety lab in Houston for examination although it was doubtful that they would be able to identify the make of gun.

"I wish we had that damn bullet," Thornton said.

"I do too," I said. "But it went all the way through."

I'd just switched off when Keith came out once again. "We're taking him to Tyler," he said. "The helicopter is on the way here, and I'm going to ride over with him." He turned to me. "Dad, could you have somebody pick me up at the hospital there and bring me back to Sequoya?"

"Sure. I'll call the office."

Toby's wife looked stricken, like she'd lost her last friend. Reverend Parsons put his arm around her.

"Don't buy trouble before you have to," Keith told her gently. "Most people come out of comas, and many return to a completely normal life. The neurologist believes he suffered a mild cerebral contusion when he fell. That's a slight bruising of the brain from striking the inside of the skull. He thinks the damage is minimal, but we won't know for sure until they do an MRI over in Tyler. I wish I could tell you more, but that's all I know except that physically he's really bouncing back. His vital signs are better than would normally be expected. Like Dr. Andrews said earlier, he's got a strong constitution."

"Thank you, Keith," she said. "I just . . ."

"I know," he said.

She gave him a wan smile, squared her shoulders and said, "I need to pull myself together and get ready to go to Tyler."

"You're not in any shape to drive right now," Walter said. "But you'll need your car. Why don't I drive you over there in it, and maybe I can ride back with whoever picks up Keith."

"Sure," I said. "That'll work fine."

"I need to go by home and pack a few things," she said.

"Y'all go on," I told Walter. "I'll take Reverend Parsons home myself."

On the way back to Sequoya I called Linda at the office to update her on Toby's condition. I also told her to dispatch somebody over to Tyler to pick up Keith and Walter. It was late, but I called Agent Don Hotchkiss on his cell phone to ask him to check the FBI's national database for crimes in the last few months involving gray minivans.

He was still up. "I'll come by the office in a couple of days with the info," he said. "I'm working a case with another agent, and we both need to talk to you, anyway. We've got a favor to ask."

"Need help?" I asked.

"Yeah. And it's a big mess."

CHAPTER TWELVE

I dropped Toby's dad off at his house and went on home and fell into bed. I was vaguely aware when Keith came in and sacked out in his old room. I awoke at my usual time to find a note on the kitchen cabinet saying he'd gone back to Dallas to begin getting his house in order for the upcoming move. First thing I called Bud Sample and told him I'd take the house at the price he'd offered it. I also asked him to deliver the survey and field notes to Walter some time that day so he could draw up the deed.

Deputy Otis Tremmel and I spent the entire morning canvassing the area where Toby had been shot. It was a stretch of farm-to-market road with a house every quarter mile or so, typical of thousands of miles of country roads in my part of the world. Several people had heard what they thought was an auto backfiring about the time the incident happened, and one man, a seasoned hunter, had recognized the sound as gunfire. But as he pointed out himself, an occasional gunshot in rural East Texas was nothing out of the ordinary.

Finally about three miles up the road I found what almost certainly precipitated the incident. An elderly couple named Hayes ran what was one of the last mom-and-pop stores in the county.

"The power company was putting in a new transformer a ways down the road," Mr. Hayes explained. "And they had our electricity turned off. One feller come in here all mad that the gas pumps weren't working, and gave me a terrible cussing when I told him there wasn't nothing I could do about it. Then Toby come in right on his heels and bought himself a Coca-Cola. I told him about the cussing, and he lit out after the feller."

"Could you identify this man again?"

"I dunno if I could or not. He was a great big rascal, and he looked kinda hippie to me."

"How so?" I asked. "Did he have long hair?"

"Yeah. And I remember that he had a beard."

"What kind of beard? Goatee? Full-faced, what?"

He shrugged and looked around at his wife, a thick-bodied, stolid woman who occupied a sagging armchair behind the counter. She shook her head morosely. "I got cataracts," she said. "With the lights off the way they was, I never really did see him all that good. I sure heard him cussing, though."

"I think it was one of them full-face beards," Hayes said. "But I ain't sure. I'm a peaceful man and the language he used just sorta stunned me. I did see his car through the window as he drove off, though. It was one of them vans."

"What color?" I asked.

"Kinda silver gray. And there was a couple of other fellers in it, too."

Later that afternoon I made a quick trip to Tyler and visited with Latoya in the ICU waiting room. There had been no change in Toby's condition. She'd checked into a motel not far from the hospital and was preparing herself mentally for a long vigil. There was nothing I could say or do to make things better.

I came back to Sequoya, checked in at the office, and then went on home to a light supper. I fell into bed early that evening, still semiexhausted from the night before. As I drifted toward sleep my mind found its way back to that magazine caption that said "Legendary East Texas Sheriff Bo Handel."

"Legendary my ass," I muttered, disgusted both at myself and the boy who'd written it.

CHAPTER THIRTEEN

Life went on. The weekend came and went. The county suffered one residential burglary and a tractor theft on Sunday night. Early Monday morning, I worked the tractor case myself while Linda and one of the other deputies covered the burglary. Once back at the office, I forced myself to put my anxiety about Toby aside and buckle down to the routine tasks of my job. By late morning I was deep in the department's projected budget for the coming year when Maylene buzzed the intercom to tell me that Hotchkiss was in the outer office asking to see me.

"I've been expecting him," I said.

"He's got a buddy in tow," she replied.

As the pair came through the doorway, Hotchkiss held a big mug of coffee in one hand and cradled a handful of Maylene's home-baked oatmeal cookies against his chest with the other. His companion was both coffee-less and cookie-less, but he was decked out in a dove-gray pinstriped suit that hadn't come off anybody's rack. He was about forty or maybe a couple of years past, and fit-looking, with dark blond hair, hazel eyes, and a ruddy face. He also had a gold pig tiepin. The Porcellian pig, for heaven's sake. The most exclusive club at Harvard. As the meeting developed, he came across as just a little supercilious and patronizing. I don't think he meant to be, but that damned tiepin got the best of him.

"This is Special Agent William Winthrop," Hotchkiss said around a mouthful of cookie.

I leaned across my desk to get a firm handshake and a perfunctory smile. I motioned for the pair to sit. "Pleased to meet you, Mr. Winthrop," I said. I looked over at Hotchkiss. "Nice to see you too, Hotch."

He was a muscular kid in his early thirties with dark hair and a dopey earnestness about him that made it impossible not to like him.

"It's nice to be back, Bo. And I've got the results from national on that minivan. In the last six months eleven crimes involving silver-gray minivans have been reported across the country. All but one have been cleared, and that was an armed robbery in Fairbanks, Alaska."

"When was it?" I asked.

"Three months ago. Two perps did a convenience store. One stayed in the van, the other came inside and did the robbery. Both wore ski masks. The clerk knew that because he saw the one behind the wheel through the window."

"Doesn't sound like it could have been the same van, but I would like to know if they catch them."

"I put a note to alert me if it was cleared. Any other help you want on this business of the attack on Toby, just let us know."

"I appreciate that, Hotch," I said. "Right now I think we've got our bases covered. So what do you have in mind?"

Winthrop spoke. "It will take some explaining."

"I've got the time and need the distraction."

"What do you know about a group called the Aryan League?" he asked.

The question didn't come as a surprise to me. I'd been well aware that this or a similar conversation loomed somewhere on my horizon. "I know they bought a couple of hundred acres up in the northwest part of the county," I said. "I know that they're building some sort of compound up there. I also know that so far they haven't done anything to draw my ire. Other than that, I haven't had the time to concern myself with them."

"What do you think about white supremacist movements?" he asked.

"I don't agree with their views, if that's what you're asking."

"In general, I mean. From a law enforcement perspective."

"Well, I've done a little reading about them online. It seems that they run the gamut from harmless cranks to really dangerous nuts like that outfit up in the Northwest. What did they call it? the Silent Brotherhood, I think. Robert Jay Matthews and David Lane and all that bunch. Also known as The Order. As I recall they did over a million dollars worth of armored car robberies and murdered a couple of people. They weren't too silent, either. When the whole thing blew up a couple of them ratted out the rest."

"That's right. But that usually happens, doesn't it?"

"Almost always, but you asked my thoughts from a law enforcement perspective. The Constitution guarantees them the right to believe and advocate anything they want. The problem is that when you get a whole coven of people like that living in one of these compounds like they had in Idaho and in Arkansas and like they seem to be setting up here, then the potential for problems escalates. It's like having an outlaw biker gang headquartered in your town. A civil libertarian might say we're obliged to ignore them until they commit specific crimes, and my own sentiments are pretty much in agreement. But my mind and experience say otherwise. You know as well as I do that as cops we need to stay a little ahead of the curve on situations like this, and that means we have to walk a fine line."

"You're absolutely right," Winthrop said. "And that's what brings us to you."

"So let's hear it," I said. "What do you want me to do?"

"First of all, what I tell you here today has to stay in this room. Be aware that we need to be very careful because we've put a man in deep out there, and some of these people probably won't hesitate. If his cover gets blown, he may be dead."

"Are they that bad?" I asked.

"We think a couple of them may be."

"Then I'd like the particulars on those two," I said.

"I'll copy everything we have on them and bring it back by later this afternoon or first thing in the morning."

"I also suggest you have this same conversation with Bob Thornton, the Ranger who covers this county. Bob will hold his mud on the subject, but you need to let him know."

"I will, but right now let me give you a quick rundown on the whole white supremacist movement in this country. No one knows for sure how many true believers there are among them. The best estimate we can come up with is about thirty thousand, of which maybe ten percent are hardcore—"

"By 'hardcore' you mean what, exactly?"

"Willing to risk life and limb and commit felonies for the cause. We're not certain of that figure either. It's probably larger since on its lower level the movement overlaps with the remnants of the Ku Klux Klan, and a lot of those guys are criminals with prison records. Then there is the Aryan Brotherhood, which is strictly a prison organization. The AB is what they call a 'blood in, blood out' affair. Do you know what that means?"

"Sure. You have to kill to get in, and you are killed if you try to leave."

"That's right. The AB is a problem, but it's a specifically criminal problem with no real political overtones. We're mostly concerned with what I call the 'respectables,' by which I mean groups like the Aryan Nations, Christian Identity, and the White Patriot Party."

"From what I've read, those outfits aren't too respectable. At least not by my standards."

"You might be surprised who you find when you start looking behind some of these groups. For example, the fellow who founded the Aryan League is Afton Spencer the fourth, Ph.D. At one time this gentleman was the country's leading authority on Old Icelandic and Old Norse, which he taught for thirty years at one of the top universities in the Midwest. That's in addition to giving graduate level courses in Greek and Roman literature in the classics department. He speaks seven modern languages fluently and has published scholarly articles in four of them. Besides that, he has an encyclopedic knowledge of medieval Germanic dialects including Anglo-Saxon, which I'm sure you know is the root language for English."

"God almighty," I said. "You mean a scholar of that stature . . ."

"That's exactly what I mean. When he was about sixteen he got bored with high school, so he took a couple of months to teach himself Anglo-Saxon so he could read *Beowulf* in the original. While he was in his second year of college he produced a translation of a cycle of East Anglian poems that's still the standard work in the field. You could go to the college bookstore over in Nacogdoches right now and pick up a copy if you were so inclined."

"I think I'll pass," I said.

He smiled and nodded. "So will I, now that you mention it. But you really need to get online and look him up. Take a look at some of his essays on politics and race. He writes the most elegant and erudite prose you can imagine, and sprinkles it here and there with words like 'kike' and 'sheeney' and 'nigger.' Coming across terminology like that while reading him has the same emotional impact as finding rat turds in a bowl of ambrosia, which I think is the effect he's after. He also refers to President Franklin Roosevelt as 'the great war criminal' and calls Eisenhower a 'filthy mongrel.' Claimed Ike had black blood."

"Funny that he should call Eisenhower filthy," I said. "One time at a law enforcement seminar in St. Louis I ran into an elderly black bartender who had been one of Ike's orderlies during the war, something he was very proud of. He showed me a photo of the two of them together. He also mentioned that the man was almost a fanatic about personal cleanliness."

"Spencer would probably claim that was Eisenhower's symbolic way of trying to wash away his Negro blood, which is the sort of pronouncement he's well known for."

"Is Spencer still around?"

Winthrop nodded. "He lives out there at that compound. He's in his midseventies and suffering a little from emphysema. He bought two hundred acres about eighteen months ago and built himself a nice house. Then he started organizing."

"Organizing what?"

"That's the question," Winthrop said. "You see, the white supremacist movement is splintered into a dozen or more competing factions. The Aryan Nations—that's Richard Butler's old group—split and then fell apart. Law enforcement put the Covenant, Sword, and Arm of the Lord out of business, but those of its members who didn't go to prison either formed or joined other groups. In turn these groups split and resplit over minor points of ideology and administration. The two factions are about as congenial toward each other as Baptists and Hindus. Spencer is what one specialist on the subject calls a 'vanguardist.' The other element in the movement the same fellow calls the 'mainstreamers.' Spencer wants to build an umbrella to coordinate the political activities of the racist right as a whole, with an eye to the eventual seizure of power by an elite group. This would be bad enough, but several of the guys he has living in that compound have some marginal connections with a couple of domestic terrorist groups. For example, one man out there named Delbert Hahn was real close to another fellow who was real close to Terry Nichols, Timothy McVeigh's coconspirator."

"Damn!" I said.

"My sentiments exactly," Winthrop said with a cold smile.

"And if that jerks your chain, then try this on for size. Does the name Richard John Snell mean anything to you?"

I nodded. "Sure. He was executed in Arkansas in 1995. Murdered a black highway patrolman and a white pawnbroker he mistakenly thought was Jewish."

"Correct. The story is that several times before his execution he told prison officials that something big would occur on the day he died—the beginning of the end for the Zionist Occupation Government."

"And?" I asked.

"He was executed just a few hours before the Alfred P. Murrah Federal Building in Oklahoma City was bombed. April nineteenth, 1995."

"But I thought that was supposed to have been done in retaliation for the Branch Davidian massacre. It was on the anniversary of that debacle."

"Right. But what do you make of the accuracy of Snell's prediction?"

"It's spooky."

"Worse than spooky," Winthrop said. "Think of how difficult it would have been for McVeigh or whoever was behind the bombing to get information about what he was planning to a man on death row in a maximum security prison . . ."

He stopped speaking and rubbed his face tiredly for a moment, then said, "I've been working this business exclusively for over a year now, and I keep running into these vague connections, like the one between Snell and McVeigh. Snell had been associated with the Covenant, Sword, and Arm of the Lord up in Arkansas. McVeigh had some marginal connections with the same group, but he wasn't openly racist, whereas Snell's whole world revolved around race and the so-called struggle for Aryan survival. So why would McVeigh blow up a federal building to avenge Snell's execution? It's easy enough to say he didn't, but how do we explain what Snell told the prison people? That's why I always say this whole damned mess is like a spiderweb in the moonlight. Look directly at it, and it vanishes. It's only out the corner of your eye that you can get a glimpse of its pattern. If there is a pattern."

"And then there's the gunrunning," Hotchkiss said.

"What kind of guns?" I asked.

"AKs. Fully automatic," he said. "Or at least that's the intel we've been getting."

"How many?"

"They seem to have an unlimited source," Winthrop said. "That's the main reason for federal interest in this particular bunch. The Aryan League itself would probably be relatively harmless, but . . . Well, I'll let our informant brief you on this side of the operation. I was hoping we could meet with him to-night."

"Sure. Where?"

"A Mexican restaurant called El Charro on the East Loop over in Tyler. Ever heard of the place?"

I nodded. "Yeah. I've been there several times. Great food."

"Good. I'll come by about five and pick you up."

"No, let me meet you there at six. I want to go by the hospital afterward and check on Toby."

"Suits me."

"By the way," I said. "Who is your informant? One of the crew who turned against them?"

He shook his head. "Have you ever heard the name Jasper Sparks?"

"The Southern police character?"

"That's our man."

I wouldn't have been more surprised if he'd said George Bush. Books had been written about Jasper Sparks. In his early years he'd been associated with the old Dixie Mafia, which had been nothing but a gaggle of redneck thugs who'd been tagged with that lurid name by the press. Nevertheless, he was as bad as any

Italian mafioso who ever walked in shoe leather—a stone psychopath with a measured IQ of over 150 who'd been the prime suspect in a half dozen contract killings and numerous high-profile robberies. He'd also been involved in a shootout still famous in Southern law enforcement circles. Back in January 1971, he and his confederates had tried to rob a wintering carnival a few miles north of Biloxi. The only problem was that the Mississippi State Police and the Texas Rangers, working together as an interstate task force, had a man undercover in Sparks's crew. That crew ran into an ambush that turned into a savage shootout when they hit the trailer park where the carnival owner was holed up with the money. Six of Sparks's accomplices were killed that night, but Sparks managed to escape, leaving behind nothing to tie him to the robbery. There was no way to nail him without outing the informant, so Sparks walked on that one. A week later he tried to rob a wealthy hardware wholesaler in Jackson. The affair went bad, the wholesaler was killed, and Sparks himself got a 9mm slug in the belly for his trouble. He also got life in Parchman penitentiary, largely because his conviction came three days after the U.S. Supreme Court moratorium on capital punishment went into effect, which eliminated the death penalty as a viable option for the jury. Otherwise, there's little doubt that he would have died many years ago in the Mississippi gas chamber.

"You look shocked, Bo," Hotchkiss said.

"Well, hell yes I'm shocked. I thought the man was still in prison. What in the world?"

Winthrop laughed a real belly laugh, something that made me think better of him. "I'll let Sparks tell you himself this evening," he said. "It sounds more plausible coming from him, anyway."

"And this is the guy you want me to keep an eye on?"

"That's right."

I sat lost in thought for a minute, then said, "I don't see why you just don't just assign one of your own men to cover him."

"Manpower problems," Winthrop said. "I'm coordinating the investigations of this and three other radical groups, and since Nine-Eleven, we just don't have the agents to spare. Also, one of our men wouldn't have the immediate resources you have with your whole department here on the ground. He would just have to call on you or the Rangers if he needed heavy backup in a hurry, so . . ."

"Besides," Hotchkiss said dryly, "Mack Reynolds told us to come to you about this. He didn't want us mounting this kind of operation in your county without your knowing about it. Also he wanted you briefed on the Aryan League."

I nodded in understanding. Mack was the main reason I had such a good working relationship with the Bureau. In addition to being a crackerjack lawman in his own right, he was the nephew of a legendary agent named Dennis Muldoon who'd been one of Hoover's golden boys back in the forties and fifties. The Bureau's culture had changed a great deal in the decades since Hoover passed from the scene, but some of the old ways still lingered. As did the influence of some of the families who had been connected with the FBI for many years.

"I'm not actually working under Agent Reynolds," Winthrop said. "But—"

"But it pays to keep the local commander happy," I said. "Especially when he's wired into the high brass like Mack is."

"Touché," Winthrop said with a tight smile. He looked about the room as though he was seeing it for the first time. His eyes came to rest on my wall-mounted gun rack. "Is that your shotgun?" he asked, pointing at my Browning Superposed.

"It is indeed."

"Beautiful. My dad has a couple of them." He rose and walked over and reached up to hold it around the pistol grip. "Ahhh, to handle the handles that Handel handled," he intoned. "I bet you don't know who said that."

"Virgil Fox."

I thought his teeth were going to fall out of his head. "You're familiar with Virgil Fox?"

"Sure. He was one of the world's top concert organists. I heard him play a couple of times, and both times he told that same story. He was talking about playing George Frideric Handel's organ when he was in England."

"I must say you have surprised me again," he said good naturedly.

"Don't let that bother you. Sometimes I even surprise myself. But while we're on the subject of music, you might try Schubert's String Quintet. Have you ever heard it?"

"I don't think so."

"I can't recall the number, but he only wrote one quintet, so you won't have any trouble finding it. A man who was pretty famous once remarked that 'The adagio will tear your heart out.' Know who that was?"

"I have no idea," Winthrop said.

"Reinhard Heydrich. He was the top-dog Nazi who set up the Holocaust."

"Amazing that such an individual should have that sort of sensitivity."

I stood and shook my head firmly. "Not really. All it proves is that the ability to appreciate fine music means nothing beyond the ability to appreciate fine music. In fact, I bet you would find a few guys out at that compound who like Schubert too."

Winthrop nodded. "You're right. Spencer, for one. He's big on classical music since practically all of it was written by his precious Aryans. So we're on for dinner in Tyler tonight?"

"I wouldn't miss it for the world. Jasper Sparks, secret agent man, is something I have to see."

CHAPTER FOURTEEN

El Charro Restaurant sat on a big corner lot on the east side of Loop 323 in Tyler, a city of some hundred thousand that lay about forty-five miles northwest of Sequoya. Winthrop knew one of the owners, who had reserved us a booth in the rear not far from the kitchen. He and Sparks were a little early and were waiting when I arrived. In person, Sparks was not what I expected. I have had my share of experience with professional criminals, some of them boss hoods like him. Much to my surprise, he was free of the aggressive arrogance I had come to associate with his kind. Instead, I saw a seemingly healthy individual about ten years my senior, with a still agile body and a businesslike demeanor. Usually thirty years in prison humbles most men and gives them a bit of a hangdog air, but not Sparks. While there was about him none of the implied challenge so characteristic of his breed, neither did he exhibit any of the little telltale quirks that identify the long-term convict. This, coupled with what I knew of his early career, convinced me that Jasper Sparks was one tough-minded hombre. "Strongly centered," as the psychologists say.

I'd barely sat down when the waitress appeared with our menus and baskets of chips and bowls of salsa. As soon as she scurried off with our drink orders, I looked him right in the eyes and asked, "What brings you into this line of work?"

He gave me a wry smile. "It does seem pretty unlikely, doesn't it?"

"I can't think of anything less likely. Agent Winthrop here says you have quite a story, so let's hear it. What turned you into a responsible citizen, provided, of course, that you really are?"

"Religion."

"Ah!" I said, the skepticism intentionally heavy in my voice. "I suppose some stump-and-thunder evangelist was working the prison and you got saved, whatever that means."

He smiled and shook his head. "No, it was nothing like that at all. It all started with a mandatory visit to a new psychologist named Dr. d'Errico. I was about to put the con on him, just for the hell of it. I mean, prison is boring, and trying to con the shrinks is viewed as recreation. But for some reason I realized it wouldn't work with this guy. What told me that, I don't know. Maybe it was his eyes. He was a big man, about six-four, with hard, dark eyes that seemed to bore right into you. Not your normal upbeat prison shrink. He had my number too, and I remember exactly what he said to me that day: '*I have often wondered about people like you, Sparks. Why did Ed Gein skin his victims? Why did Stalin banish so many of his own countrymen to the Siberian gulags? Why did Hitler murder the Jews? Why does a cobra spit venom through the air? I honestly don't know, but it is not a bad thing that I don't know. I am glad I don't understand you, for you and people like you are a subject upon which one should consult theology and leave psychology strictly alone.*'

"Then he reached in his desk and pulled out a copy of *The Confessions of St. Augustine* and tossed it across the desk to me and said, 'In the unlikely event you should ever wish to change, something like this is your only hope.' All of which was rather strange since I later learned that he was neither particularly religious nor Catholic."

"And you actually remember that word for word?"

"Yeah. I have a nearly eidetic memory, and what he said was so unlike standard psychobabble."

"So I guess you took his advice and read the book," I said.

"Not for several months. But when I finally got around to it and finished it, I felt unsettled in a way I never had before in my life. Since Augustine was Catholic, I started talking to the Catholic chaplain." He shrugged. "After that, one thing led to another, but that's all I want to say. The rest is between me and my confessor. As you can see, I am trying to work out my redemption."

I decided to go ahead and voice my doubts. "I don't want to belittle any man's honest attempt to find peace with himself and God, but I'm having a little trouble swallowing this."

He nodded in understanding. "I'm not surprised, given my record. But for the first time in my life I really want to be honest with me. That's what's really important. Not whether or not I'm taken seriously."

The waitress appeared and took our orders. As soon as she left, I said, "It's well known that you mobbed out a few times with black hoods on some of your scores. In fact, you were unique among your cohorts in that regard. In light of that, how can you pass yourself off to these people as a white supremacist?"

It was as though a veil lifted and the old Jasper Sparks of his Dixie Mafia days sat there before me. His pale blue eyes were diamond bright and reptilian, and as he spoke his head weaved a little from side to side like that cobra his shrink friend had mentioned. Even his voice was different. "I just tell them, 'Listen, you put in a few years in a joint where the niggers are seventy percent of the population, and you'll get your head straight on the race question.' Then I read all the right stuff, things like Madison Grant's *Passing of the Great Race* and Houston Stewart Chamberlain's *Foundations of the Nineteenth Century. Mein Kampf.* It didn't take me long to figure out that the Jews are behind it all. A parasitical race, those kikes. Feed off us Aryans and contaminate our bloodlines by encouraging us to interbreed with coons and spics."

He smiled and the veil dropped once again. "Get the picture? I say things they want to hear."

"Did you actually read all that business?" I asked.

"Sure. Prepping for this job. Ripped through them and several others in a couple of weeks. Some really strange stuff there. Remember that giant dome Hitler had Albert Speer design for Berlin?"

Winthrop and I both nodded.

"No one really knows what its purpose was, but some of the more mystically inclined Nazis like Himmler had the idea of finding the Holy Grail—you know, the cup Jesus drank from at the Last Supper—and having a ceremony once a year in that dome where it was filled with pure German blood. In fact, Himmler actually spent a good bit of money on expeditions to try to recover the thing. Now think about it for a moment. The largest enclosed space on earth built for the sole purpose of holding a cup of blood. If such sheer pointlessness and waste of human effort isn't the Logos of hell, I don't know what would be."

His insight surprised me, though given his intelligence it shouldn't have. "You make a good point," I said. "Are some of the people out at Spencer's compound inclined toward that sort of Germanic mysticism?"

"A couple are, but in an ignorant, countrified way. Some of them are into a revival of Wodenism and the old Norse gods. Not Spencer, though. He's a thoroughgoing atheist and materialist. No Nordic hocus-pocus for him."

"And you think your cover will work?"

"It's working right now. Political fanatics are quite adept at seeing what they want to see, and what these people want to see when they look at me is a guy with a big reputation and a genius level IQ who's come around to their way of thinking and who is ready to work for their cause. In fact, it was an easy con."

"I'll take your word for it," I said. "I'm curious about how you got hooked up with the Bureau."

Winthrop spoke. "That's something neither of us are at liberty to discuss. Just be assured that we have confidence in him."

"They tell me they want me to be your primary contact," I said.

Sparks nodded. "I can live with that if you can."

"They also think that since I'm close at hand I might be able to get you out of there if things go sour on you."

"That's right, but neither of us should count on it."

"Why so?"

"There are a few pretty rabid guys out there. They may act first and sort it out later."

"I thought this Professor Spencer was the head honcho."

"He is, but he doesn't have complete control. There are a couple of other intellectual types out there besides him, and I'm sure that's the kind of group he had in mind when he first started out. Sort of an academy of theorists mentoring political activists. But you know how things go. This kind of group attracts people, and before he knew it he had some outright criminals on his hands. So to some extent he's the prisoner of his own creation. They respect him and his intellect, but some of them have their own projects going."

"Projects like this gun trafficking business," Winthrop said.

"Exactly," Sparks said. "You see, Spencer's great dream is to unite the whole white supremacist movement, which is badly fractured into a dozen or more factions. I've heard him say several times that Christianity, with its ideals of tolerance and compassion and charity, is nothing but a Jewish plot to emasculate the Aryan warrior."

"No joke?" I asked.

He nodded. "That's what the man believes. On the other hand, many other white supremacists consider themselves religious in their own goofy way—an Aryan Jesus, Aryan apostles, et cetera. But Spencer doesn't argue the point with them because he realizes that to have any political clout they have to present some kind of united front. He's not too enthusiastic about close ties with the militia movement because most of those guys aren't racially oriented, and race is everything to him. Spencer is a long-term thinker, and he's trying to build a structure that will begin to have an influence long after he's gone from this earth. But a few of these younger guys need to feel that they are making some kind of progress *now*. Hence, the gunrunning. They would like to be able to arm every supremacist group in the country with fully automatic weapons. AKs and M-sixteens."

"Why doesn't he just run their asses off?" I asked.

"For one thing, that would be contrary to his ideas of unity. Secondly, they might not run. They respect him, but they could well decide to override his decisions. They look at him as an aging and much-loved grandfather who still runs the family business, but who is slipping enough that they need to double-check everything he does."

Winthrop spoke. "By the way, Sheriff, I've got the files on the two characters I promised you. One is the Delbert Hahn guy I mentioned this morning. The other is named Leroy Fancher."

"You know these two birds?" I asked Sparks.

"Sure."

"What are they like?" I asked.

"Fancher has a sort of court jester persona about him. Still, there's something about the man that raises my hackles."

"You think he's more dangerous than he acts?" Winthrop asked.

He nodded. "He could be. On the other hand, Hahn seems more benign until you bring up ZOG. You know what they mean by ZOG, don't you?"

"Sure. The Zionist Occupation Government, which is what those birds all call the federal establishment."

"Well, with Hahn it's ZOG, ZOG, ZOG. Hate, hate, hate.

Jews and blacks and Mexicans. He doesn't say much, but when he talks that's what you get. Ever heard of the Fourteen Words? Hahn lives by them."

"I've run across them in some Internet reading I've done lately," I said. "But I've forgotten exactly what they are."

"'We must secure the existence of our people and a future for white children,'" Sparks said. "David Lane of The Order dreamed them up, but they have become the signature slogan of the whole white supremacist movement. Lane died in federal prison but his venom lives on."

"How about drugs?" I asked. "Are these people into the drug trade at all?"

"They claim not to be. The movement as a whole views heavy drug use as a degeneracy, and they advocate the death penalty for cocaine and heroin dealers. Some of the guys do weed, and a couple have sources for amphetamines. They like to amp up a little."

"How about Spencer?"

He shook his head. "Absolutely not. He's a cognac man. Hennessy VSOP."

"How does he view the weed usage among his minions?"

"I think he considers it a relatively harmless vice, though I imagine he would prefer that they don't do any drugs at all. But after all, he likes to get an occasional buzz on with his brandy."

Service was quick and our food soon arrived. Conversation lapsed while the three of us applied ourselves to steaming platters of enchiladas, refried beans and Spanish rice. When the meal was finished, Winthrop paid the check, and then we walked outside and around to the back where we had parked.

"So how about it, Sheriff?" Sparks asked. "Can I count on you to bring in the cavalry if things go bad out there?"

"Sure. But how do we stay in contact?"

"I've got a cell phone, and I'll give you the number. I'll need yours too. But I would prefer that you don't call me unless you absolutely have to. It's safer. Somebody might see the caller ID."

"You don't need to tell me that. In fact, I'll get a second one and register it in a female name. Then if anybody sees it the logical inference will be that you have something going with some lady."

He nodded. "Good idea. And if I need to talk to you at more length than we can manage over the phone, then we can meet somewhere. Maybe here, if that suits you."

"Good enough," I said. "One last question about Delbert Hahn. Is he as dangerous as you were back when you were his age?"

Jasper Sparks smiled. "Is that intended to be a sort of back-door compliment?"

I shook my head firmly. "No, not really. I'm just asking for your comparative estimate based on what we both know to be true. So how about it?"

He didn't even pause to weigh the question, and when he answered his eyes were bright and unworldly in the dim light of the streetlamps, his face was coldly impassive. "Not quite. He could be dangerous enough under the right circumstances, but I think he'd roll to save his own skin. I never did."

"That's right," I said. "You never did. But I don't know whether that's admirable or stupid."

He shrugged. "It is what it is."

"How about Fancher?"

"Maybe, but he's not nearly as smart as I am."

I jotted down my contact numbers for him. We shook hands, and Sparks climbed into a brand-new, coal-black Lexus coupe.

"How did he manage a vehicle like that?" I asked as the sleek car whisked away into the night.

"Inherited money," Winthrop said. "His family was wealthy. Makes me wonder why he chose a life of crime in the first place."

"Because it was in his nature to do so."

I went by the hospital to check on Toby. There was no change. I visited a few minutes with Latoya, then drove back home. Before I went to bed that night I went over the files on Hahn and Fancher. Hahn was ex-army with a couple of assault charges. A skilled welder, he'd bounced around the country from one job to another, acquiring and abandoning in turn a wife and several live-in girlfriends along the way. He'd first surfaced among the white supremacists in Ohio where he'd been hauled in and booked for felony assault when a neo-Nazi rally had turned into a full-scale street brawl with a black nationalist group. A plea bargain dropped the charge back to a class-A misdemeanor that cost him a fifteen hundred dollar fine and thirty days in jail. He'd also been one of the suspects in a Cleveland synagogue bombing, but since hard proof was lacking, he was questioned but never actually arrested in the case.

The report on Fancher was thin gruel. He billed himself as a high school graduate and held a Social Security card and a valid Texas driver's license, but beyond that nothing was known of his origins or background. He'd managed to stay off law enforcement radar until two years earlier when his name was linked with an Indiana Klan group. He'd never been arrested as a result of his activities, staying, as one investigator put it, "safely near the comfortable outer fringes of the white nationalist movement." My guess was that both men were reasonably intelligent but poorly educated, with mental lives that played out in that gray wonderland where paranoia meets lower class white resentment. A dangerous brew.

"Just what we need here in Sequoya," I muttered to myself as I tuned off the light and rolled over to go to sleep.

CHAPTER FIFTEEN

I dragged myself out of bed a little after five without my usual eagerness. I was beginning to feel like a man who had lost his edge, and the thought crept into my mind that maybe I'd stayed on the job too long. I had two unsolved murders on my hands, and now my chief deputy had been shot right on my doorstep, so to speak. Then there was the white supremacist problem. I also found myself mildly annoyed at Hotchkiss and his buddy, admittedly for no good reason since they were just doing their jobs. But monitoring a killer-turned-snitch within a neo-Nazi cult was a little more than I needed on my plate at the moment. Illogical and irrational of me, I know. Yet in thinking back to that day when Linda and Sheila had jokingly demanded wisdom from me, I wished I'd told them that one thing I have learned in my sixty-three years is that we don't live in a world dominated by logic and reason. We live in a world of sensation and emotion, and for better or worse that's just the way we are. "And there ain't no two ways about it," I muttered as I cranked my pickup and backed out into the street.

Just then my cell phone beeped and Texas Ranger Bob Thornton's name came up on the caller ID. "Where you at, Bo?" he asked.

"On my way to the Caravan to get an early breakfast."

"I'm already there. See you in five."

I found him in a corner booth at the rear of the dining room. "What's up?" I asked, sliding in opposite him.

"I went down to Houston myself yesterday to check out that address on Bissonnet. I figured I owed it to Toby to get personally involved. The apartment was rented to a young woman named Crystal Henderson. She moved out about a month after the title to that van was mailed. No forwarding address, no nothing. The manager said she only lived there about six months, and never was any problem to him."

"How old was she?" I asked.

"Twenty-six. The contact info on her application was bogus. I'm going to have Austin do a complete rundown on her."

"Let's have Hotchkiss check her out with Social Security and see if anybody is paying into her account."

"Good idea," he said.

"Did the manager say anything about any of her friends and associates?" I asked.

"Only that she told him she was moving out to move in with her boyfriend. According to him the boyfriend was about ten or fifteen years older than her."

"Could he identify the boyfriend if he had to?"

Thornton shook his head. "He got that information from a college boy that worked for him doing maintenance. The kid tried to chat her up a few times, and the boyfriend got rough with him and told him to get off her case. Kinda scared the kid. He claimed he never said anything out of line to her. She was a pretty girl and he was a horny young buck. You know how that goes."

I grinned at him. "Do I? I'm not too sure I remember."

He laughed. "Me either, now that you mention it. I may have a faint glimmer of a recollection way back yonder in the back of my mind somewhere, but that's about all."

"We're over the hill, Bob."

"Maybe so, but when it comes to these old criminals we can still kick at their ankles as they run by us. Anyhow, this college kid finished his education last fall and moved back to Odessa. I got him on the phone, and he thinks he could ID the guy if he ever saw him again. Said he was a tough-looking bastard."

"How about the insurance on the vehicle?" I asked.

"It was in her name and paid in advance for the year. The van was bought from a used car dealer there in Houston, and had been previously owned by a doctor's wife."

"Thanks for the help, Bob," I said.

"Glad to do it. But there's something else I need to ask you about."

"Shoot."

"Have you got anything on this neo-Nazi outfit that's setting up out in the north end of the county?"

"Funny you should ask. You remember Don Hotchkiss, don't you?"

"Sure."

"Well, yesterday he was in my office with another agent, an older guy named Winthrop. They came by to brief me on that bunch. They also wanted my help. I told them they needed to bring you on board too."

"Winthrop called me last night. We're supposed to meet later in the week."

We stopped talking as the waitress came by to take our orders. Once she was gone, Thornton asked, "What did they want you to do for them?"

"They've got an informant out there. They thought that if things clabbered up on him I'd be in a better position to bail him out than they would. Apparently the Feds are mounting a nationwide multiagency investigation of this whole white supremacist movement, but at the moment they've only got two agents assigned to this local outfit, and even they're not here all the time."

"Were you supposed to tell me this?" he asked with a twisted smile.

"I don't know. I assume Winthrop will tell you when he briefs you. If not, screw 'em. But you'll never guess who the informant is. It's a name you'll recognize, though."

"Yeah?"

"Jasper Sparks."

"*The* Jasper Sparks?"

"The one and only."

He seemed to reflect for a few seconds, then said, "I've probably heard something stranger than that in my life, but I can't recall what it might have been. Did they give you any idea why he's working for them?"

I shook my head. "They claimed they weren't at liberty to discuss that, but it seems that he's run point for them before on a couple of other operations, and they're satisfied." I went on to tell him about Sparks's conversion to Catholicism and the gun-running suspicions the Feds had.

"Do you think Sparks's religion is for real?"

"I don't think it matters, Bob. He has to stay with their agenda or he goes back. He'd never bolt and go fugitive because he's just plain too old to go skulking around back alleys. Besides, as it is I think he's having plenty of fun."

"Eh? How's that?"

"Just look at his record. Supersmart, bores easily, and addicted to thrill-seeking behavior. This way he can get his kicks inside the law. And I'm willing to admit that there's a chance he's for real about the religion. Some really bad people have been known to completely change course. Years ago I knew the retired Dallas deputy sheriff who used to come up here and fish a lot with his wife. He was the officer who went undercover on that famous trailer park robbery down there in Biloxi, Mississippi. That was back in the Dixie Mafia's heyday, and he knew

Sparks real well. He said if Sparks had a trait that even bordered on redeeming it was his attitude toward women."

"Yeah?"

"He told me that Sparks simply will not tolerate a woman being bullied or abused. While this deputy was down there working undercover, a well-known pimp roughed up one of his girls that Sparks was particularly fond of. My friend heard Sparks tell him it better not happen again. The pimp told him to mind his own business. A couple of days later this girl showed up at one of those clubs where the characters hung out, and she was all beat to hell and back. Two black eyes, split lip, bruised ribs. Sparks just nodded and said, 'Okay, if that's the way that sucker wants to play it.' About a week later the pimp's body was found in the trunk of a stolen car abandoned in the woods about thirty miles north of Biloxi. The pimp was supposed to have been a real badass himself, but according to my friend he was way out of his league when he tangled with Jasper Sparks."

Thornton laughed. "Hell, you almost have to like a man who killed a damn pimp."

"I feel the same way. Listen, earlier you mentioned the Aryan League. Anybody in particular out there you're concerned with?"

"One bird named Delbert Hahn," he said. "DPS intelligence links him with the meth trade out of Mexico. As you know, these local labs we bust from time to time are just a small part of the problem. The really good stuff comes from south of the border."

"Sparks didn't think he was heavily involved in drugs," I said.

"Well, I would imagine he plays it pretty close to his vest. Wouldn't you?"

I nodded. "I've got a copy of the FBI file on Hahn if you want to look at it."

"I sure as hell do."

Just then my cell phone rang. I listened for a few moments and then snapped it off. "They found that minivan," I said.

"They did?" he asked, beginning to rise from his seat. "Then let's go. I'll have a DPS forensics team on it before you can sneeze."

"There's no hurry, Don," I said. "We may as well finish our breakfast in peace. It's been torched."

The burned-out carcass of the van was surrounded by the smoking ruins of what had once been a very nice garage at an uninhabited farmstead two miles across the county line in Nacogdoches County. According to the fire marshal, several gallons of an accelerant, which had almost certainly been gasoline, had been poured in and around the vehicle and then set afire. The paint was gone from the license plates, of course, but they were still readable.

"We're not going to get any fingerprints or DNA out of that mess," Thornton said bleakly.

"Not hardly," I said.

"Still, I'm going to have the team to check it out. Something might turn up."

"Thanks. You asked about the file on Hahn. I've got it on disk so drop by the office and I'll make you a copy. There's a pretty recent photo in it. While we're at it, why don't you e-mail it to the Ranger out there at Odessa and have him show it to that college boy."

"Sure," he replied. "Have you got some reason to suspect Hahn?"

"No, but I've got no reason not to suspect him either. It just seems like a lot of violence has accompanied that bunch's move to Caddo County."

CHAPTER SIXTEEN

B ack at the office I made Thornton a copy of the file on Hahn, and he went on his way. While at the scene of the arson, I'd noticed a local Realtor's "For Sale" sign on the property. I knew the Realtor and gave him a call. I learned that the property was owned by a trust at Fredonia National Bank in Nacogdoches, and the trust beneficiaries were a pair of respectable heirs who had long since left East Texas. However, the garage had been leased out for a year by the Realtor, who was also the property manager. I gave him a call. After the exchange of pleasantries, I asked, "Leased to who?"

"A young lady named Crystal Henderson."

"What did she look like?"

"I have no idea. The transaction was handled by mail and by phone. We agreed over the telephone to the details, and I e-mailed her a contract. She signed it and snail mailed it back along with a bank money order for the full year's rent. You see, the pasture is rented by a local cattleman who didn't want the garage. The previous renter had kept his tractor there in the garage. It's really a very substantial building, and I was able to get a hundred dollars a month for it even in such a remote location."

"It's not a substantial building any longer," I said. "It was torched this morning."

"Really? I wonder who would do such a thing?"

"Hasn't anyone from the fire marshal's office contacted you?"

"I just got to the office and my secretary is out sick today. You said it was torched?"

"Right."

"Well, I suppose it was just vandalism. It's really no problem, although I will have to return part of the rent. Actually, the tract is being bought by a developer, and the garage was slated for demolition anyway as soon as the lease was up. He'll be happy to have it out of the way."

"Oh, but it is a problem. When the thing went up in flames it contained a car I'm pretty sure was used by whoever shot my chief deputy a few days ago."

"My gosh . . ."

"Did she say what she wanted it for?"

"Storage. She said she and her boyfriend had some things they needed to store there. She mentioned a couple of motorcycles they were restoring. The advantage it would have over a commercial storage building was that they would have the room to work on their restoration projects there."

"Do you lease things sight unseen very often?" I asked.

"No, but she seemed like a nice young woman, and I didn't pry too far into her business. If it had been a residence I would never have made the deal without meeting the people."

"I don't suppose you made a photocopy of the money order."

"No, but I imagine my bank did. They seem to copy and computerize about everything these days. I do recall that it came from Chase Bank in Houston."

"Thanks," I said.

A dead end. The chances of a teller at one of the largest banks on the Gulf Coast remembering who had bought a particular money order months earlier were nonexistent.

I called Hotchkiss and gave him Crystal Henderson's Social Security number and asked him to check it for me to see if anyone was paying into her Social Security account.

"Sure thing, Bo," he replied. "But it will probably be tomorrow before I can get back to you on this."

"That's fine," I said and hung up.

Just then Maylene stuck her head in the doorway. "Lester Prichard came by just after I got here and wanted to see you."

"Lester? What in the Sam Hill was on his mind?"

"He claimed he's been threatened."

"Well, is he coming back?"

She shook her head. "He said he'd wait for you across the street at the café."

On my way down the basement corridor I met Eva just coming back from an early call. "Let's go," I told her. "This interview will give you some insight into the culture of Caddo County."

"Yeah? How's that?"

"We're going to meet with the head of the DPS."

"The DPS?" she asked in confusion. "You mean the Department of Public Safety?"

"No, I mean the Dead Pecker Society."

The DPS consisted of a crew of ill-tempered old coots who met most mornings at the back corner table of the Texan Café and often lingered on until noon, cadging free refills on coffee and complaining about everything under the sun. Their main stock in conversation consisted of the shortcomings of the modern world as personified by crooked politicians, loose morals, short skirts, uppity women, smart-mouthed young folks, and rising prices. All of which, in their view, made the imminent collapse of civilization a foregone conclusion. They also loved to rail against something they called "socialism," despite being the eager recipients of various farm subsidies, Medicare, Social Security, assorted veterans' benefits, and anything else they could wheedle from the government. And Lester Prichard was the lead fiddle in that dreary orchestra. He was seventy-five years old and dealt in anything legal that would bring him a dollar—land, cattle, used farm implements, and whatever else came his way—activities that had made him a millionaire, something you could never tell by looking at him. He wore rumpled khaki pants and threadbare shirts and an old 1940s-era fedora whose color hovered somewhere between tan and gray, depending on the light. His eyes were rheumy blue buttons that peered suspiciously out at the world through black plastic-framed trifocals that had probably been new about the time Kennedy was sworn in. He also had a long, pointed, beaky nose that he never hesitated to poke into anybody's business that suited him, and a face that held the perpetually sour expression of a man who had just discovered a dead skunk in his refrigerator.

There had once been a Mrs. Lester, but she had long ago passed on to her reward, leaving the marriage "without issue" as the genealogists say. Which meant that Lester was now wifeless and childless with nothing to occupy his time except making money and being a horse's ass, both of which he was extremely good at.

We found him and two of his cronies at their usual table. "What's on your mind, Lester?" I asked after I'd introduced Eva.

He examined her through the various lenses of his glasses, then nodded a brief hello. "I been threatened," he said.

"That's what Maylene told me. Let's hear about it."

"You know that Dr. Spencer feller that's bought the old Douglas place out in the north end of the county?"

"I've never met him, but I know who he is."

"Well, I own a piece of land just north of his, and he wants to buy it. I asked him two thousand an acre, but he only offered twelve hundred. It's worth about fifteen, so I guess he thought we'd meet somewhere in the middle, but I won't come down none at all. That's how come those two fellers came and threat-ened me this morning."

"What two fellows?" I asked.

"Hell, I don't know their names. They said they were friends of his."

"Did you talk to both of them?"

"No, now that you mention it only one of them spoke. The other one stayed in the truck. He was the one with the beard."

"Okay," I said. "Let's back up here and tell me the whole story from the beginning."

The waitress came over and Eva and I both ordered Cokes. Lester rooted around for a while in his ear with his little finger, belched, and then asked her for a refill. When she was gone, he said, "I was out in the front yard this morning when this pickup pulled up—"

"What kind of pickup?" I asked.

"It was a GMC. Pretty new too."

"What color?"

"Dark blue. Long-bed model. Kinda fancy. Had one of them chrome toolboxes in the front part of the bed up against the cab."

I nodded. "Go on."

"Well, this guy got out and asked if I was Lester Prichard. When I told him I was, he smiled right nasty like and asked me if I wanted to go on being Lester Prichard. I told him I reckoned I'd have to because I didn't know how to go about being nobody else. That's when he said, 'Oh, you can be something else all right. You can be dead.' I started to edge toward the house, but he got between me and it. That's when he said he was a friend of Dr. Spencer's and that I'd better sell them that tract of land at their price if I knew what was good for me."

"What did this guy look like, Lester?" I asked.

"Well, he was clean shaved and maybe a little taller than you are. I'd say he was about forty or so."

"How about his hair? Was it long, short, what?"

"It was just normal. Kinda dirty blond. Longer than I wear mine but not hippie long."

"How about the one in the truck? What did he look like?"

"He had a beard."

"How about his hair?"

"It was brown and shorter than the other feller's. Not army short, but short like men used to wear it before all this hippie business come along."

"How were they dressed?"

"Like anybody else their age would dress, I reckon. The one that got out was wearing jeans and a green shirt and a jacket. I don't know what the guy in the truck had on in the way of pants. He was wearing a brown shirt."

The waitress was back with the coffeepot and our Cokes. Lester's two cronies were listening with rapt attention despite no doubt having heard the story all morning long.

"Go on," I urged.

"Well, I told him I'd think it over. He told me I'd better think fast and come up with the right answer. Then he got in his truck, and they left. That was about all there was to it."

"Are you? Going to think it over, I mean?"

"I sure as hell don't want to sell at his price. Ain't there anything you can do?"

"Of course. It would help if you'd file a formal complaint, though."

He shook his head. "I don't want to do that. I'll sell before I do that and get crossways with these rascals. I mean it ain't like it's gonna kill me financially if I do."

"You're not going to have to sell. I promise you that."

"Thanks, Bo," he said, sticking out his hand to shake mine. "I've always voted for you, and now I reckon I'll get something for my trouble."

I laughed. "You've been getting something all along, Lester.

I've been in office almost thirty years, and nobody's bothered you before, have they?"

He indulged in some more deep ear exploration before reluctantly admitting, "I reckon not."

"Well, there you go."

CHAPTER SEVENTEEN

I returned to the courthouse and read over the evening shift's reports to learn that the county had enjoyed a quiet night. In the late morning, just as I ran out of busywork, the sense of dissatisfaction I'd been feeling the last few days became oppressive. I realized then that I was tired of things happening to me. I decided to happen to somebody. Originally I'd intended to put a stop-and-hold on the blue pickup and have whoever was driving it brought in to me. Instead, I decided to go to the source.

I buzzed Maylene and told her to scare up a phone number for Professor Afton Spencer. "Call Hotchkiss if you can't get it any other way," I said.

A couple of minutes later she appeared in my doorway and said, "I got his number from information, which you could have done for yourself if you'd been of a mind to. Now what do you want me to do with it?"

"Call him and tell him I need to talk to him. Today."

"Do I tell him why?"

"He'll know why, so he won't ask. And don't take no for an answer."

Puzzled, she nodded and said, "Okay. It's your funeral."

"Not yet it ain't."

A few minutes later she was back at the doorway. "Mission accomplished."

"What was he like?"

"Very polite, as a matter of fact. He said he'd be happy to see you any time after noon. He also said he'd tell the man at the gate that you were expected and that he was to extend you every courtesy."

"Good," I said with some surprise.

"What's that business about the gate?"

"Security."

"Security for what?" she asked. "Who is this Spencer guy, anyhow?"

"A damned old Nazi. Haven't you heard about that crew of white supremacists who are building a compound out on the north side of the county?"

She shook her head. "You're not joking, are you?"

"I wish I was. Is Linda on duty today?"

"No, she's off today."

"Then call Eva back and tell her to meet me at one at the Caravan for lunch. Now that I think about it, her being Mexican means she's better for my purpose than Linda anyway."

"And what purpose would that be?"

"I want her to help me make a nuisance of myself."

"You don't need any help for that, Bo."

"It's nice to feel appreciated, Maylene."

"I call 'em like I see 'em," she said and spun around on her heel and stalked out of the room.

After a pleasant lunch, Eva and I were on our way. "They have a guarded entryway out there," I said. "According to the Bureau, they enclosed the compound with a chain-link fence six feet tall. They also put up a booth at the entryway and hired a man named

Lyndon Till to man it in the daytime. Then they go into lockdown at night. It's an electric gate and all the honchos have gadgets that open it. I know the man, and I imagine he fits in real good with that crowd."

"Sounds like the two of you have a history. Any of it fit for my ears?"

I sighed and told her the story. My dad had been a fine man, but his one glaring fault was too much sympathy for the wrong sort of people. He would work hard to find some reason not to fire a man who needed firing. One such individual was Lyndon Till. He was a tall, red-faced fat man who'd been timekeeper at the mill when I was in high school and college. He was a full-tilt son of a bitch who came by it naturally and worked hard to build on what fate had given him. He always sat at a small desk in a little portable building beside the mill gate where his job was to check the clock and note the exact time each employee arrived and left and then mark it down on his big yellow tally sheet. Other than checking in any visitors who came to the mill, that was his sole duty. The rest of the day he lounged back with his feet propped on the desk, drank Coca-Cola, ate MoonPies and leered his way through a foot-tall stack of what passed for girlie magazines back in those innocent days. The magazines resided in a big cardboard box that sat permanently beside his chair, which also held a few tattered paperback novels with plain brown covers and titles like *Honey's Delight*. Occasionally Till would be in a literary frame of mind and could be seen perusing one of these masterpieces rather than his magazines. One time when I passed I noticed the words "Paris, France" stamped on one of the books' spines, and I had a pretty good idea what kind of honey the book was talking about.

The summer before my dad died, a black mill hand, a dependable fellow who had been working for us for years, came in the gate and gave his name just as he always did. "Coy Presnell," he said.

Till looked up with his little suet-ringed fat man's eyes and said, "You weren't here all last week, were you? Did you get leave from Mr. Handel to miss work?"

Presnell nodded and said that his father had passed away, which was the reason for his absence.

"Is that a fact?" Till asked, raising his eyebrows. "Well, I expect you'll get over it soon enough. We both know he was the most useless damn nigger in this county, and there ain't nothing more useless than a useless nigger."

Even the two rednecks who told me of the incident a couple of days later thought Till was beyond the pale since Presnell was a hardworking, church-going man who was respected by all his coworkers, black and white alike. But such cruelty was typical of Till. When I came back home to take over the business, the first thing I did was fire him.

"Fired?" Till had asked. "How come?"

"I don't like you," I told him.

"That's not reason enough to a fire a man."

"It is for me," I said.

"This ain't fair."

"Maybe not, but if you're not packed and off the property in thirty minutes I'll have a couple of the colored mill hands throw your ass right out the front gate. Then you'll really have something to whine about."

Needless to say, he'd held a grudge to this day . . .

"And that's why I've got no use for Lyndon Till," I said.

"Good for you."

I shook my head. "Don't make me out into a saint, Eva. Because I'm not. My own ideas about race were very traditional in my younger years. The assumption of black inferiority—and for that matter Mexican inferiority as well—was just a part of the world I grew up in. But Till's kind of abuse was something no decent white person would even think of heaping on a black man. So you can see why Lyndon Till is the perfect man to be working for an outfit like this. I'm sure it suits him just fine."

I was right. It did. He was full of self-importance and bluster. The guard booth was a portable building that appeared to be about ten feet square. A propane tank sat beside it and no doubt served a small space heater inside. Till opened the sliding window and peered out. "Well, Bo," he said. "I don't guess I need to ask for your ID. But I would like to know who your lady friend is."

"Shut up and open the damned gate, Lyndon," I said. "Be a good little boy and maybe this bunch will let you wear a helmet with a spike on top."

"You always were too smart-mouthed for your own good," he said with a snarl and pushed a button beside the door facing, lifting the crossbar and allowing us to drive in.

As we drove slowly up the winding drive to the house, I noticed one of Kaiser Trucking Company's box trailers parked behind a large metal building that sat some hundred or so yards behind Spencer's house in a cluster of mobile homes. I made a mental note to have a chat with the company's owner, Buck Kaiser, a man I'd known all my life. I also noticed a dark blue GMC pickup parked at one of the trailers. I stopped, got the binoculars out of the console and focused them on the back bumper of the truck. The license number was visible, and I jotted it down.

The house was large, single story, rustic, roofed in wood shingles and encased in dark, earth-toned brick. We made our way up the walk and I rang the bell. The front door was a huge, thick wooden affair that had been carved in some sort of ancient Aryan symbols. I recognized the god Shiva, the Indo-European multiarmed god of destruction and rebirth.

The door was opened by a tiny little woman with a sweet smile and a soft voice. "I'm Mrs. Spencer," she said. "Afton is expecting you."

Inside the foyer she gazed up at Eva's face and said, "My, but you're a lovely girl. So tall. I've always wished that I was taller."

She took Eva's arm and led us back through the house to a room that must have been the library. The ceiling was beamed and tall, at least ten feet to the cornices, and every square foot of the room's wall space was occupied by built-in bookshelves that were crammed to overflowing. Spencer himself was ensconced in a low leather sofa that was one of a pair that sat on either side of a fireplace with an elaborate mantel in which a small fire burned. An oxygen tank and a breathing mask sat near the end of the sofa farthest from the fireplace, and a pack of unfiltered Camels lay on the coffee table.

Spencer rose to his feet and held out his hand. He was tall, perhaps six-four, and a bit portly with a full head of gray hair and a pencil-line mustache. Other than his smile, which I found annoyingly prissy, he seemed like an affable enough fellow—a dignified, elderly uncle who served as the family patriarch and storyteller.

"Call if you need anything," Mrs. Spencer said.

"Don't trouble yourself, dear," he said. "We'll be fine."

"I'm County Sheriff Bo Handel," I said. "And this is Deputy Eva Mendoza."

"Welcome to you both. Please sit down and make yourselves comfortable. I'm more than happy to have a little company. I'm taking a break from a treatise I'm working on about the disease of liberalism."

"Oh, really?" I asked.

"Yes, and I don't mean just liberalism as the word is commonly used today, that is to designate those to the left of center on our current domestic politics. I'm talking about the whole rickety edifice of contemporary political thought that began in the eighteenth century with all those declarations of the so-called natural rights of man. If one is astute, one realizes that what passes as conservatism today is merely the right wing of liberalism. There simply are no true conservatives anymore."

"You don't believe in human rights?" I asked.

"I believe in those rights a man can secure to himself and his race by the force of will. All other notions of rights are delusions that originated in Christianity, which is nothing more than a Jewish plot to enslave the Aryan peoples."

He looked across at Eva. "You are Catholic, are you not, Miss Mendoza?" he asked.

She nodded.

"And you, Sheriff?" he asked.

"Fifth-generation Presbyterian."

He nodded sagely. "Both are relatively dignified as salvation shops go, but both are destructive of our culture."

"What do you have against churches?" Eva asked.

"What I have against them is that Christianity encourages belief in the redemptive value of meekness and forgiveness and other such hallucinations. Also, Christianity manifests a fascination with whatever is lowly, inferior, deformed, and degenerate. This perverted obsession with biological refuse wouldn't even make sense if there actually was a god who urged it on mankind, which, of course, there isn't."

"Are you talking about retarded people when you say 'biological refuse'?" Eva asked.

"Among others. The malignantly deformed as well. A sane society would euthanize such creatures shortly after birth if they had not already been diagnosed and aborted in the womb. Sympathy with such waste is alien to the Aryan temperament. However, this misplaced sympathy is only one of the weapons the Jew uses against us. There are others."

"What might they be?" I asked.

He was warming to his subject. Obviously he was a man who loved to hold forth on his theories. "The most effective is liberal guilt. The Aryan is a natural warrior. It is in his genetic makeup to conquer nature through philosophy and science, both of which he invented, by the way. It is also in his makeup to conquer and enslave the lesser races through the force of arms. However, the Aryan has a finely developed sense of compassion toward others that is lacking in his inferiors. Through the diabolical manipulation of this noble quality, the Jew has been able to make the Aryan ashamed of his greatest accomplishments."

He stopped speaking for a moment, then quoted in a sonorous voice, "'Blessed are the strong, for they shall possess the earth. Cursed are the weak, for they shall inherit the yoke.' Do you have any idea who said that, Sheriff Handel?" he asked me, no doubt rhetorically, not expecting an answer.

"Ragnar Redbeard," I said.

His face showed surprise. He was so accustomed to knowing more than anyone else that it was disconcerting for him to find anyone who knew anything at all.

"That's right, but—"

I cut him off. "Ragnar Redbeard was the pen name for somebody who wrote a book called *Might Is Right* back in the late nineteenth century. Some people claim Redbeard was really Jack London, but I don't buy that. I think he had to be some pencil-necked little clerk, vicariously indulging his fascination for the kind of violence you couldn't have paid him to get within a mile of. I always imagined him there at his cubbyhole at work, scribbling away on his lunch break, sipping his tepid bullion and nibbling his watercress sandwich, writing about starlit Valhallas and victorious warriors drinking mead from the skulls of fallen adversaries. Then the bell would ring signaling the end of lunchtime, and he'd slip his masterpiece back into his bottom desk drawer and go back to nitpicking columns of figures for the benefit of other men."

"I suppose you could be right," he murmured. "Regardless of who wrote it, though, the philosophy is correct. Force and fear rule this world, and if we are to ever have world peace it will come through Aryan man imposing his peace on the lesser races. Of course, this can only come after the extermination of the Jewish blight. Have you ever read Yockey's *Imperium*?"

"No, but I know it's a fascist screed," I said.

"Fascism is merely another name for 'meritocracy,' which is rule by the fittest and the most able. But in his book Yockey points out that even the Jews, who work assiduously to preserve their own racial purity, have a scale of racial hierarchy. We can see clear examples of it all around in our contemporary world. Take Richard Snell up there in Arkansas. I trust you know who he was?"

"Of course."

"Snell was convicted of two murders, one a Congoid highway patrolman, the other a Jewish pawnshop owner. He drew life for the cop and death for the shop owner, thus proving that our would-be masters value a Jew pawnbroker more than they do a nigger state trooper."

"That trooper had an enviable record," I said. "Are you aware the he rescued a white baby from a burning car at considerable risk to himself? It was a little girl about fifteen months old."

He gave us a little laugh and the patronizing smile of a wise and worldly grandfather dealing patiently with his idiot offspring. "I would suspect that cannibal rescued her merely because the flames had awakened his ancestral dreams, and he fantasized baking her in his own oven."

"Why do you hate blacks so much?" Eva asked.

"I don't hate them at all. I just know that they are a separate and inferior species that doesn't warrant the same consideration I give my own. That is the great error the Aryan has made. He should never have accepted the Jewish fairy tale about the brotherhood of man."

"Nonsense," I said. "The proof that two animals belong to the same species is the ability to mate and produce fertile offspring. Donkeys and horses are different species, and while they can breed, their offspring are sterile. Humans can mate across racial lines, and the children they produce are just as fertile as the parent populations."

"That's old science," he said, waving his hand dismissively.

"Lamentably out of date, although such swill is still fed to youngsters in high school biology classes, which are nothing but propaganda parlors run by racketeers. No doubt that's where you heard it. However, even if you hadn't imbibed such drivel you would have still felt the same way because your attitude on the question of race is dictated not by reason but by your Jewish blood."

I was truly surprised. "My what?" I blurted out.

"Your Jewish blood," he repeated and treated us to another of his prissy little smiles. "I have researched your background rather well, Sheriff Handel. Are you familiar with your great-great-grandfather Johannes Handel?"

I shrugged. "Marginally. What about him?"

"He came to Texas in 1826 with Adolphus Sterne. I presume you know who Sterne was?"

"Of course. He was a close friend of Sam Houston. He helped finance the Texas Revolution."

"That's right. He and your ancestor were first cousins, and both were German Jews. He married your great-great-grandmother, and no doubt as a matter of convenience converted to Christianity. I have the documentation to prove it. Would you like me to produce it?"

"There's no need because I don't care."

"You should care because race is the main determinant in one's behavior."

"Oh, really? My maternal grandmother was half Cherokee, but I've never had the urge to scalp anybody."

"Perhaps not, but such a mixture makes you a mongrel, just like your pretty Mexican friend sitting there beside you. I'm not trying to be unnecessarily offensive, but that's the best word for it . . . 'mongrel.' Indian blood is Asiatic blood, and mixing Asiatic blood with Aryan blood never leads to anything good. In your case, Sheriff, the Asiatic component merely reinforces your Jewish genes."

"And how do you know you're pure Aryan?" Eva asked.

"One indication is my finely tuned sense of racial identity and my sensitivity to racial differences. You see, one of the strongest indicators of mixed blood in an individual is racial tolerance. True Aryans have a strong aversion to other races."

I laughed. "So in your view, being a bigoted jackass is a sign of superiority? Right?"

His face froze for a moment, but then he smiled again and gave me a minute bow of his head. "I wouldn't phrase it in quite that fashion, but yes."

"You don't believe in hybrid vigor?" I said. "All the agricultural people seem to believe that crossbreeds are more vigorous than the parent stock."

"Among the higher animals that idea is a myth. But take heart, Sheriff. Even mongrels have been known to achieve remarkable things. In fact, I do believe your ancestor may have been related to the famous composer, George Frideric Handel. You may not have heard of him, but you can look him up. There is no doubt that he too was part Jew."

"And just what makes you think that?"

"Certain structural factors in his music are very Jewish and not at all Aryan. But I won't bore you with technical details you wouldn't understand."

"Please don't bore me," I said. "Especially since music's not the main thing on my mind today. This morning I got a complaint from an old friend of mine named Lester Prichard. It seems that someone had come by his house and threatened him to try to make him take your offer on that twenty acres up behind your place that you're trying to buy."

"Why come to me? I had nothing to do with it."

"Maybe not, but a couple of your resident acolytes did. It was two guys in a blue GMC pickup. As it happens, I noticed a blue GMC parked beside one of those mobile homes out back."

"That's hardly proof of—"

Hi, Buck."

He pointed at the chair in front of his desk and continued spooning sugar generously into a large mug that held a couple of Constant Comment tea bags. A box of cream-filled doughnuts from the boutique pastry shop on the square rested on his desk beside the mug. In the place of honor in the center of the desk blotter sat a large prescription bottle that must have held a hundred caplets.

"You back on that crap?" I asked, indicating his pill bottle.

He gave me a serene smile. "I do like my Percodan," he said, pronouncing it "perky-dan."

"I thought you'd quit all that foolishness and joined the church."

"Well, I did. But that was a couple of wives back there, if you know what I mean. You didn't come out here to hassle me about it, did you?"

"Hell no."

"Glad to hear that," he said cheerfully. "Have a doughnut. There's coffee on that credenza over there. I like tea better when I'm cruising, though."

"Why not?" I said and filled myself a cup and grabbed a doughnut. I took a chair, and after he'd poured boiling water into his cup, he seated himself in his high-backed executive throne and stirred his tea languidly.

"Buck, how many times you been strung out on that stuff?" I asked.

"Lordy, I don't know. Whenever it gets burdensome to me I just lay it aside till the next time I get bored."

"Isn't getting off of it awful rough?"

"Not really. Kinda like the flu for three or four days. A little anxiety and a few stomach cramps. No big deal."

"Where on earth did you get a prescription for that many of the damned things?" I asked.

"The VA clinic. The Feds are apt to hassle a private doctor

"Let's be frank, Dr. Spencer. I know you don't have complete control over everything these clowns do, but you better get a handle on this before it gets out of hand. I won't tolerate that sort of threat made against a citizen in my county. By the way, who owns that blue truck?"

"A fellow named Delbert Hahn. I'm sure he would be happy to speak to you."

"Happy or not, he's going to have to talk to me anyway. You tell him to be in my office by noon tomorrow of I'll have him stopped and hauled in and his truck impounded. And tell him to bring his buddy too. The one who went to Prichard's house with him."

I rose to my feet and motioned Eva to follow. At the door I stopped, turned back and said, "That pawnbroker Snell shot? He wasn't Jewish. Snell thought he was, but he was wrong."

"I . . ."

"One other point. You obviously didn't research me as well as you thought. If you had you would know that I was only one semester away from a degree in classical piano from Rice University when I had to come home and take over the family business. As for old G. F. Handel, there's nothing alien in the structure of his compositions, either. But I won't bore you with technical details you wouldn't understand."

Once we were past the gate, I said, "That wasn't the sort of experience you have every day in Sequoya, Texas."

"It was the strangest conversation I ever heard in my life," Eva said. "No prelude and no fanfare, he just launched into his ideology right off the bat. Did you notice that one minute he was advocating the extermination of retarded people and the next he was babbling about how compassionate Aryans are?"

"Yes, I sure did."

"I think he's crazy. And probably miserable too."

I shook my head. "I don't think he's crazy. Or especially un-happy, either. Oh, no doubt he has some bitterness from some-where in his past. Maybe back along the line he was passed over for a promotion and some Jewish professor got the job instead. Who knows? But I think that all in all he's pretty satisfied with himself. The Feds say there are about thirty thousand of these hardcore white supremacists in this country, and he's famous among them. The intellectual godfather of the whole shebang, with all of them looking up to him because he's the most accom-plished of the lot. A great whale of learning in a tiny pond of ignorance, a man whose academic reputation lends credibility to their crackpot beliefs. Or so they think. I bet he gets a bunch of those guys over on Friday night, builds up a big fire, has a few snorts of brandy, and then lectures away while he basks in their admiring gaze."

"So you're saying that he's . . . What, exactly?"

"An asshole."

She laughed. "But that's hardly a scientific observation."

"Don't be too sure. A therapist friend of mine down in Austin says in some cases that's the only possible diagnosis."

CHAPTER EIGHTEEN

The next morning I found Buck Kaiser in his office at Caddo County Livestock Commission Company. Know locally in East Texas parlance as the "sale barn," it was a ver successful cattle auction owned jointly by Buck and Walter Durbin. He also traded in cattle and quarter horses and dealt in farmland. A hometown boy who'd been a year ahead of me in high school, he'd been my friend most of our lives. He was tall, slim, weathered, and prosperous enough to be called wealthy in a small community like ours.

That day he was dressed in a Resistol 100X beaver western hat that would have cost close to a thousand dollars and a pair of dark, hand-lasted boots that probably set him back at least twice as much. In between he wore faded but starched and well-pressed Wranglers and a red checked gingham shirt. The watch on his wrist was a simple, stainless Timex electric. All this was signa-ture Buck—the way he'd dressed all his adult life. Another of his signature characteristics was the bulge in his left front pocket, which I knew would be several thousand dollars in hundred dol-lar bills. The man liked to be prepared to move quickly when moneymaking opportunities presented themselves, and he well knew that nothing can cinch a deal quicker than the sanctifying presence of pure cash. He looked up and smiled. "Hello, Bo."

that writes a script for more than thirty at a time, but they let their own croakers dole it out by the bucketful. Ain't life a hoot sometimes?"

"Indeed it is," I said and sipped my coffee. It was excellent, some kind of fancy gourmet blend.

"So what can I do for you this morning, Bo? You aren't planning on going in the cattle business, are you?"

I shook my head. "I was out at Dr. Afton Spencer's place yesterday. As I was leaving I happened to notice one of your trailers out there. Just curious."

"No mystery to it. Spencer hired me to go up to Arkansas and bring a load of stuff down here for him. I left the trailer out there so they can unload it. Gave 'em three days since I got no other business for it right now."

"What kind of stuff?"

"Office furniture and computers, mostly." He rooted around in a stack of papers on his desk and came out with a yellow sheet of crumpled paper. "Here's the manifest. You're welcome to look at it if you want."

I scanned the sheet quickly. It listed several desks, chairs, computers, and filing cabinets along with sixteen crates.

"What about these crates, Buck?" I asked, pointing at the sheet in my hand. "What did they look like?"

"Hell, I don't know. I never saw the things. I just sent a couple of my hands up there, and they didn't even have to load the truck. Some other guys met them and loaded it up, then signed off on the manifest. That was all arranged before they left here."

"I really need to know about those boxes."

He gave me a baffled shrug and nodded, then swung around to the credenza and picked up a microphone. A few seconds later his voice boomed out all over the grounds. "Tyrone, I need you up at the office!"

A couple of minutes later the door opened and a big, tough-looking black man named Tyrone Mosby stepped into the room.

Tyrone was about forty, and except for two years in the army he'd been working for Buck since he was a kid. He not only looked tough, he was tough, and his devotion to his boss was legendary. "Hello, Sheriff Bo," he said in a voice that was surprisingly soft and gentle.

"Hi, Tyrone. I need a little information."

He grinned. "If I can, I will."

"That load you brought back from Arkansas—" I stopped speaking. His face lost its smile and grew hard. "What?" I asked.

"Those folks where we picked up that load don't like blacks. Not one damn bit. In fact, one of them called me a nigger right to my face."

Buck's feet came off the desk and he leaned forward. "Why didn't you tell me about this?"

"No need to. It ain't like it was the first time."

"Bullshit," Buck said firmly. "I don't aim for none of my hands to have to take abuse like that. Not black nor white nor Mexican. I'm going to have a little talk with this Dr. Spencer."

"Let it lay, Buck," Tyrone said. "It's business, and we still got another load to pick up from that place. I don't want to see you lose money on account of me."

"Wait!" I said. "You have another load to get for them?"

"Yeah," Buck said. "Some time next week or maybe early the week afterward. They say they have to get the rest of the stuff packed first."

I tuned to Tyrone. "Could any of those crates have held guns? Specifically, military-type rifles?"

His face showed no surprise at the question. "Damn right some of them could. In fact, they looked a lot like those heavy crates the gun makers pack M-sixteens in for the army. To tell you the truth I thought about that at the time."

"What kind of outfit has Spencer got going out there, anyway?" Buck asked.

"You mean you don't know?" I said.

He shook his head.

"It's one of those white supremacist, neo-Nazi setups."

"You don't mean it."

I nodded and said nothing.

"Who the hell is this Spencer?" he asked. "What's the story on him?"

"For one thing he's an internationally recognized literary scholar who speaks and reads about a half-dozen languages. The Feds tell me he's more or less the intellectual godfather of the whole white supremacist movement in this country."

"Then I know I'm having a talk with the man. I don't need to get mixed up in this kind of crap."

Tyrone spoke. "If that's all you want to know, I need to get back to work." He looked at me. "Tomorrow's Saturday. Sale day, and we already got several trucks waiting to unload."

I nodded. "Thanks, Tyrone."

"Sure," Kaiser told him. "You go ahead on."

Once Mosby was out the door, I said, "Buck, don't talk to Spencer. Go up there and get that load. I'll get a search warrant and be waiting when you pull in."

His face showed doubt. "I dunno, Bo. I mean, your say-so holds sway here in our county, but there's a lot of ground to cover between here and Arkansas. I don't relish the notion of transporting illegal weapons across state lines, if that's what's in those crates. I'd rather play it safe on this one. The Feds, you know."

"Buck, can you promise me you won't say anything if I tell you something?"

"You know I won't if you don't want me to."

"This *is* a federal case. Or joint federal and state I guess I should have said. You'll be perfectly safe on this one. I guarantee it."

He sighed and nodded. "Okay. If that's the way it is I don't see how I can turn you down. What do you want me to do?"

"When they call to make the arrangements, just treat it like any other business deal. Meanwhile, let me brief some people."

"The Feds?"

"Yeah."

"Then I'll go up there on this one myself," he said. "I might just crack open anything that looks interesting and have a look-see."

"I can't tell you to do that, Buck. But if such a thing happened I'd be very interested in knowing what's inside of it. I'll get back to you by phone this afternoon. And maybe you can tell Tyrone not to mention what we talked about."

"I will, but he's pretty closemouthed anyway. Here, let me give you one of my cards. It's got my cell phone number on it. That's your best bet to get hold of me."

"I owe you one for this, Buck."

He waved his hand dismissively. "By the way, how's Toby?"

I shook my head. "Physically, he's out of the woods, but he's still in a coma."

He grimaced. "I need to call on the family, Walter being my partner here in the sale barn and all. I mean with him being so close to Toby's sister . . ."

"You do that, Buck. I'm sure they'll appreciate it."

"Do you think his shooting might have something to do with this Nazi bunch?"

"At the moment I've got no reason to think so."

In retrospect, I wish I could have come up with a better answer. It was not the last time I was destined to have to deal with that question.

CHAPTER NINETEEN

I arrived at the courthouse to find Delbert Hahn and Leroy Fancher waiting for me. I waved them into my office, took my place behind my desk, and gave them a close examination. Both men were about six feet tall with regular features and neat clothes, and both appeared to be in reasonably good physical shape. Fancher was a little bulkier than his companion, and looked like he might have played football at one time. His face held a goofy grin, while Hahn looked a little apprehensive and suspicious.

Before I could say anything, Hahn blurted out, "Dr. Spencer says you're a Jew."

I shook my head with amusement. "Dr. Spencer is completely full of bullshit, and it wouldn't surprise me to learn that you sport at least a half tank of that wondrous substance yourself."

"Huh?"

"I'm Presbyterian, but that doesn't matter to us here today. What does matter is that I'm sheriff of this county and that I have almost three decades of experience dealing with guys like you. I also have the power to throw your asses in jail and charge you with a felony should I choose to do so. That's where you need to focus your attention. Not on my religion."

Hahn actually seemed surprised. "What felony?"

"Threat of grave bodily harm or death. That constitutes felony assault in this state. I'm talking about the threat you made to Lester Prichard."

"Hey," Fancher said, "Del didn't mean anything by that he just—"

"Did I speak to you?" I asked coldly, turning to look at him. He shook his head.

"Then shut up until I do."

I looked once more at Hahn. "Uh . . . Do we need a lawyer?" he asked.

"Only if I arrest you. As it stands now we're just having a conversation. So what do you have to say for yourself about your meeting with Mr. Prichard?"

"That old man wants way too much for that tract of land and we—"

"That's his right. Just like it's your right to put any price you want on your own possessions."

"I just thought a little friendly persuasion would—"

"You call threatening a man with death friendly persuasion?"

"You can't prove I did that," Hahn said.

I leaned back in my chair and regarded him with an amused smile on my face. "It would be your word against Mr. Prichard's, a man who happens to be a respected citizen of this county. Our DA is one of the most skilled in the courtroom I've ever seen. How long do you think it would take her to convince a jury of locals that a couple of out-of-town neo-Nazis had threatened him? See the problem you have?"

"I got a lawyer too."

I chose to ignore this childish statement. "Right now Mr. Prichard doesn't want to file charges, which is fine with me for the time being. But if you mess with him again or bother another citizen of this county, I promise you I can pressure him into signing a complaint against you in no time at all. After that your ass is mine. Is that clear?"

He nodded reluctantly. I turned to Fancher. "And what was your part in this affair?"

He shrugged and his goofy grin got even goofier. "I had no idea Del was going to get rough with the old man. I thought he was just going to . . . Well, you know, like he said. Friendly persuasion. I just went along for the ride."

"Did Spencer know what you were doing?" I asked.

Hahn shook his head. "No, and he was pissed off about it too."

"Good for him. That proves nobody can be wrong all the time."

"I think he's right about a lot of stuff," Hahn said.

"Nobody gives a shit what you think," I said. I turned my gaze to his companion. "So what brings you to this motley crew of Hitler wannabes, Fancher?"

"A meeting of the minds, I guess you might say."

I nodded. "What's the matter? Afraid that you and yours are going to be permanently relegated to the bottom rung of the ladder if blacks keep making progress?"

"Nah, I just don't like niggers, and I really don't like them mixing with whites."

"Well, you need to get over it," I said. "There're twenty-five million African Americans in this country, and they're not going anywhere."

"We'll see."

"What do you expect out of all your political involvement? What's the windup of it to be? I promise you that blacks aren't going back to being 'good darkies,' happily picking cotton for two cents a pound and crooning reassuring spirituals in the twilight of the day."

"Like I said, we'll see."

"Indeed we will."

He gave me another goofy grin and said, "So where are we on this deal, Sheriff? Can we go?"

I nodded. "But I promise you that if either one of you birds step out of line again you're going in the slammer and Lester

Prichard is signing that complaint. I won't abide threats against the citizens of this county. That's something you better believe."

As they rose to leave, Fancher said, "Really sorry about all this, Sheriff."

When they were gone I sat for a few moments in thought. Fancher might seem to be a clown, but one thing about him was disturbing. The whole time nothing anyone said touched his iron-gray eyes in the least. They were remote and icy, almost like they belonged to someone who wasn't even there.

CHAPTER TWENTY

About an hour after lunch Hotchkiss stuck his head in the door. "Come on in and sit down," I said. "Take a load off."

He dropped into his accustomed chair across from my desk and said, "You wanted to know about Crystal Henderson. Nothing has been paid into her Social Security account for over three months."

"Hmmm . . . Do you have a last known address on her?"

"Yeah, it's in Waco." He rattled off the address while I jotted it down. "But there's more. About a month ago her parents reported her missing."

"I'm not surprised."

"What's this all about, Bo?"

"I'm not sure. It may have something to do with that guy who shot Toby."

"Let me know if I can help."

"I will. By the way, I went out to see Dr. Spencer yesterday."

"Do you think that's a good idea? I mean we don't want to ring his bells and—"

"I really didn't have much choice in the matter. A couple of his goons leaned on a local citizen." I quickly told him about Lester Prichard and the subsequent meetings with Spencer and later with Hahn and Fancher.

"What's your opinion of Spencer?" he asked.

"I had read some of his essays online before I met him. No doubt that he's brilliant, but he isn't really mindful of details. For example, he'd done some research on me, and knew all about my great-great-grandfather, but he completely missed the fact that I'd been to college. And he builds scenarios that are plausible only if you buy into the completely unfounded assumptions they're based on. Did you know he testified before the Warren Commission?"

"Yeah, but I don't know what it was all about."

"He wrote an article in December of 1963 in which he claimed President Kennedy was a communist agent. If you buy that, then it becomes reasonable that the Soviets killed him because he was about to 'turn American' and expose the big plot, which is exactly what Spencer claimed was behind the assassination."

"I have a hard time with the idea that Kennedy was a communist," he said.

I laughed. "Well, hell yes you do, and so does anybody else with a lick of sense."

"Do you think Spencer really believes it himself?"

"I wonder about that," I said. "His followers certainly do. A quick Web search proves it."

"He really is a sort of a god to those people, isn't he?" he said.

"If not a god, then at least he's their Delphic Oracle."

"Well, Mack's my oracle, and he insists I get a few things done today. See you later."

After he was out the door, I called Bob Thornton to tell him what I'd learned about Crystal Henderson, but he didn't answer his cell phone. I made myself a note to call him again later.

A few minutes after Hotchkiss left, Maylene buzzed to tell me that Gabe Jordan, a local small-time businessman, wanted to see me.

I felt sorry for Gabe. The poor guy manifested all the glib, self-sustaining ignorance found so often in men of his sort. You knew just by looking at him that if asked to speak to the Rotary or the Chamber of Commerce, his talk would be a litany of half-baked ideas gleaned from hasty readings of *Reader's Digest* and various self-help books that had come his way. He'd quote at least one famous football coach, maybe Bear Bryant or Vince Lombardi, and when he did it would be in the hushed and reverent tones you'd expect from a scholar of ancient Greek deciphering the inscriptions on the Parthenon. In closing, he'd almost certainly make mention of some long-dead captain of industry once renowned for his dime-store wisdom, and then go on to leave his listeners with the impression that this worthy individual was at the very least the equal of Socrates, and perhaps even of Moses himself. He would also make frequent pious references to the "free enterprise system," which, while not really free, was, in his case at least, enterprising in the same sense that rodents may be said to be enterprising.

Besides his limping real estate business, Gabe owned the town's only advertising agency, a cubbyhole operation a block off the square that specialized in printed matchbook covers, cheap give-away ballpoint pens, and parking lot flyers. I knew he'd never be very successful. I knew that he'd never drive that big fine car or live in that big house or have any of the other outward trappings of wealth so many of his kind push themselves into early graves scrabbling after. I knew too that despite all his hustling and huck-stering, he'd probably remain a noisy little mouse nibbling around the outer edges of the Great Capitalist Pie—a little tired, a little baffled, and ultimately, more than a little sad. Yet, damn it all, he had a good heart and I couldn't help but like him.

As he came through the door, he gave me a big, manly wave.

"What's up, Gabe?" I asked.

He came across the room and treated me to his most vigorous handshake. I motioned for him to sit.

"How's life, Bo?" he asked.

"Busy, busy. What's on your mind?"

"I heard you're buying that custom home Bud Sample got stuck with," he said. "I figured you must be getting it as a rental property, and I thought maybe you'd need a little help with the property management."

I shook my head. "I'm selling it to my son and putting the note in his kids' trust. He's moving back to town."

His face fell. "Gee, I'm happy for Keith, but I'd hoped . . ."

Seeing his crushed expression, I dived impulsively into something I'd been thinking about doing anyway. "I've got a better deal for you," I said.

"Really?"

"Damn right. I intend to cash a couple of CDs, but I'm going to have to either sell some stocks in a down market or borrow about twenty thousand over at the bank to come up with the last of the purchase price. Remember that fifteen acres I've got over on the north side of Nacogdoches you asked me about last year?"

"Sure."

"I think it's about time to let that tract go. Want the listing?"

"Hell yes. I may already know a buyer. There're developments planned within a half mile of that acreage already. How much do you want for it?"

"What do you think?"

"I wouldn't think of taking less than ten thousand an acre if I was you."

That was more than I'd expected. I nodded. "Do you really think you can get that much?"

"I do. And pretty quick, too."

"If worse came to worse, I would take eight."

"Let's not think about that happening," he said.

"Then bring me a listing contract by here tomorrow and we'll do it."

"Gee, Bo, this is great. This will be my biggest commission ever, bigger even than the fee I split with Joe Duncan on that tract we sold to that Dr. Spencer out there on the north end of the county."

"Whoa! You sold that tract to Spencer?"

"Yeah, sure. They came to me, and I took the deal to Joe. He had the property listed."

"But why didn't they go to Joe?"

"His sign had got knocked over, and they didn't know he had the listing. They just picked the first local Realtor they came to. Joe cut me in on the deal because I was free to do all the legwork. He had to go to Houston for a few days, and they wanted to move fast."

"You said 'they' came to you," I said. "Who did you mean?"

"Dr. Spencer and Mr. Scobine."

"Who in the hell is Mr. Scobine?"

"Herman Scobine. He's from up north. Vermont, I think. He and Spencer seemed to be partners."

I quickly jotted down the name.

"Did I do something wrong, Bo?"

"No. Don't worry about it."

"You know, somehow I got the notion that Scobine was the money man. Yeah, Vermont! I just remembered that it was a Vermont bank the check was drawn on. Spencer was moving down here from Arkansas, so the money must have come from Scobine . . ."

"Whose name went on the deed?"

"Spencer's. I just figured Scobine was financing the deal for him, and they were taking care of their mortgage arrangements privately."

"Good enough."

"Say, I heard Spencer was building some kind of foundation out there. Do you know anything about it?"

"Yeah, it's a neo-Nazi outfit. Don't worry about it. You didn't do anything wrong. Just go get our contract drawn up."

CHAPTER TWENTY-ONE

Gabe had been gone about thirty minutes when I got a call on the phone I'd bought to communicate with Jasper Sparks. "Sparks here," he said as soon as I switched it on.

"I assume you're in a safe situation or you wouldn't be calling."

"Bank-vault safe. I'm in my car coming back from Tyler. I'm about ten miles out."

"Then what you got for me?" I asked.

"Ever heard the name Jackson Knapp? It's spelled with a 'K' like 'knife'."

"No, don't believe I have."

"You need to get Winthrop to run it. The guy's been around for a month or so, but I just had my first real conversation with him early this morning."

"Describe him."

"Late thirties, tall, well muscled, short dark hair, mean face. He looks like he was weaned on a dill pickle."

"Anything else?" I asked.

"He's something of an instigator. I've heard that he likes to get these other guys all worked up with his bullshit. I've also heard that he's supposed to be a real heavyweight in the movement. I mean, you can hear anything, and some of these guys are full of it, but . . ."

"But you have doubts?"

"I don't know. Whatever his story is, he's serious enough to give me the creeps. And brother, there aren't many people walking through this old world who can do that."

I called Winthrop and left a voice message when he didn't answer. An hour later he returned my call, and I explained what I needed.

"I'll run this Knapp guy for you," he said. "As a matter of fact I was hoping to see you in a little while if possible."

"Sure. Come on by. What's in the works?"

He sighed a long sigh. "Would you believe the ATF is now involved in this investigation?"

"How come?"

"The attorney general's office wanted it that way. In Washington they seem to have infinite faith in the multiagency approach to things."

"No," I said firmly. "They have faith in the old nostrum that it's safer to share the credit so you can spread the blame if things clabber up on you. Did anybody in Washington think of asking if I'd be willing to work with them?"

"Apparently not. Are you?"

"If I have to, but my last ATF joint operation left a sour taste in my mouth. I'll tell you about it when you get here."

"Maybe you ought to wait on that until we have a little time alone. I'll have the agent they assigned to the case with me."

"I won't let that inhibit me one damned bit," I said. "In fact, I welcome the opportunity to let my feelings be known."

He sighed once again, this time in resignation. "Then I'll see you about four. It should be interesting."

A few moments later, acting DA Liddy Snow stuck her head in the doorway. "What's on your mind?" I asked her.

"How are things going on the investigation of Toby's shooting?"

"They aren't," I said, and ran down to her the story of the gray minivan.

"Maybe you should broaden the scope of your inquiry."

"How's that?"

"The Aryan League."

"Grand idea," I said sarcastically. "Do you happen to have any evidence linking them to the crime?"

"No, but considering that Toby is black and they're white supremacists it just seems logical there could be some possibility that—"

"Do you think that hasn't occurred to me?"

"Perhaps, but I just want to go on record as having advised you to look into the group in relation to the assault. That's all."

"What record?" I asked.

"I'll talk to you later, Sheriff," she said softly, giving me a departing wave.

I leaned back in my chair and pondered for a few moments. She was obviously laying the groundwork for something, but the question was exactly what? Tom Waller was right: It looked as though the time was coming when I would have to trim her sails a little, and I certainly had the means at hand to do it.

CHAPTER TWENTY-TWO

Winthrop arrived a couple of minutes before four with a young lady he introduced as Agent April Dee of the Bureau of Alcohol, Tobacco and Firearms. With a name like that, you'd think she'd be just a little bit bouncy and pleasant. If you did you'd be wrong. Everything about the woman gave the impression that she'd been stamped out of tin. About Linda's size, age, and build, and adorned by neither makeup nor jewelry, she was dressed in a gray pantsuit and a plain white blouse and had a face that looked like it would shatter into a thousand pieces if she tried to smile.

She treated me to a perfunctory handshake. After I invited the two of them to sit, she perched tensely on the edge of her chair like she expected the meeting to be unpleasant. Which made me determined to see that it lived up to her expectations.

I gazed at her quizzically for a few seconds, then said, "Why do I get the feeling that you are with us in body but not in spirit? Like maybe you're a little hesitant to get with the program?"

She shook her head and tried to make light of the question with a dismissive wave of her hand. But I persisted. "No, I don't sense that you're fully engaged here. If you've got a beef I'd like to hear it."

She gave me an offhand shrug and said, "Okay. Since you

insist, I must admit that I question the usefulness of your department to this investigation. I certainly don't mean to be insulting, but the truth is that I don't have much confidence in small-town, self-taught lawmen. I think this is a job for trained professionals."

"So thirty years experience doesn't count for much with you?"

"Thirty years of doing what? Chasing moonshiners and mediating domestic disputes?"

"Those domestic squabbles can teach you a lot about human nature," I murmured softly. "But never mind that. Since we're airing the sheets, let me give you *my* take on *your* agency. Are you familiar with a fellow named Albert Packer?"

"I've heard the name in passing."

I nodded. "Yeah, I bet you have. And not just in passing, either. Here's the story on Al. Five years ago we worked a major case together. He screwed up bad, and a young agent died because of his mistake. Understand that this wasn't a reasonable error of judgment that anyone might have made. It was sheer jackassery on Packer's part because he wanted to make a big splash and get a lot of publicity. I could have taken the fall for it and survived since I'm an elected official, and that was what he wanted me to do. But I have a few hard and fast rules. One is I won't hog another man's credit, and another is that I won't shoulder his blame. A woman's either, for that matter. Al had to bite the bullet and take his licks. The agency let him stay on, but it was a dead-bang certainty that he would never rise any further. Be aware that this was a man who'd once had big ambitions. A real golden boy."

She started to speak, but I held up my hand to silence her and continued. "As a result of my refusal to play ball, he harbored a grudge against me for three years. Then he tried to set me up for a drug bust by planting a meth cooker in a barn on my farm. Fortunately—"

"Meth?" she asked, interrupting me. "Why meth? We don't usually get involved with narcotics."

"Why indeed?" I said. "That's an interesting question, isn't it? But as I was about to say, one of the two young dopers he'd turned out as informants was a kid who'd snitched for me before and was more afraid of me than he was of your agency. He came to me, I went to Mack Reynolds, the FBI chief in Houston who's an old friend of mine. From Mack I learned that after his career cratered, Packer went on the take feeding info to a major gun dealer on the coast and my former snitch met with Packer several times wearing a wire. We had him dead to rights. There was a short standoff at the barn in which Packer forced a couple of young Bureau guys to kill him rather than face the music."

"You shouldn't hold it against a whole agency because of one rogue agent," she said.

"Maybe not, but I do because Packer should have been fired after he screwed up the way he did. Letting him stay on was setting a time bomb. So in my view you have to prove yourself to me instead of the other way around. Now if the pissing match is over, what can I do for you?"

It was obvious that she didn't like the way the conversation had developed, but it was equally obvious that she didn't see any profit in continuing in the same vein. Instead, she buckled down to business. "As you might expect, my agency's main interest is in the reports we've been getting about fully automatic weapons in the white supremacist movement. There seems to be some pretty strong evidence that these groups all over the country are arming themselves against what they see as possible oppression on the part of the government."

"I have reason to believe that you're right," I said. "It comes from inside information I've developed myself."

She looked surprised. "Really? How so?"

"A friend of mine hauled a load of office furniture and other stuff down here for them, along with several crates he claimed were very similar to the ones the government packs M-sixteens in for shipment."

"You must mean someone connected to Kaiser Trucking."

I nodded and went on to tell the two of them what I had learned from Buck. I also mentioned the load he was to pick up in Arkansas.

"I'll need to talk to him," she said.

"You'll get to talk to him. With me and Winthrop present."

"Why not see him on my own?"

"You do that and he's liable to sull up on you as sure as the world."

"What the hell does 'sull up' mean?" she asked.

"It means he's liable to freeze up on you like an old mule and refuse to go forward."

"Why?"

"Why? Because he's Buck Kaiser, and that's just what he does sometimes. He's got plenty of money and a damned good lawyer, and he relishes any opportunity to get ornery with people who try to push him around. He would especially relish bowing up at an aggressive young female Fed from up north."

She rolled her eyes. "Jesus! What is *wrong* with you people down here?"

I grinned at her. "Appomattox."

"Huh?"

I leaned forward and tried to be as sweetly persuasive as possible. "Look, joking aside, we're not going to have but one shot at this thing, and it's a godsend. Don't screw it up, please."

"I really think we should follow Sheriff Handel's advice here," Winthrop said.

"Then I guess I'm outvoted," she said. "But then he's not my informant, anyway."

I shook my head firmly. "Buck's not an informant. He's a solid citizen who just doesn't like an outfit like Spencer's roosting here in our county."

"So what do you have planned?" she asked.

I gave her a cold smile. "I don't have anything planned, but Buck does. On his way back from Arkansas he intends to pull off to the side of the road somewhere and see what he's carrying."

She shook her head. "You can't do that."

"I'm not going to. Buck is."

"But it's an illegal search . . ."

"I don't know that it is, but one way or another we'll know what's in those damn creates, if there are any in this load. Then we just get a warrant based on the info of an 'unnamed source' and hit 'em as soon as he pulls in."

"I doubt that we can get a federal warrant on something that flimsy," she said.

"Maybe not, but I can sure as hell get a state warrant. The judge here in town will give me one in a New York minute."

"I still don't like it."

"Can you come up with a better option?"

She sat lost in thought for a moment. "Not off the top of my head. But I wonder why they would trust a commercial trucker with the things."

"Deniability," Winthrop said. "That's my guess. If the truck was to happen to get stopped and searched between point A and point B, then it's their word against Mr. Kaiser's. Who's to say he wasn't hauling them for himself, or for a third party?"

"But the inventory," she said. "Surely there was some sort of paperwork on the load."

"Of course there was," I said. "But we all know that paper-work can be forged. It's not airtight, but it would give them a better chance of sliding by than if they were caught red-handed with the things in their own truck."

"I guess you're right," she said and glanced at her watch. "I'm afraid I'll have to cut this short. There's someone I need to see."

I gave her one of my cards with my phone numbers, including

my cell number, and said, "Call when you need to. And please stay the hell away from Buck Kaiser."

She gave us a two-finger salute, nodded, and said with a touch of rancor in her voice, "And now I'll leave the two of you to carry on your male-bonding rituals without me."

"Not a chance," I said. "We'll just be sitting here mourning your absence."

CHAPTER TWENTY-THREE

As soon as she was gone and the door firmly shut, I asked Winthrop, "What in the hell is wrong with that girl? She's got a chip on her shoulder as big as Kansas."

"God, who knows?"

"One more thing," I said. "I've got another name you need to check out."

"Okay . . ."

"Herman Scobine."

"I don't need to check him out. He's pretty well known up on the East Coast, and the Bureau has a file on him, which I've read. He's a billionaire newspaper publisher and financier who is headquartered in Vermont. Long known for both editorial and financial support of far right–wing causes. He comes from an old Puritan family that used to virtually rule the northern third of the state like a private fiefdom. Over the last three generations they've grown richer but less powerful politically, largely because the family is extremely reactionary. Herman himself hasn't come to terms with the twentieth century."

"Ha!" I said. "We're already in the twenty-first."

"That's what I mean," he said. "But how did he come to your attention?"

"A Realtor I know here in town handled the sale of that two

hundred acres to Spencer. Scobine was down here when the deal went through, and my friend swears he was the money man behind the transaction."

"Now that does surprise me. This is the first time I've come across any connections between him and the white supremacist movement. I'll need to let Washington know about this. This is what I meant when I said it would surprise you who you might find hiding in the neo-Nazi woodshed."

"How old is Scobine?"

"About Spencer's age. Midseventies."

"I wonder what happened that made him get in bed with these people," I said.

"My guess would be what the shrinks call 'progressive radicalization.' It's an old story, and it happens to people on the left, too. No doubt he felt forced to move further and further to the right by the social changes we're undergone in the last fifty years. Civil rights for blacks, women's rights, the gay rights movement, the Great Society . . . Most of us adapt, but to guys like Scobine all these things have destroyed the America he grew up in. Then take his own family, which was heavy in manufacturing at one time. When he was a kid their workers were compliant proles and the Scobines took a paternalistic attitude toward them. They didn't pay them worth a damn, but . . ." Here he broke off and smiled cynically.

"But they'd see them through hard times," I said, "and provide a little money for medical care and so forth. Hell, I've seen that same pattern time and again here in East Texas."

"Sure. Then their employees finally unionized and turned what had been a familial, paternalistic relationship into a wholly economic arrangement. To the benefit of the workers, I might add, but the Scobines didn't see it that way. They saw it as a betrayal of an ancient and traditional social arrangement. It must have been traumatic for the squire to have to step down from his squiredom."

I nodded. "I bet it is." I paused. "I just thought of something else I meant to ask you. Are there other agencies besides the ATF involved in this investigation at the moment?" I asked.

"I don't think so."

"But you're not sure?"

"I don't know if I'm sure of anything anymore in relation to this mess," he said with a rueful smile. "Why do you ask?"

"Because I think Miss Dee and her bunch have a man on the inside out there at Spencer's place too. You know anything about that?"

His expression showed considerable surprise. "Hell no! What makes you think so?"

"She let it slip when she brought up Kaiser Trucking. Buck left one of his trailers out there for them to unload, and his name and logo are painted on the side."

"So?"

"You can't see the damned thing from the road."

"Ah-ha . . ."

"How long has the ATF been involved in this investigation?" I asked.

"Less than a week. Why do you ask?"

I quickly filled him in on what Jasper Sparks had told me about Jackson Knapp. "I thought he might be their man, but Sparks says he's been around about a month or longer."

He took a small notebook out of his inner coat pocket and flipped it open. "There was only one Jackson Knapp in the national crime data computer, so this must be him. His full name is James Jackson Knapp, but he goes by Jackson or Jack. He's been connected with Spencer quite some time. About fifteen years ago, he was one of the old man's students, but he never finished college. Born and raised in Minnesota. Ex-army Special Forces, small weapons expert. He's got a long list of minor offenses, mostly hell-raising stuff along with two class-A misdemeanor assaults. Been hauled in a time or two on suspicion of high-line burglary. Plus there's one other thing . . ."

"Yeah?" I asked.

"Word around the Twin Cities area is that in the past couple of years he's worked as an occasional hit man for a bunch of badass drug dealers out of Chicago who run the Midwest–Ciudad Juarez connection. Crystal meth and Mexican heroin. According to his file, he's the main suspect in at least three drug-related killings."

"Well, Sparks did say the guy gives him the creeps."

He smiled ruefully. "Isn't that something? You start out to investigate a few racist cranks, and before you know it you're up against a guy who spooks the toughest character the Dixie Mafia ever produced."

"Where's your sense of adventure?" I asked.

"Never had one. I just signed on to get a paycheck and a fancy job title to impress the ladies and make them a little more pliant."

"Did it work?"

"Well enough to get me soundly married to a Tennessee debutante. But since she's a competitive pistol-shooter, I haven't experimented any further."

I laughed. "If you had sense enough to marry a Southern girl I guess there's hope for you yet."

CHAPTER TWENTY-FOUR

Once again the weekend was upon us. Carla and I went to Tyler to visit with Toby's family at the waiting room, and Sunday she accompanied me to church for the first time since we'd been together. The county was quiet with only a few disturbance calls and one tavern fight.

Monday morning Winthrop and I met April Dee at Buck's office at the sale barn. She came in her own car while he and I drove out from the courthouse in my pickup. The conference didn't go as I'd expected. Instead, Buck had Miss Tinfoil cooing and burbling in no time. I shouldn't have been surprised, since he'd always had a courtly charm about him that many women found irresistible. I'd just introduced them when she noticed his desk and said, "That's a magnificent piece, Mr. Kaiser."

"It's rosewood," Buck said. "Mid-Victorian, made in New Orleans about 1875. I found it in a junk shop in Shreveport years ago."

"Did you refinish it?"

"Oh, Lordy no. That's the finish the maker put on it. It was hidden under about a half-dozen coats of old varnish when I got it. I started out with white gas and steel wool. When I got close to bedrock, I went to turpentine and burlap. Just worked it off layer by layer. Once I'd exposed the original, I brought it back to life with lemon oil and persistence."

"Antique furniture seems to be a strange enthusiasm for a man who runs a cattle auction."

Buck smiled at her. "Well, ma'am, I've got any number of odd-ball interests I've acquired from various wives along the way. I'm kinda like a piece of litmus paper where the ladies are concerned. I just soak up whatever they want me to soak up and take on any coloring they need."

She actually giggled at this like a schoolgirl. From then on the meeting went smoothly. She voiced no objections to Buck's plan to search the load for guns. After thirty minutes during which we each had a couple of cream-filled doughnuts and enjoyed plenty of that fine coffee of his, she showed no signs that she was interested in getting on with her day. Winthrop and I left the two of them there, chattering away contentedly.

"I thought they were going to go at it right there on that antique desk," he said once we were in my truck.

"You may think you're joking, but don't be surprised if you drive by Buck's house about midnight tonight and see her car there."

"Really?"

I nodded and laughed. "They broke the mold when they made Buck Kaiser. But if she hadn't complimented his desk right off the bat the whole thing might have gone south just as quickly."

"He's old enough to be her father."

I nodded and said nothing. It had just dawned on me that, strictly speaking, I was old enough to be Carla's father as well.

CHAPTER TWENTY-FIVE

Another week passed. Gabe Jordon came by early Monday in a state of ecstasy. The buyer would pay ten thousand an acre provided I would agree to cover the closing costs and provide him with a new survey. I was willing, and Walter was able to get a surveyor out to do the job the next day. The buyer signed a sales contract and put down a deposit. We scheduled both closings—the house and the Nacogdoches acreage—for a week hence at Walter's office.

Each day when I got to the office I called Latoya Parsons to check on Toby, just as I'd been doing since he'd been shot. I learned that there had been no change. During the week I fielded several calls from the media, one coming from CNN and another from one of the major networks. The presence of a white supremacist group in a county where a black lawman had been shot no doubt made the story worthy of a bit of national attention. I had nothing to report on the case and said so. Still, that did not stop the questions. My lack of progress made a small spot on CNN Wednesday evening. It took note of the Aryan League and showed a panning shot of the compound's entryway complete with Lyndon Till and his guardhouse. The segment also carried the announcement that the network was planning to air a lengthy program on the white nationalist movement early in February. In turn, this broadcast generated several calls from the local press—a strange case of the news itself making news. I had nothing to tell them, either.

Monday morning I went over a half-dozen reports, dealt with some scheduling problems, and then about eleven-thirty the phone rang. It was Toby's sister, Nelda Minton, calling from Walter's office just across the street in the old Sequoya National Bank building. "Bo, are you going to be there for a little while?" she asked. "I need to see you."

"Sure. Do you want me to come over?"

"No, I'll be there in a couple of minutes."

At a very young forty, Nelda was about five foot four, trim, sexy, and the same shade of café au lait as Toby with an added sprinkling of freckles across her nose and cheeks. For the past ten years she'd run Walter's office, managed his finances, signed most of his checks, and dealt with a clientele that was predominately white and often unreasonably demanding. Endlessly diplomatic, she could even handle those elderly female dreadnoughts who come in unannounced wanting to change their wills for the ninth or tenth time in order to disinherit whichever niece, nephew, or grandchild had been the most recently inattentive. She carried all this off in a fashion that left the client feeling like he or she had gotten valet service, yet she did it without wasting Walter's valuable time on the mundane and the pointless. I'd once heard her describe her job as walking a tightrope over a pond full of hungry alligators, which was not an inapt way of putting it.

"Coffee?" I asked her as soon as I got her seated in front of my desk.

"Please," she replied.

I poured us each a cup and made my way around behind my desk. "What's on your mind?"

"You've heard of Reverend Lucas Dawkins, haven't you?" she asked.

"Oh, shit," I said with a groan as I lowered myself into my chair. Dawkins was a sort of bush league Al Sharpton, a man determined to profit from the rapidly fading remnants of the Civil Rights Movement by stirring up racial unrest and discontent wherever he could. I'd first become aware of him when he tried unsuccessfully to insert himself into the media frenzy that accompanied the dragging death of James Byrd Jr. down at Jasper a decade or so earlier. Since that time he'd improved his approach and had become fairly adept at attracting press attention, as much as anything because he made allegations far wilder and more outrageous than even Sharpton was prone to make. He'd been featured a couple of times in the national press, and had even enjoyed a short tenure as a network commentator until a blizzard of lawsuits forced his employers to let him go.

"Dawkins called my dad last night," Nelda said. "He was fishing around to see if the family had any complaints about the way you'd handled the investigation of the shooting. Daddy told him to take a hike. It might not go any further than that except that one of the major networks is doing a feature story on that group of white nationalists who've set up shop out on the north side of the county. That means the network reporters are in town, and Dawkins is trying to generate as much attention for himself as he can. He's making an announcement at noon today, right outside on the front portico of the courthouse. He also told Daddy that he got CNN to send a crew down to cover it."

"What kind of announcement?"

"From what he said, Daddy thinks he'll charge that you're dragging your feet on the investigation because some of that Aryan League bunch is involved and you're afraid of them. Either that, or that you're a racist yourself."

"About what I would have expected."

She nodded. "You need to prepare a press release of your own."

"No."

"Why not?"

"Because that's exactly what he wants. He hopes to engage me in a war of words through the press, and if I fall into that trap there's no end to it. All I'd be doing is generating more publicity for him by defending myself. Besides, I don't answer to Lucas Dawkins or to CNN. I answer to the voters of this county."

"Bo—"

"No," I said with a shake of my head.

"You'd think that the media people would have sense enough to know you would never have made him chief deputy in the first place if you were a racist."

"You'd think so, but sensational allegations sell better than facts."

"I still feel like I should do something," she said. "This isn't right."

"You can. Have lunch with me at the Caravan."

We finished our coffee, ducked out the side entrance, and drove to the restaurant in my pickup. Thirty minutes later the media followed us there in the person of my niece, Sheila. We were half-way through our meal when she slid into the other side of the booth beside Nelda.

"Can I buy you lunch?" I asked her.

"Coffee, maybe. I'm not hungry."

I signaled the waitress to bring over the pot and another cup.

"Is the big media event all over?" Nelda asked.

Sheila nodded.

"Don't keep us in suspense," Nelda said. "What did he say?"

She laughed. "He took the high road and inferred that Bo's a coward instead of a bigot."

"I'm mighty happy about that," I said. "Thrilled to death."

"Well, actually he said that his *preferred* interpretation was that the Aryan League is just too much for you to handle. He left the possibility of bigotry on the table for future use if you don't come up to his standards. He also suggested that you call on the state and federal authorities for help."

"I've already got the state and federal cops helping. Bob Thornton has been on the case from the beginning, and Hotchkiss has assured me the Bureau's resources are at my disposal. The problem is that we have very little to go on, and it all seems to lead nowhere."

"Then my story will say they're helping you," Sheila said.

"Did you come to interview me?" I asked.

She shook her head and said, "I don't need to. I know you're doing your best, and that's just what I'm going to say. Maybe the wire service will pick it up."

"I wish you wouldn't," I said.

"Bo—"

"I'm doing my job, and I don't need to be defended by anybody."

"Has he always been this stubborn?" Nelda asked her.

"Ever since I can remember. But you've known him as long as I have."

"Not really," Nelda said. "I've known who he is all my life, but I've just gotten to know him personally in the years since I first started to work for Walter. I remember back when I was a little girl I was scared to death of him."

"Really?" I asked, truly surprised. "Why?"

She nodded at me solemnly. "A big white lawman with that big hat and fancy gun? What are you talking about? When you'd come campaigning to a church picnic in the black section of town, I'd hide behind my mama's skirt and peep out at you."

"I hope you don't feel that way any longer," I said.

"I don't, but it helps that you're close friends with Walter. Back when I was little I was terrified of you, and so were a lot of others. Some still are."

"I've always carried the black vote three to one," I said.

She regarded me with a patronizing amusement. "People can

vote for you and still be frightened of you too, you know. That's just the nature of the black-white situation here in the South. It's not you, Bo. It's what you represent."

"I represent the law."

"That's right," she said with a nod. "You do. And for a long time that law said that black people had to go to substandard schools and use separate restrooms and water fountains in public buildings and ride at the back of the bus. That law was enforced by white men in big white hats with fancy pistols, and woe unto any black man who got too uppity because there was no shortage of rope and plenty of limbs to hang him from."

"Nelda, I don't know what to say except that things aren't like that any longer, and I'm glad of it. We all should be."

"Of course things are much better now. For one thing, the three of us can sit here and enjoy a meal together without winding up in jail." She reached across the table and patted my hand. "I'm not dumping on you, Bo. I'm just giving you a little insight into something you obviously weren't aware of."

"I'm sure sorry I ever scared you. I sure didn't mean to."

"Don't worry about it."

Before I could insert my foot any further into my mouth, Reverend Dawkins and his entourage came into the dining room. As the waitress was pushing two tables together to accommodate them, he looked around, saw me, and headed our way. He was a tall man, impressive in his own manner, with a long face, graying hair, and gold-rimmed glasses.

"Sheriff Handel, I believe," he said and stuck out his hand. I shook with him and said nothing. Next he looked at Sheila and said, "And here we have a member of the press, do we not?"

"My niece, Sheila Warbeck," I said. "She writes for the *Daily Sentinel.*"

He gave her a pleasant smile and looked at Nelda. "And you might be?"

"I suppose I might be anybody," she said, her voice tart.

"Ah, I see," he said. "Perhaps if—"

She cut him off. "But who I am is Nelda Parsons Minton."

"Then you're—"

"Toby's older sister."

"So you're the one who . . ." His voice tapered off.

"Who what?" she asked pointedly.

"I was about to say the one who works for the prominent white attorney here in town."

"Is that what you were about to say?" Nelda asked.

"Of course. What else could I have said?"

"What else, indeed?"

Apparently seeing no profit in continuing in this vein, he turned to me. "I just want you to know that there is nothing personal in my attitude toward you, Sheriff. It's just that when a black officer is wounded and—"

"I don't care," I said.

"Huh?" he seemed surprised.

"I don't care if it's personal or not. Attack away and have fun doing it. You don't live here, you don't pay taxes here, and you don't vote here. Therefore I don't give a damn what you think, and I won't be responding in any way to your allegations. Understood?"

"I would think—" he began.

"Understood?" I asked, more firmly this time.

He held up both hands placatingly. "If that's the way you want it."

"That's the way it's going to be. Now I see the waitress has your table ready. If you would excuse us we need to finish our meal and get back to work."

"Of course," he said with a minute bow. "It was a pleasure."

When he was out of earshot Sheila said, "You could have been a little more diplomatic, Bo."

"I'm not in the mood for diplomacy."

"I see Bo's point, Sheila," Nelda said. "After all the man came to town to attack him, so why be friendly with him? Besides, the very worst that could happen is that he might lose the next election, and it's not like he really needs the job."

"No, Nelda," I said with a firm shake of my head. "The worst that can happen is that I never find out who shot Toby. That would pain me a whole hell of a lot more than losing an election."

No sooner had I got back to the office than B. B. Holcomb, a detective with the Nacogdoches County Sheriff's Department stuck his head in the door. "Hey, Bo," he said.

"Hi, BB. What's on your mind?"

"I may have a way to help me and you both. I'm on my way to Marshall to pick up a prisoner we've got a warrant out on, and I'm a little pressed for time."

"Sure. What can I do for you?"

"Yesterday we had a guy cop to a bunch of burglaries, and he turned these over to us."

At that point he set a cigar box on my desk and flipped it open. Inside were two finely wrought bronze figurines—a bull and a horned ram.

"He took these from that Spencer guy's house out at that compound several months ago. Word is that you're looking at those people, and I thought you might like an excuse to get in there by returning these to their owner. You can save me about an hour of my time if you will."

"Be glad to," I said. "It may be a couple of days before I have a chance, though."

"That's no problem. Just sign this property receipt and I'll be on my way."

After I bade him good-bye, I put the cigar box in my lower desk drawer and promptly forgot about it.

Later, in the middle of the afternoon, I was about to leave the office to go feed my horses when Maylene appeared in the doorway and said, "Some young fellow named Mike MacAffee from the governor's office wants to talk to you."

Gritting my teeth, I picked up the phone to hear an eager, brisk voice say, "Sheriff Handel, I'm Mike MacAffee with the governor's office and—"

"My secretary already told me that. What do you want?"

"Oh, well . . . Yes, as a matter of fact the reason I was calling is that the governor would like to feel that everything possible is being done to bring Deputy Parsons's assailant to justice."

"Then tell him to go ahead and feel that way. I'm not stopping him."

"Uh . . . Did you happen to see the early afternoon spot CNN did on Sequoya and the situation up there?"

"No, I didn't see it. We generally work in the afternoons. And we don't have a situation here."

"Reverend Dawkins was featured and—"

"Reverend Dawkins is a horse's ass. Why would the governor care what he has to say?"

"Sheriff, you're not being reasonable. The governor wants—"

"The governor wants to cover his butt with the public, and particularly with the state's black population. I can sympathize with his problem, but it's not my problem. So here's what you can tell the governor. Tobias Parsons is the best chief deputy I've ever had. He is also a personal friend of mine, and so are his father and his sister. His dad is a prominent local minister who's been one of my strongest supporters since I first ran for office almost thirty years ago. I just had lunch with his sister. She's office manager and paralegal for my closest friend. In light of all that, can you think of any reason I wouldn't be doing my dead-level best to find out who shot him?"

I'd found myself getting progressively madder as I spoke and was just about to explode.

"But, Sheriff—"

I cut him off once again. "Son, at this point I'm going to hang up before one of us says something we'll both regret."

I slammed the receiver down and yelled, "Damn, damn, damn, damn!"

A moment later Maylene stuck her head through the doorway and said, "What in the world?"

"Politics," I said.

"I suppose you were rude to the governor's aide?"

"I suppose you're right."

"Well, I can't say that I blame you. We can tend to our own knitting up here without any help out of Austin."

I stared at her with frank astonishment. "Do you mean you're actually agreeing one hundred percent with something I've done?"

"Yeah, I am, but don't let it go to your head, Bo." With that announcement she executed a perfect about-face and stalked from the room.

I was just about to leave fifteen minutes later when Bob Thornton appeared in the doorway, his face grim. "What's going on?" I asked.

"Crystal Henderson has turned up. Dead, as a matter of fact."

"I'm sorry to hear it, but it's no big surprise."

"No, I've been expecting it since her parents reported her missing."

"Where did they find her?"

"An old boy was doing a little late season deer hunting down in Montgomery County, and he came across the body. It was pretty decomposed, but she had her driver's license in her pocket and her parents have identified a bracelet and a ring she was wearing. They're going to do dental and DNA, but it's her all right enough."

"How long ago was she killed?"

"About three weeks the pathologist says. She was shot twice in the back. There's not enough evidence to tell if she was killed at the site, or if she was hauled there and dumped. The local Ranger is working the case, but he doesn't have much to go on. They found one bullet and the Feds are running it against previous crimes. But you and I both know who did her."

"Yeah," I said. "Bart Simpson."

He nodded thoughtfully. "So we have the silver minivan connected to the Henderson girl and to Dual's murder as well. Same guy, but he doesn't know that we know about the van. And even if he did, he has sense enough to know that there are plenty of silver vans and knowing is a long way from proving."

"Right you are."

"So given all that, it's pretty obvious why he shot Toby."

"I'm already there, Bob. He's not worried about getting convicted on Dual or the Henderson girl. He shot Toby because he can't even afford to get arrested. There's something else back down the road behind him a ways that could really turn around and bite him if he was hauled in and had his prints run through national."

"I wonder what in the name of thunder it could be," he said.

"Something bad enough that he didn't think twice about trying to kill a cop over it."

A little before my bedtime, Carla knocked on the kitchen door. "You need to watch the ten p.m. news out of Lufkin," she said.

"Sure. Come on in and watch it with me."

The first pertinent segment came halfway through the broadcast. It was Reverend Dawkins and his press conference. He said nothing I hadn't expected, but actually hearing it with the Caddo County courthouse portico in the background was grating. The segment that immediately followed Dawkins's spot was even more grating. It showed Acting DA Liddy Snow in her office on the third floor, and the gist of the matter was her claiming that Dawkins's charges were superfluous because she had *instructed* me several days earlier to widen my investigation to take in the Aryan League.

"Aren't you going to blow up?" Carla asked once the spot was over.

"No, but I'm going to have a drink. Do you want one?"

"Why not? I thought I'd stay over tonight."

"Wonderful," I said and put my arm around her and steered her toward the kitchen.

"Are you going to have a talk with her?"

"Of course."

"What will you say?"

"Nothing she wants to hear, I can promise you that."

CHAPTER TWENTY-SIX

The next morning Carla was gone when I woke up. I rose late and had a leisurely breakfast at the Caravan. The day before I'd noticed that the court docket was empty for the day, and I had every reason to expect Ms. Snow to be in her office. When I arrived at the courthouse I first read over the evening reports, had another cup of coffee, then called her secretary and told her I would expect her boss in my office in five minutes, no excuses accepted. Then I hung up before I got a response I might not like.

In her midthirties, Liddy was tall, slim, blond, and stylish. Unlike most attorneys who adopt more aggressive persona inside the courtroom than out, she was at her most abrasive in her day-to-day business. Once before the bar, she became the Girl Scout with the most merit badges, the hospital candy-striper who delighted in helping the old ladies with their breakfasts—calm, feminine, and sweetly brilliant—just what East Texas juries liked in a female lawyer. She was also possessed of boundless ambition, and I knew for a fact that she had her eye on a congressional run in a few years when our aging congressman finally retired. Now it was time for her to acquire a little prudence and restraint to complement her other virtues.

"I'm not used to being summoned like some servant," she said, her voice cold.

"Calm down and sit down. When I have something unpleasant to communicate, I prefer to do it on my own turf."

She took the chair across from my desk and perched uneasily on its edge. "And this is going to be unpleasant?" she asked.

"For me it is. Do you remember a thug named Farley Mott that you prosecuted two years ago?"

"Sure. Felony larceny. I lost the case, but I shouldn't have."

"Well, Mr. Mott felt that you went after him a little too aggressively. Afterward he was so hell-bent on revenge that he hired a Mexican PI to do a considerable amount of clandestine photography of you when you were on vacation down at Cancún. Even to the extent of putting a fiber optics camera in your room."

She turned pale. "Oh my God!"

I nodded. "Right you are."

She buried her face in her hands and shook her head. "I'm not . . . I mean, I'm dating a man now. That trip was right after my divorce, and I was hurt and confused. I thought that woman was my friend, but she took advantage of me."

"We all do foolish things at times. But I didn't have you come down here today to lecture you on morality."

"Then what is your purpose? Blackmail?"

I shook my head. "Absolutely not. No one will ever hear it from me. Or from Toby. But I did want to impress on you the fact that you just flat owe the both of us."

"Toby? Why?"

"Mott knew that you and Toby had clashed a couple of times, which made him think that Toby would like to preside over your undoing. Damned foolishness on his part. Toby played along and convinced him that I had several bones to pick with you as well. Then he set up a meeting for the three of us here at the office. Once we got him in here, we locked the doors and pecked him on the head a few times to focus his attention on the business at hand. After that, we were able to get across to him that Caddo County was about the last place he wanted to take up permanent residence. The long and short of the matter is that we got the photos, and we got what I hope was his only storage disk."

I stopped speaking and gave her a shrug. "I can't guarantee that, of course. But I do believe we were persuasive enough that we got our point across. I think we also convinced him how unhappy we'd be if he popped back out of the woodwork to bother you in the future. I recall Toby saying something about deep East Texas being the 'land of midnight burials in unmarked graves.' That's one of his favorite phrases, you know. He used it to scare the hell out of a black drug dealer from up north last fall."

"Did he really?"

I nodded. "I still laugh every time I think about the look on that fool's face when he said it."

"I thought Toby hated me."

"Not at all. You're a hometown girl, and Mott was an outsider. Aside from being a decent man who would never do something like Mott was proposing, Toby's natural sympathy is with the people he grew up with. The two of you were in the same class in school, weren't you?"

"He was a year ahead of me. We always got along fine until—"

"Until you became a pushy young assistant DA who wanted to run his business," I said.

She didn't respond to that. Instead she asked, "What happened to the photos and the disk?"

"I took them home that same afternoon and burned them in my barbecue pit."

"Thank you for that. I'm so embarrassed that the two of you saw me . . ."

"We didn't spend a lot of time ogling them if that's what's worrying you. In fact, we were both ill at ease just seeing them."

She gave me a deep heaving sigh of resignation. "Okay, fine, I'm in your debt. So what do you want me to do in return?"

"I'll get to that in a minute. First I want to tell you something that you need to keep under your hat for a few days."

She looked puzzled. "Sure . . ."

"Tom Waller's condition is terminal. Pancreatic cancer. He's never coming back to work."

"Don't say that!"

I nodded. "It's true, and it means that you'll be appointed to serve out the remaining two years of his term."

"But I don't want to profit from his misfortune. Tom's my boss. Hell, he's more than that. He's my friend. He brought me into the DA's office when he was first elected."

"I understand how you feel, but the only way for you not to profit is by resigning. Since you love the job, and since you are by far the most competent of the three assistants, that wouldn't do either you or the county any good at all. Tom would tell you the same thing."

"How long has he got?"

"Three or four months, barring miracles."

"That's so awful . . ."

"Yes, it is. I've known Tom all his life. His family goes to my church. My parents were his sponsors when he was baptized."

She nodded absently, her eyes fixed on some point of the wall behind me, her face stricken.

"But we need to be honest here," I said. "You're very ambitious, and I expect you to run for the office after you fill out Tom's term. You'd be a fool not to. All of which means that you and I have to come to some sort of understanding."

"I asked you want you wanted."

"I know you did. What I want is to be able to run my investigations without having to worry about your interference. I want your legal advice when I need it, but I want you out of my hair the rest of the time. That includes any attempts to manipulate me through impromptu press conferences like you pulled yesterday. And no more statements that you've directed me to do this or that. I don't work under you, and you don't give me orders. Do things my way, and in return I promise you you'll get all the publicity and credit you can stand. And believe me when I tell you that's the way you want it because sometimes I do things that you can't afford to know about."

"I don't guess I have much choice, do I?"

"Sure you do. Cooperate with me, and you can count on my behind-the-scenes support when you run for DA in two years. On the other hand you can jam me up and . . ."

"Expect the opposite, huh?"

"You said it. I didn't."

She nodded and stood and stuck her hand across my desk. "Okay. Deal. I don't like it, though. I can't help but resent being strong-armed."

"Which is exactly what you were trying to do to me yesterday with that press conference."

"Not really. I was trying to convince the world that we're capable of handling our own affairs here."

"We don't need to do that because we're doing our jobs. We answer to the voters and not to Dawkins or the press."

"If you say so."

As we shook hands I said, "By any chance do you remember what Mr. Sam Rayburn used to say about political debts?"

She shook her head. "He was way before my time."

"It was a favorite of his. 'In politics you've got to go along to get along. You've got to give a little to get a little.'"

"So you think that's a lesson you think I need to learn, eh?"

"It's one we all need to take to heart if we're going to stay in this business."

CHAPTER TWENTY-SEVEN

About an hour before lunchtime, Maylene buzzed me on the intercom. "Lyndon Till is out here asking to see you," she said.

That was a strange new wrinkle. He'd never come to me about anything in all the years that had come and gone since I'd fired him. "Send him in," I told her.

Till came through the door with some hesitation, ducking his head and moving slowly like a fifth-grader called on the carpet by the principal.

"Sit down, Lyndon," I said jovially.

He took one of the chairs in front of my desk and sat uneasily, twisting and turning his feed store gimme cap in his hands.

"What's on your mind?" I asked.

"Bo, it's hard for me to come to you. I mean in the past we ain't seen eye to eye on some things. Is there any bad blood between us from your angle?"

I shook my head. "Not from where I sit."

"Me either . . ."

He remained silent and stared off some place over my left shoulder. I'd been here before with country people hesitant to unburden themselves. I gave him my standard speech for such occasions. "Lyndon, I'm the sheriff of Caddo County, and I've been in office almost thirty years. I haven't held on to the job by playing favorites. You're a lifelong resident, and if you've got a problem with something you'll get the same time and consideration my best friend would get. Now out with it."

He nodded slowly, his mind somewhere far away. I opened the desk drawer and took out the V.O. and a glass. I had reasons for keeping a little whiskey in the office beyond self indulgence. Many a time over the last thirty years a dram or two had made talking easier for some frightened or embarrassed citizen. I poured him a couple of inches and pushed the drink across the desk toward him. Just having the glass in his hand seemed to give him courage. "It's that bunch I been working for out there at Dr. Spencer's place," he said. "I hear things."

"What things?"

"Stuff about guns and drugs. A couple of them old boys been down to the gatehouse a time or two. You know how it goes. They'll bring a bottle, we'll have a few, and they get to talking. Nothing specific, but I think they got some illegal guns out there."

"What gives you that idea?" I asked.

"A couple of times I've heard what sounds like machine gun fire up in them woods behind Spencer's property."

"Fully automatic weapons, huh?"

"I don't see how it could have been anything else. Then there's the dope. What do you call that stuff that gets you all excited and wild eyed?"

"Amphetamines?"

"I dunno," he said. "They called it something else."

"Speed?"

His head bobbed up and down like a fishing cork. "That's it. That's the very word they used. One feller called it 'amping up.' Said he likes to stay a just little amped up all the time. They offered me some, but I wouldn't take it. Hell, I don't need none of that shit."

"Have they actually mentioned the guns?"

"Nothing specific, but they talk around in circles. Just hints here and there. One time one of them said they'd be ready to take on ZOG when the time comes. What in the hell is 'ZOG,' anyhow?"

"ZOG stands for 'Zionist Occupation Government'—"

"Don't that Zion business have something to do with the Jews?"

I laughed and said, "Yeah, Lyndon, it sure does. They think Jews are running the country and plotting against gentiles."

He nodded again. "That fits. I heard one of 'em say that he can't wait to kill himself a Jewboy."

"Any of these guys got names?"

"The one talking about ZOG was a feller named Delbert Hahn. Another one they call Jack Knapp, and he's one mean-looking rascal, let me tell you. He likes to egg Hahn on and get him going."

"How do you react to all this?" I asked.

"I just sit there and listen. I ain't got nothing against Jews."

"I know, Lyndon," I said softly. "With you, it's blacks."

"You know, Bo, here lately I been doing a little rethinking in that area. I mean, I know colored folks right here in Sequoya I'd trust with my life, and I wouldn't trust that bunch out there with my fingernail clippings, even if they are white men. This whole business has given me some . . . What is it they call it?"

"Perspective?" I said.

"Yeah, that's what it is." He finished his drink and I poured him another. "Have you had any trouble out of any of those guys?" he asked.

"A little. Hahn threatened Lester Prichard over selling that twenty acres of his that adjoins Spencer's property. That was what I came to see Spencer about the day I ran into you at the gatehouse. Lester declined to press charges, but I think I put the fear of God in Hahn about bothering local citizens. So unless they actually do something overt that breaks the law, I have to leave them alone."

He nodded in understanding. "I'd like to quit," he said. "But I'm afraid that if I do they'll think I know too much about their business and come after me. Some them old boys are really bad-ass. I wish I never had gone out there, but I needed a little something to supplement my Social Security."

"Don't quit. Just be pleasant and act dumb. Socialize with them when they come out to the gatehouse, but don't seek them out and don't ask any questions. I don't want you trying to play secret agent, so don't seem too curious."

I stopped speaking and handed him one of my cards. "If you do happen to hear anything you think I should know about, call me on that cell phone number. Wait and do it from home in the evening where you'll be safe. Hang on for a couple of weeks and I'll arrange you some plausible reason for quitting. Maybe a bogus health problem. Until then, just act like a happy-assed old fat man, sympathetic with their views but unwilling to get involved."

"If you say so."

"Who's handling the gate today if you're here in town?"

"The guy that does it on weekends. He only wants to work a couple of days a week. I told him I needed to take care of some business here at the courthouse, so he said he'd fill in for me."

"Who is he?" I asked.

"Name's Boyd Bright. He's a retired security guard that lives out at the Corinth community. I don't think he's involved with their business, either. To him it's just a part-time job."

"I see. How much traffic do they get out there?"

"Not a whole lot. Some days nobody, then some days eight or ten visitors. When Spencer is expecting people, he calls down to the gate and gives me their names."

"What sort of people do they appear to be?"

"Well, some are women coming to see some of those guys.

And some of the folks that come look pretty well off. I mean, they drive fine cars and dress nice and whatnot."

I nodded. "You be careful. If it comes to it, I'll ask Dr. Dotty Fletcher to sign off on some health problem for you. She'll give you something you can show them."

He rose from his chair and stuck out his hand. "Bo, I really appreciate this. I probably didn't deserve this much consideration."

I reached across the desk and shook hands with the man for the first time in forty years. "Lyndon, if we started getting what we deserve they'd hang us all."

Not long after he left, Bob Thornton came by the office once again. After I'd poured us each a cup of coffee, he said, "That bullet out of Crystal Henderson's body didn't match up with any known crimes, but the Bureau's ballistics people think it came from a Browning Hi Power."

"Not much to go on," I said. "Not unless somebody gets arrested with an illegal gun and it matches."

"One other point I need to bring up," he said with a grimace. "I got a call from my captain this morning. He'd gotten a call from the director, who'd talked to somebody in the governor's office—"

"Aw, shit," I said in disgust. "Does it never end?"

"It has ended as far as the Rangers are concerned. This young fool from out of Austin was demanding that we take the investigation into Toby's shooting away from you. He made it sound like it was the governor's orders, but I don't buy that."

"Even so, the governor has no such statutory authority, Bob. And we both know it. You can run a parallel investigation, or we can do a joint investigation like we've been doing. But you can't take over without a court order, not that you would want to anyway."

"I know that, and now that young jackass knows it. The captain just wanted to make sure you were getting enough help from us."

"I hope you told him that I am," I said.

"I did. He offered to assign an extra Ranger to the case, but I told him that so far we haven't got a case. Are you going to issue a press release of any kind?"

"Hell, no! I won't give Dawkins the satisfaction. One of the city cops told me that only about a dozen blacks showed up, and they weren't applauding the man."

"He sure had 'em piddling their knickers down in Austin, though."

"Anything new on Delbert Hahn?" I asked, changing the subject.

"No, not a thing. You?"

"Yeah. He threatened a local citizen." I told him about the incident with Lester Prichard and my trip to talk to Spencer. "Lester didn't want to file charges. He's afraid of that bunch, and I don't blame him."

"What was your impression of Hahn?"

"He's an idiot. Sparks says he really believes that there's such at thing as the Zionist Occupation Government running the country, and he's obsessed with it. You mentioned him being tangled up in the meth trade, but I can't see it. If I was dealing in that stuff Delbert Hahn is one of the last people I'd want to know anything about any of my business."

"How about the other guy? I believe you said his name is Fancher."

"He'd like for people to think he's an idiot too. He may not be an Einstein, but he has a lot better grasp of things than his buddy does. I doubt that he buys into all that ZOG business. Sparks described him as a court jester type, and that's pretty accurate. But I think it's just a front, something he hides behind."

"The question is, what else is he hiding behind it?"

"Your guess is as good as mine, Bob."

"Did Sparks say anything else about him?"

"Just that he thought the man could be a real badass if the need arose."

"How about Spencer? What's he like?"

"Smart, well read, and full of crap. Full of himself, too. A little arrogant, a little patronizing. He's what I think of as a ninety-five percenter."

"Eh? How's that?"

"In order for ninety-five percent of his philosophy to make any sense, you have to believe the five percent that it all rests on. And that five percent consists of nothing but unfounded assumptions and crackpot allegations. In his case those assumptions are that the Jewish people are genetically programmed to scheme and plot against what he calls 'Aryans,' by which he means Europeans and their descendants."

He shook his head in bemusement. "You know, Bo, I'm your age, and back when I was younger I thought the coloreds ought to stay in their place. Now after all these years of fighting these old criminals, I've changed. I don't care what race a man is. If he acts decent, then I'm in his corner. What's wrong with people, anyhow?"

"Some of 'em are misguided," I said. "Led astray by people like Spencer."

"I reckon so . . ."

"And some of 'em just ain't no damned good to start with."

CHAPTER TWENTY-EIGHT

Later that afternoon Jasper Sparks called and wanted to meet that same evening. We decided to get together once again at El Charro in Tyler. As it turned out, it was the same time, the same booth, and the same waiter. And as he had been before, Sparks was waiting when I got there.

"I thought it wise to come over here," he said. "I knew this was going to be a longer conversation than I'd be comfortable with on the phone."

"The trip was no trouble for me," I said. "What's on your mind?"

"For one thing, I just learned that Spencer and company are hosting a conference in April. White supremacists are coming from all over the country."

"They had a few blowouts like that up in Idaho."

"Right. But this time it's for serious people only. No skinheads, no Nazi uniforms, no burning crosses, none of that silly symbolic crap. It's going to be a three-day affair aimed at the mind instead of the emotions. Just speeches, lectures, slideshows, movies. A learning experience. This is the function where Spencer plans to make his big appeal for unity. They hope to bury a lot of hatchets."

"Do you think they will?" I asked. "Bury the hatchets, I mean."

He laughed. "It would take a miracle. These guys are like medieval scholars arguing over how many angels can dance on the head of a pin."

"How many people are they expecting?"

"Around two hundred and fifty. Supposedly these people are the crème de la crème."

I shook my head in annoyance. "This poses a real problem for law enforcement. What if a couple of hundred black nationalists or La Raza members decide to show up and crash the party?"

"They have more sense than these goons. And another thing," Sparks said. "You're right about the fully automatic weapons."

"How did you find out about that? You must have penetrated the inner circle enough to get somebody to talking."

"I split a quart of Brandy with Delbert Hahn, is what I did. This was a couple of nights ago. The man does like his grog, and it gets his tongue moving. He says they have some more rifles coming in soon."

"How many are already out there?"

"I think about a hundred. AK-forty-sevens. The story is that they're getting them from some place in Eastern Europe."

"Where in Eastern Europe?"

"Hahn didn't know. My guess would be either the former Yugoslavia or one of the republics that broke away from the old Soviet Union. From what I've read both regions have sizable neo-fascist movements that are made up mostly of former military people. Guys nostalgic for that old-time discipline."

"How do they get them into the country?" I asked.

"Hahn claims they come through some East Coast ports. If that's true, I imagine some customs people are bribed to look the other way. Apparently some of the weapons are going to groups other than the white supremacists. Hahn says the people who are actually importing the damned things will sell to anybody with the money."

"I wonder how they think they can do crap like this without eventually attracting attention."

"I can tell you how," he said. "They feel omnipotent, just like I did in my younger days. And they don't really have a clear picture of the resources available to law enforcement these days. Particularly federal law enforcement."

Sparks leaned forward. "I'm not saying anybody is smarter than anybody else. I'm just saying that's the mind-set."

I laughed. "It's still the sheriff's posse versus the outlaw, as always. In the cowboy movies, I suppose I used to root for the outlaw whenever he seemed outnumbered and outgunned."

"It's still no less a game than it ever was," Sparks said. "You merely have to pick your side and start playing."

"Since you brought the subject up, how in the hell did you ever pick that side? I mean a man with your brains and all the advantages you were born with? Just what were you after that you couldn't have gotten . . . uh, honestly?"

He smiled, and I swear it was a smile full of sadness. "The lure of the money and the big cars and the easy living were part of it, of course. But back then what I wanted more than anything else was a big reputation in the character world. I wanted to strut around those old joints down in Biloxi and places like the Fan Tan Club in Dallas where the people hang out and have them all say, 'There goes Jasper Sparks. He's one boss outlaw, man. Mess with him and he'll take the bark off of you.' "

"That was rather childish, wasn't it?"

"Very childish, but since when did a high IQ necessarily match up with emotional maturity?"

I nodded. "Thanks for being frank with me. For the better part of my career I've wondered why criminals do the things they do. I'd say your insight is at least helpful."

"I had to be frank with you, Bo. I have no choice these days. My redemption, remember?"

His theological references made me uneasy. I was beginning to think he might be for real. "Back to the Aryan League," I said. "Are these guys planning some sort of immediate insurrection? I mean, with this many weapons—"

He shook his head. "Absolutely not. They're looking several years down the road, but they think it's coming, and they think it will start with racial unrest. This is just the beginning of their arming themselves since they think ZOG's ultimate objective is to incite the blacks and the Mexicans into rising up and exterminating enough whites to impose an openly Zionist dictatorship. Or at least so says Hahn, and he's in a position to know their thinking and begin doing some of it for them. Besides, this isn't the only white nationalist group getting and distributing these same rifles."

"Distributing? Exactly what do you mean by that?" I asked.

Sparks smiled a cold smile. "Spencer is calling this rally as 'a plea for nationwide unity.' That's *his* purpose, but do you remember when I told you at our first meeting that some of these guys had their own agendas that he didn't know anything about?"

I nodded. "Sure."

"They're making two lists of the attendees at the upcoming conference. Their objective is to separate out the more intellectual types who are committed mainly to political action. They're not interested in them. What they're after are the hardcore true believers. It'll be like one of those lakefront developments where they sucker a bunch of people to their grand opening by promising a nice set of steak knives or something as a door prize."

"You mean . . ."

"That's right. Each of the chosen goes home with a brand-new AK-forty-seven."

CHAPTER TWENTY-NINE

Back at home I stretched out on the sofa and called Winthrop. He didn't answer, but I left a voice mail for him to call me. I'd dozed off to sleep an hour later when the phone rang. "Winthrop here," he said as soon as I answered.

I filled him in on what I'd learned, including the rifles, the spring meeting, the whole ball of wax.

"Damn!" he said.

"What's the problem?"

"I'll have to relay this to Washington, and those people are already too deep in my soup as it is. God only knows what sort of aggravation this will lead to."

"You want aggravation, you need to move to Texas and get elected sheriff. Then in addition to having to sidestep you Feds, you'll have to put up with interference out of Austin, and you'll fight for every dollar of operating money with a bunch of pinhead county commissioners who want to spend it all out in their districts filling in potholes to keep their constituents happy. On top of all that, you'll have your own voters to think about—"

"I get the picture," he said dryly. "I'll let you know what the reaction is when I talk to them."

"You're getting awfully open with me to criticize the bosses the way you do."

"I'm beginning to think you're the only real ally I have in this mess."

"There's Hotch," I said. "He's of like mind. And Mack."

"Yeah, but Mack's in Houston and Hotch has marriage on the brain."

I laughed. "Good for Hotch. That's what life's really all about, anyway. Family and friends."

"I know. Talk to you tomorrow."

As I was getting dressed for work the next morning Buck Kaiser called. "I'm off to Arkansas to pick up that load," he said.

"Be careful, Buck."

"I'm just a trucker doing a job. Don't worry about me. I'm taking one of my Mexican hands with me. I thought that might rattle their chains a little less than Tyrone would."

"Which one?"

"Pecos Bill."

I smiled at Buck's curious nomenclature. The young man's real name was Alonzo Alejandro IV, but Buck called him Pecos Bill because his previous job had been at a ranch that lay just beyond the Pecos River out in West Texas.

"That's a good choice," I said. "He's easygoing, but you still need to tell him these people may not like him on account of his race."

"He already knows that. I'll call you when I know something."

An hour later Maylene buzzed to tell me that the governor's office was once again on the phone. Muttering dire imprecations, I raised the receiver to hear a cheery voice say, "Hello Sheriff Handel, I'm Mark Wilson with Governor—"

"Are you higher up the food chain than that little peckerwood who called me a couple of days ago?"

"Uh . . . Well, sir, I'm deputy chief of staff. I wanted to clear up any misunderstanding that might have grown out of your previous conversation with our office."

"There was no misunderstanding," I said. "I understood perfectly."

"Sheriff, if you would—"

"I understood that the governor or somebody on his staff was trying to get a quote out of me you people could use with the press. I wouldn't do it then, and I won't do it now."

"Sheriff, if you would just be reasonable for a moment you'd see that I'm trying to apologize—"

"You should be. I don't meddle in your business, and there's no reason for you to meddle in mine. By the way, do you really know anything about law enforcement?"

"No, but there's always a political angle to everything government does. Being an officeholder yourself, you should be aware of that."

"I am," I said. "But with me politics stops at the Caddo County line. Good day to you."

With that I slammed down the phone.

I looked up to see Maylene standing at the door, listening. "Did that feel good, Bo?" she asked.

"You have no idea how good."

Late that afternoon I was poring over my proposed budget for the year when I heard a soft knock on the door facing. I looked up from my paperwork to see Winthrop standing in the doorway. "Got a minute?" he asked.

"Sure. "What's on the burner?"

He took his accustomed chair in front of my desk and said, "Just what I expected to happen when we talked last night. The people in Washington want to wait until that big April conference for the bust."

"Why? More fish in the net?"

"Sure."

I snorted in exasperation. "Don't they realize how risky that is? These clowns are volatile. They could change plans at the drop of a hat and move those rifles out of there any day. If we wait and pull the bust in April and the guns aren't still there, what are we going to find? A few lids of weed and some diet pills? It's going to be hard to stretch that to cover a dozen guys, some of whom are theoretical types with no criminal records."

"I know, I know," he said, shaking his head. "To forestall any possible undetected removal, they suggested that you keep the place under round-the-clock surveillance."

"Bullshit!" I said hotly. "You tell them I don't like that suggestion at all, and I'm not about to do it. I don't have enough deputies to cover what I need covered as it is."

He gave me a tight little smile. "I have already informed them of your probable reaction."

"How about Mack? Can't he convince them we need to strike while the iron is hot?"

"No. The assistant AG who's running this operation is eager for a big splash."

"May the good Lord protect us from such folks," I said. "Okay, let's assume that by some miracle the weapons are still there in April when the bust goes down. What are the possible charges?"

"Possession of fully automatic rifles to begin with. The number present will be taken as proof of the intent to distribute. That will allow the government to invoke the RICO statute and charge everybody out there with an ongoing criminal conspiracy, though I have some doubts about getting a conviction in Spencer's case. Charge everybody except Sparks, that is. He refuses to even be jailed briefly to protect him."

"Refuses?"

Winthrop nodded. "We knew that going in. We don't hold all

the cards with Sparks, and we've had to accommodate him a little. Hell, it's reasonable. He doesn't want his name linked with Nazism in the papers, and I can certainly understand that. He's what the Brits call a 'decent, ordinary criminal.' He wouldn't want to be charged with child molestation, either. Not even to protect himself."

"That's fine with me, but I can tell you for certain that there's nothing ordinary about Jasper Sparks."

He nodded in agreement. We sat for a few moments, neither saying anything, both lost in thought. After a while I asked, "If the government is going the RICO route, I guess they'll invoke asset forfeiture?"

"Absolutely," Winthrop nodded. "Spencer and Scobine incorporated the Aryan League and deeded the two hundred acres to it. All Spencer owns is the house and the two acres right around it. No doubt the government will confiscate the two hundred acres under the RICO forfeiture provision. One of our forensic accountants traced the transaction. You were right. Scobine paid for the acreage. It won't really hurt him financially, but it will piss him off. He doesn't believe in taxes, and it boils his blood for the government to get a nickel of his money."

"How about the house?" I asked. "Will it be confiscated too?"

"I imagine they'll take that too, even thought the accountant says Spencer built it with his own money."

I shook my head and rolled my eyes. "That's what I thought."

"You have a problem with that?"

"I sure do. Let me tell you a little story—"

Winthrop smiled. "I've been expecting this. Mack said you like to teach in parables."

"They get the point across, so here it is. I was in the last year of my second full term in office when a woman who'd been raised here in town and had left forty years earlier moved back home and demanded that I open an old, unsolved case. Her husband had been killed, and the killer had never been caught.

Without boring you with the details, I'll just say that I rooted around in the matter and put some pressure on some people, and I found out that the old boy had met his end in a drunken brawl with a good buddy of his. Just a bunch of young bucks in their late twenties, cutting up on a Saturday night. Too much whiskey and too much testosterone. Technically, it was manslaughter. Morally speaking, it was self-defense since it was just a drunken fight, and the dead man threw the first blow. So what was I to do?"

"Follow the law," he said.

I nodded. "That's easy enough to say, and that's just what I did. The problem was that the incident had waked the perpetrator up. He never touched another drop. Became a model citizen, started going to church, and eventually had his own business. Everybody in town liked and respected him. I confronted him and he confessed. Since this state has no statute of limitations on manslaughter, I filed the charges expecting that forty years after the fact the fellow who was DA back then would be willing to go for a probated sentence. He didn't. He was a hard-ass, ambitious for better things, and five years was the best he would offer on a plea bargain. Even the victim's wife, once she knew the whole story, asked him to go easy on the man. He wasn't listening. Higher office beckoned, and he had his eyes on his scorecard. Walter Durbin was a young lawyer back in those days, and he thought he could try the case and get probation. He was wrong. A rogue jury came back with twenty-five years, and the windup of the matter was that a decent man died in prison for a crime he'd long since atoned for."

"And exactly how does this apply to Spencer? You're not expecting him to repent and become a model citizen, are you?"

"Of course not, but you've said from the first that he wanted nothing to do with gunrunning or any of the rest of that illegal crap. So when you boil it all down, no matter how much you and I both dislike him, the only things he's really guilty of are being a jackass and holding some toxic opinions. That's why I don't see any need in taking the house and turning an old man and an old woman out on the road with nothing. Twenty-five years wasn't a proportional sentence in that manslaughter case, and complete confiscation isn't proportional here."

He sighed. "What do you suggest one lowly field agent like myself can do about it?"

"At least talk to the assigned prosecutor and talk to the people from the attorney general's office in Washington. Try to get them to settle for the two hundred acres and leave the house intact."

"I'll give it a shot, but I don't know how much good I can do."

"You do your best, and I guarantee that you'll feel better about it in the years to come. I know because when that case was all over with, I realized that as smart as John Nightwalker was, he was bound to have known that old boy killed his buddy, and he knew the circumstances surrounding the incident, too. But he decided to show a little mercy. I've wished a thousand times since then that he'd still been around to advise me before I filed the charges."

"I don't doubt that you're right. But I think the AG wants to send a message."

I regarded him bleakly. "Tell him to try the post office. Or e-mail. Law and law enforcement should be for redress and equity. Justice, in other words. The notion of the government kicking the shit out of one guy to impress a bunch of other folks doesn't appeal to me at all."

"Between the two of us, I agree completely. But in this case I may not have any say in the matter."

"Just speak up and do your best. Then you can sleep soundly at night. Besides, that RICO statute is too damned broad in the first place."

"You're right." Winthrop stopped speaking and rubbed his face. "Hell, Spencer is crazy anyway."

"I don't know about that, but he sure as hell has some curious notions. He thinks I'm Jewish, you know."

"What?" he exclaimed.

I nodded. "He claims that my great-great-grandfather, Johannes Handel, was a German Jew. And he may be right, not that I care one way or another. I do know that he came here from Germany with a prominent Jew who was important in early Texas history."

"What difference would it make if he was?"

"Spencer goes by the one-drop theory. One drop of Jewish blood and my attitudes on social and racial questions are genetically fixed. He claims that's why I get along with blacks and Mexicans so well."

"I think if you go back far enough everybody has at least one drop of everything."

"Of course," I said and glanced at my watch. I swung my chair around so I could open my lower desk drawer. "Speaking of drops," I said, "the clock just passed five, so let's have ourselves a drop or two of whiskey."

"Best idea I've heard all day."

I got out the bottle and glasses and poured us each a drink. As I pushed his across the desk, I stared at him for a moment. "You look a little down today," I said.

He shook his head. "It's nothing."

"Out with it," I growled.

"I don't know how you've stood thirty years of this," he said.

"Thirty years of what?"

"The underbelly of humanity. People like these neo-Nazis. And what's just as depressing is all the damned political maneuvering that orbits around law enforcement. How do you cope?"

"Well, I'm pretty well grounded in the Presbyterian Church. The old doctrine of the complete depravity of the human race, you know. I just don't expect too much out of people." I stopped speaking for a moment and raised my glass. "Then there's the soothing effects of a dram or two of good whiskey every now and then. That and music. By the way . . . Did you get a chance to listen to the Schubert String Quintet yet?"

He shook his head regretfully. "No, and I've been trying to remember exactly what Heydrich said about it."

"He said, 'The adagio will tear your heart out.' "

"I'll get online tonight and order it. I'll talk to Washington about Spencer's house, too."

I nodded and we sipped our drinks in silence. No more was said on the subject. I had no doubt that Winthrop would do his best. On the other hand, I had little hope that it would do any good. Nevertheless, I'd kept a promise I'd made to myself many years earlier on the way home from the Walls Unit of the Texas prison system after making the most reluctant delivery I ever made.

CHAPTER THIRTY

I was just about to head off to bed that same evening when the phone rang. It was Buck Kaiser, but the Bowie County Sheriff's Department showed on the caller ID.

"What's wrong?" I asked.

"Well, Bo, I've got some good news and some bad news. How about giving you the good news first?"

"Sure, Buck."

"I decided to wait until we were back in Texas to check out that load. We pulled in at a little truck stop café just a few miles south of Texarkana, and I told Pecos Bill to go on inside. I figured that there wasn't any reason to get him involved in this business."

"That was prudent."

"The good news is that you were right about the guns. We picked up eleven of those crates. I pried one of 'em open and found an even dozen fully automatic AK-forty-sevens."

"You're sure they were fully auto?" I asked.

"Hell yes. I saw plenty of 'em in Vietnam. The fully auto models have a switch on the side right above the trigger housing to go back and forth between auto fire and semiauto. The semiauto version doesn't have the switch. Anyhow, I nailed the crate back shut and went inside to eat my supper. That's the good news."

"And the bad?"

"We got hijacked. The truck stop was crowded, and we'd had to park over to one side where it was pretty dark. When we got back to the truck there were two guys waiting for us with sawed-off pump shotguns. They took my cell phone first thing and then made us get in the truck cab. Then they dropped us off about fifteen miles down the road halfway between Nowhere and Even Worse. The south end of Bowie County is deep woods and not much else. It took better than an hour to walk to a house, and then we damn near got shot when we knocked on the door. Not that I blame the feller."

"I assume they had their faces covered," I said.

"Yeah, ski masks."

"Do you think you would recognize either of their voices if you heard it again?"

"One guy sounded a little familiar, but I can't place him. The other one was just a voice."

"Could it have been the guys up there where you loaded the truck?" I asked. "I can't help but think the rifles were the point of the hijacking. Who'd bother to steal a load of used office furniture?"

"It wasn't either one of the men we met when we picked the stuff up. I can promise you that. They were a couple of stumpy little critters, and both these old boys were big."

"How's it going with the law there in Texarkana?"

"They're nice guys. They're going to take us to a motel here in a few minutes."

"Call me collect when you get there and give me the address. I can have a car pick you up tomorrow morning if you want."

"I'd sure appreciate it," he said. "I don't relish the notion of getting on a bus since I've still got my thirty-eight in my coat pocket."

"You mean they didn't take it?"

"They never even searched us. I never got a chance to use it, though, and I wouldn't have anyway. One guy kept the muzzle of that damned pump in my ribs the whole time. One handgun against two assholes with shotguns ain't my kind of odds."

"I'm glad you didn't, Buck. This isn't worth getting killed over."

"My thinking exactly."

"You didn't let the Bowie County boys know about the AK-forty-sevens, did you?"

"No. I just gave them the manifest and they didn't ask about the load. And they gave me this little cubbyhole office I'm in now to make my call in private."

"I'll call and thank the sheriff tomorrow. Just let me know when you get to your motel."

"Sure. I'm going to ask them to stop along the way so I can get Pecos Bill a bottle of popskull."

"That won't work, Buck. Bowie County is completely dry."

"Damn, I hate to hear that. Bill's awful shook up."

"And you aren't?"

"Not particularly, no. Perky-dan does have its virtues, you know."

"I don't want to know, Buck," I said with a laugh. "I might like it a little too much."

"To each his own. I guess I'll just have to give Bill a couple of my pills. That'll take the edge off for him."

"I hate that this happened."

"Don't worry about it. I'm bonded and the rig was insured, so I'll come out okay. Hell, they might abandon the truck anyway. I think you're right about them being after those guns."

"Still . . ."

He laughed a little and when he spoke his voice was full of ironic reproach. "Just 'cause I'm a dope fiend don't mean I'm void of community spirit, Bo. If I have to lose a few bucks to help get this bunch out of Caddo County, then so be it. I'll make it back quick enough. Besides, it'll give me a good story to tell my grandkids."

I was already in bed when my cell phone buzzed once again, and when I looked at the caller ID, Latoya Parsons's name came up. I grimaced. I'd been over to the hospital in Tyler three more times, and I'd been calling every day, but this was the first time she had called me. With considerable apprehension I switched the phone to talk and said, "Hello?"

"He's coming out of it, Bo," she said. I could tell she was near tears.

"Thank the Lord," I said. "What do the doctors say?"

"It may take a few days for him to be fully back with us, but he's going to make it."

"I'll get over there to see him as soon as I can."

"There's no hurry. They won't let anybody but immediate family in there now, and then only for a couple of minutes."

"I don't care. I'm going to come anyway whenever I can catch a break in this mess I've got here."

"Thanks, Bo."

"No, thank *you*."

After promising to keep me posted on any changes she hung up. I switched off my phone with a tremendous sense of relief. Now if I could only nail the man who shot him.

CHAPTER THIRTY-ONE

The next morning I called Sparks as soon as I crawled out of bed. There was no answer, but he returned my call an hour later as I was on my way to the courthouse. "What's up?" he asked.

"Do you have any idea where Fancher and Hahn are at the moment?"

"Not a clue. They've been gone a couple of days."

Surprise, surprise, I thought. "Are they in Hahn's pickup?"

"I think so. It's not here at the compound."

"Let me know when they show up, would you?"

"That's what I'm here for. It may take me a little while to get some place safe to call, though."

"No sweat."

I switched off the phone. From the beginning I'd been convinced the hijacking had been an inside job. The rifles made the cargo worth the trouble while a batch of used office furniture and a few computers didn't. I was also fairly certain Hahn and Fancher had pulled the job. I based this on their backgrounds, Buck's description, and my reading of them as a pair who might have political convictions but who would also be unwilling to let those convictions stand in the way of personal gain. In short, I had them pegged as two guys who would eagerly screw their ideological brethren if there was a buck to be made.

What to do about my suspicion was another matter. I could put out a bulletin on Hahn's pickup and have them brought in, but such an arrest would be meaningless without bringing up the guns, mention of which would probably blow the case the Feds were building. There was the possibility that if I moved fast enough Buck's truck could be recovered, but he had insurance, and he himself claimed his losses would be minimal. In the end I decided to wait and check with Winthrop before I did anything. He didn't answer his phone, so I left a voice mail for him to either call back or come by the office.

In the early afternoon Linda Willis came into my office. "I thought you'd want to know about this, Bo."

"About what?"

"Remember that briefing memo you sent out on the Aryan League? Well, one of the guys affiliated with it just got in a big fight at the Roundup Club."

"Really?"

"Yeah, according to the people out there this League guy and Big Earl Chalmers went at it like a couple of pit bulls."

I shook my head in disgust. Except for a pair of giant identical twins called Gog and Magog Flannigan, Earl Chalmers was the biggest and most destructive miscreant in the county. He was six feet four inches of bone and gristle and worked in construction, an occupation that had given him biceps the size of my thighs. Known for fighting cops, he was pacified the first time I was called out to handle him a decade earlier by the simple expedient of telling him that if he ever assaulted me I'd just shoot him and take my chances with the grand jury. He must have believed me because he'd always come along peacefully whenever I'd had occasion to arrest him.

"I suppose the guilty parties left before you got there?" I said.

"Yeah, but the owner wants to press charges."

"What's the extent of the damage?"

"Three tables were ruined and the mirror behind the bar was shattered. One of the faucets on the bar sink was completely knocked loose. They had to turn the water off until they can get it fixed. Then there's about a dozen bottles of whiskey and two racks of glasses that were broken. That alone comes to about three hundred dollars."

"Who was the other participant?"

"A guy named Jack Knapp. And check this out. On every call we've made since Toby was shot I've been asking about that gray minivan. The bartender told me that up until a few weeks ago Knapp was always in a gray van when he came in."

This time I decided to use a little diplomacy. The two bronze figurines B. B. Holcomb had left with me still resided in their cigar box in my desk drawer. While Linda went to get one of the JPs to give her warrants on Chalmers and Knapp, I filled out a property receipt on the figurines. Then I called Dr. Spencer to tell him I was coming out to return his property.

I took Linda with me and went in one of the patrol cars. Our first stop was Earl Chalmers's place. He wasn't home, which was no problem since I'd intended to send him out to the jail on his own to be processed, provided he was sober enough to drive, of course. I went to each of the neighbors in the houses on both sides of the surprisingly neat cottage where he dwelt alone and left word for him to come to the office. I also left a note on his front door.

I pulled up once more at the Aryan League's gate, and once more Lyndon Till let me in, only this time he was much friendlier. As before, Mrs. Spencer greeted us at the door and led us back to the library where her husband waited. He too seemed to be in a less feisty mood than on my previous visit.

I put the cigar box on the table in front of him and we sat down on the opposite sofa. He opened the box and smiled. "I never expected to see these again," he said. "How on earth did you get them, Sheriff?"

"The Nacogdoches County Sheriff's Department arrested a burglar, and he decided to clear the slate. For some reason he hadn't sold them."

"He probably couldn't get much for them around here."

"What are they worth?" I asked.

"About fifteen hundred dollars each, but you would have to find a buyer who knows pre-Christian artifacts to get that."

"Why didn't you report the theft?" I asked.

He shook his head. "I didn't see the point. We were burgled the week we moved in, while we were shopping in Nacogdoches. This was before we fenced the area and installed our security system. Other than these, little of actual monetary value was stolen, and I'm familiar with the statistics on residential burglaries. I'm not being critical, you understand. I well know what you're up against fighting this sort of crime."

"What are those things, exactly?" Linda asked.

"They're from Persia, fourth century B.C. Just common house-hold objects, really. But they mean a great deal to me."

"If that's the case," I said, "their common household objects were better than ours. Even to my untutored eye they're fine pieces."

"Isn't it amazing what posterity values?" he said. "Just think, in twenty-five hundred years the salt and pepper shakers from your favorite café right here in town may find themselves in some yet unbuilt equivalent of the British Museum."

"I need to get you to sign this receipt," I said. "It merely ac-knowledges that they were returned to you."

"Certainly." He took it from me.

"Are you a collector?" Linda asked.

"No, but I've acquired a few things over the years that ap-pealed to me." He handed me back the signed receipt and said,

"Sheriff Handel, were you pulling my leg the other day about majoring in classical piano?"

"No, not at all."

"Then let me show you something." He rose to his feet and motioned for us to follow him. After leading us down a short hallway, he pushed aside a pair of heavy sliding doors to reveal a splendidly furnished living room at the far end of which sat a magnificent grand piano. "Do you recognize that?" he asked.

"Of course," I said. "It's a Bösendorfer, the Rolls-Royce of pianos. Do you play?"

"Not really. I had some lessons years ago. It was my mother's. However, I keep it in tune. In fact, the tuner was out here just last week. Would you like to . . ."

"I'm tempted," I admitted. "Normally I only play around other people when I've had enough to drink that I don't worry about how bad I sound."

"Go ahead," he urged. "Feel free."

I adjusted the bench, sat down, limbered up my fingers, then began the first movement of the Schubert B Flat Major Piano Sonata. I played for about five minutes while Spencer listened raptly, standing beside the piano, his eyes closed. Finally I stopped.

"Sublime," he said. "I know that piece well, and I couldn't detect a single mistake."

"I can. I didn't miss any notes, but my timing is off. I play some each week just for my own enjoyment, but I don't really consider it practice because I don't try to make things Julliard perfect."

I turned back to the piano. Thinking to annoy him, I broke into "Camptown Races." Surprisingly, he laughed and clapped his hands like a child. "My mother always ended each of her practice sessions with a honky-tonk medley," he said. "My father claimed it was the best part."

I smiled and closed the keyboard. "It's a wonderful instrument, Dr. Spencer," I said. "You should be proud of it."

"I am." Then, without a bit of the previous prissy arrogance in his face and in a voice tinged with what I believe was real regret, he said, "You know, Sherriff, I've heard stories about you. Everyone says you have a great deal of physical courage. Add that to your artistic and musical sensitivity and your obvious intelligence, and you personify the ideal Aryan male. It's such a pity about that Jewish taint in your blood."

"So much for the honeymoon," I said, and nodded to Linda, who cracked a smile.

I stood up from the piano, turned, and regarded Dr. Spencer, and paused for a moment to assure the precise effect for what I was about to do.

"Dr. Spencer," I said, putting on my official voice. "I have an arrest warrant for Jackson Knapp." I reached into my pocket and showed him the front fold without giving it to him. Knapp's name was prominent. "I'm hoping you'll cooperate with me on this. Is Knapp here at the compound?"

"I think so," he said, "I wouldn't know where he is, but I do have his cell phone number. That's how we have to communicate around here sometimes."

"I'd be obliged if you'd give it to me."

"Sure," Spencer said.

We walked out onto the back patio where we could see the trailer houses on the other side of the clearing. I called the number and the man answered on the first ring. "Jackson Knapp?" I asked.

"Yeah," came the gruff reply.

"This is Caddo County Sheriff Bo Handel. I have a warrant for your arrest."

"What for?" He sounded disinterested, as though being arrested was not an unfamiliar procedure to him.

"The fight at the Roundup Club today. Come out with your

hands on your head and proceed to the middle of the clearing. And don't try anything cute."

"Why should I? It was just a chickenshit barroom brawl."

He emerged as instructed, and I held my gun on him while Linda got him cuffed. We put him in the backseat behind the mesh barrier, and I told Linda to drive so I could keep an eye on him. During the ride into town he said nothing. We hustled him into the jail where I instructed the jailers to keep him the permitted seventy-two hours even if he made bond on the disturbance charge.

Linda dropped me off at the courthouse, and I arrived at my office to find Winthrop waiting for me. I quickly filled him in on the hijacking and what I had learned about Fancher's and Hahn's absence from the compound. "It had to be an inside job," I said. "I can't see anybody stealing a load of used office furniture."

"You make them for the hijackers?"

I nodded. "Those two guys are criminals. Their political motivations are secondary. Does that surprise you?"

"No." He sat lost in thought for a few moments, then said, "Lord only knows what new burst of creativity this revelation will bring out of Washington."

"Then why tell them?"

"They have to know about the hijacking. Just the fact that I have information that over a hundred fully automatic rifles are loose in the country makes the Bureau liable."

"But do they have to know about my suspicions?"

He smiled. "Now that you mention it, I don't see why they would. After all, they're just suspicions."

Just then Big Earl Chalmers appeared in the doorway. "They said you wanted to see me," he said.

"Yeah, I did. You're under arrest for that little fracas this morning at the Roundup Club. Are you sober?"

"I never was drunk. I just had two beers and that was hours ago."

"Good. Get your ass out to the jail to get processed. I'll call out there and tell 'em you're coming."

"What about my car? I don't want to pay no impound fee."

"I'll tell them to let you park it for free. You want me to call Walter Durbin for you? You're gonna need him on this one."

"Yeah, thanks, Bo," he said. "See you later."

Winthrop stared at me in disbelief. "You arrested him by messenger? You just sent word and he came in? And now you expect him to go out and check into the jail on his own?"

"Sure. I do that with a lot of the locals. It saves time and money."

"Do any of them ever fail to come in?"

"Not more than once they don't."

He shook his head in bemusement. "Well, I suppose whatever work, works."

"It does work. By the way, I've got Jack Knapp locked up out at the jail."

"Really? What on earth for?"

"He was the other participant in the Roundup Club brawl. But there's more than that. The bartender out there says that until a few days ago Knapp was driving a gray van."

"What are you going to do?" he asked.

"Let him stew overnight and question him about it sometime tomorrow. Only this guy doesn't seem to stew. He was very blasé about his arrest."

"Want me to come by and put in my two cents worth?" he asked.

"Why not? Of course, he may lawyer up on us. I have to tell him he has the right to one, which I'm sure he knows anyway."

"Regardless, we'll give it our best shot."

CHAPTER THIRTY-TWO

The next morning Winthrop and I started in on Knapp right after breakfast was over at the jail. We grilled him for over an hour and got nowhere. I'd never questioned a cooler and more collected suspect. He claimed that he'd never owned a gray van; had never driven a gray van; nor indeed had he ever even ridden in one, and he told us all this with the indifferent, off-hand manner of a man who simply didn't give a damn whether he is believed or not. I decided that Sparks was right and that they were very similar, which made the rumors of his hit man status for the Chicago–Juarez cartel all the more plausible.

Near the end of the interview I said, "It seems like you'd at least try to remember where you were the day Toby was shot. That might provide you with a credible alibi."

"It might make your job easier, which I have no intention of doing. You prove I was anywhere near that shooting, if you can."

"I'm interested in your racial theories," Winthrop asked him. "Tell me about them."

"Hitler laid them out in his book far better than I ever could. If ZOG doesn't pay you enough to afford a copy I have an extra I'll give you."

"What do you think of Bart Simpson?" I asked, just to see his reaction to the words.

"What?"

"Bart Simpson."

"Oh, yeah. The cartoon character. I've never really been a big fan of that show, but I kinda like the little guy. See, he's obnoxious, and I like obnoxious. I do obnoxious pretty good myself."

"Is that what got you into that squabble with Earl Chalmers?" I asked. "Being obnoxious, I mean."

"You mean that guy I had the fight with?"

I nodded. "The bartender told my deputy that old Earl gave you a good whipping."

"He's a pretty tough old boy, all right. I'll admit that much. I may look him up and try to recruit him to the movement."

"Won't work," I said. "Earl likes to drink and fight and raise hell, but at heart he's a decent guy. He wouldn't piss on you Nazis if you were on fire."

This bought me a disinterested shrug. "Then I guess we'll have to limp along without him."

"I want to go back to your gray van for a moment," Winthrop said. "Why did you murder the girl who registered it for you? Her name was Crystal Henderson, in case you've forgotten."

The name didn't elicit a bit of reaction from the man. "I told you, I've never owned a gray van, and I never heard of the girl."

"What attracted you to the white supremacist movement in the first place?" I asked.

"I don't like Jews or niggers or queers. The movement doesn't like 'em either. It seemed like a good fit."

Winthrop looked across at me. "What say we hold him and bring him before the grand jury on Deputy Parsons's assault. If we get an indictment the judge will probably deny bail since he's from out of state."

Knapp laughed. "I'm no lawyer, but even I know you can't get an indictment on the testimony of a bartender who thinks he saw me driving a gray van."

"What makes you think that's all we have?" I asked.

"Because that's all there is."

I had the jailers take him back to his cell.

"Arrogant bastard, isn't he?" I said.

"I wanted to beat the living shit out of him," Winthrop said. "This is the first guy in my career that's really got under my skin that way."

I laughed at him. "You're beginning to sound like one of us redneck Southern cops."

"Is there a background check, or can I just get in on enthusiasm? Do you have secret handshakes or anything like that?"

I had nothing to justify holding the man. I told the chief jailer that when he made bond on the Roundup Club charges—and I knew that Knapp would have the resources to do so because guys like him always do—they needed to cut him loose. It was just one more disappointment in a case that was becoming increasingly frustrating.

CHAPTER THIRTY-THREE

I arrived at work a little late the following day to have Maylene inform me that I'd gotten a call from the sheriff of Johnson County, over south of Fort Worth. I returned the call and asked for the sheriff. Once he came on the line, he said, "I got a bulletin here that says you're looking for a great big hippie-type guy you thought might have shot your deputy."

"That's right," I said.

"I think we may have your man."

The county seat of Johnson County is Cleburne, a drive of almost two hundred miles. Even using the flashing lights, it takes close to four hours over traffic-laden two-lane highways and state secondary roads to get there from Sequoya. There was a chance I could do it quicker. I threw a full set of restraint chains into my battered, long-suffering briefcase and hurried across the street to Walter Durbin's office in the old Sequoya National Bank building. Nelda was at her desk and Walter's office door was open. "Hi, Bo," she said. "Need to see him?"

"Yes, please."

Before she could buzz the intercom, he heard me and stepped through the doorway.

"What's up, Bo?" he asked.

"What have you got on your plate today?"

"Just a couple of appointments. That's all."

"They've apprehended a thug in Cleburne who appears to be a good suspect in Toby's shooting, and I was hoping you could fly me over there."

He looked at Nelda. "Can you handle it?"

She nodded. "Go."

As soon as we were out in the hallway he asked, "What's the story on this guy?"

"He matches the description of the assailant I got from the people who run that store out there. The Johnson County people arrested him on an armed robbery beef, and when they caught him he was carrying a Browning Hi Power. That's the gun the DPS ballistic wizards say fired the bullet that killed Crystal Henderson."

"Who's she?"

"The girl who registered the van that Toby stopped just before he was shot. Apparently, she was the girlfriend of the van's owner. And there's one other thing."

"Yeah?"

"He had several receipts from East Texas motels in his wallet, including one from the Eight Ball right here in town that was dated the night before Toby got shot."

Walter had earned his private pilot's license back when he was in college. Over the years he'd gotten his twin engine and instrument ratings. The previous November he'd won an enormous judgment against a Metroplex defense contractor in a wrongful death suit here in Sequoya. With part of his fee he'd fulfilled a lifelong dream and bought a used Piper Twin Comanche he now kept at a private airstrip about three miles out of town.

He went carefully through the preflight checklist and warmed up the engines. We taxied out onto the asphalt and after a short takeoff roll we were airborne into the bright, sunny winter sky. He leveled the plane off at 8,500 feet and adjusted the trim.

"I'll try to get the commissioners' court to pop for your gas on this deal," I said. "But if they won't I'll pay for it myself. It's worth it not to have to spend eight hours in highway traffic."

"Forget about it. Consider it my contribution to catching the guy who shot Toby."

It was a short flight of only an hour and fifteen minutes ground to ground to the Cleburne Municipal Airport. A lone deputy was waiting to drive us to the jail.

I've always thought that if I wasn't so committed to Sequoya, I'd like to live in Cleburne. It's one of the most charming places in the state, and the Johnson County Courthouse is the jewel of the town. A classical building, it's decorated with prairie-style ornamentation and trim. Instead of the usual rotunda, it has a square tower that soars three floors above the roof and is topped by a domed skylight that contains one of the finest displays of Tiffany art glass I have ever seen.

Like Sequoya, Johnson County had built a new jail over on the north side of town a few years earlier. The sheriff had to be away for the rest of the day, but he had left instructions that I was to be given every possible assistance.

"He also said you can take Harvey back with you if you think you can make your case," the chief jailer said as he escorted the manacled suspect into an interrogation room. "His full name's Edward Axel Harvey. He goes by Axel." He handed me a file folder. "And this is his sheet we got from the Bureau."

"You ought to stay out here," I told Walter in the corridor outside the room. "As an officer of the court you can't afford to hear some of the stuff I may lay on this guy."

He smiled and nodded and said, "This side of your job has never appealed to me anyway, Bo."

While I waited for the suspect to be brought in I read his file.

He was typical of a certain breed of career criminal: too lazy to work and too unimaginative to do a good job of crime. Consequently, he'd just drifted aimlessly along, living a hand-to-mouth, day-to-day existence. Already more than half his adult life had been spent in prison serving out short sentences for minor infractions, crimes that no doubt yielded him little in profit compared to the risks involved. The longest jolt had been seven years of a ten-to-fifteen bid in Indiana for indecency with a child.

The jailer brought him in. After he'd locked his manacles to a fixture in the floor, he left us alone to glare at each other from opposite sides of a heavy steel table. Harvey was about forty-five or so, a big sloppy oaf of a man in a pair of baggy denim pants and a green checked flannel shirt worn unbuttoned over a stained T-shirt. He had blurry features, a scraggly beard, long hair—"hippie long," as Lester Prichard would have said—and a shuffling walk.

"Where you from, Axel?" I asked.

"Ohio. Who the hell are you?"

"Sheriff Handel from down in Caddo County."

"What do you want with me?"

"I've got a few questions," I said pleasantly. "What were you doing in Sequoya a while back?"

He shrugged sullenly. "Just looking around."

"Your previous criminal record leads me to believe that you were doing a little more than that."

"Have it your way."

"Was that gray van you were in yours, or did it belong to somebody else? I'm guessing somebody else."

"Huh? What gray van?"

"The one you were in when you shot my chief deputy."

He got agitated quickly. "Whoa! I never shot nobody."

"Then maybe it was one of your buddies."

"I don't know nothing about no gray van, neither."

I looked him right in the eyes and spoke slowly and clearly. "According to witnesses there were three people in that van. The one who came in the store and caused the ruckus fit your description perfectly. If we don't catch the other two, then you're left holding the bag. If we do catch the others, then one of them may roll first and still leave you holding the bag. Now's the time for you to speak up and save your own skin."

"I don't know what you're talking about," he said. "What store?"

"The store where you stopped on the north of Sequoya the afternoon after you spent the night at the Eight Ball Motel. A man who fits your description gave the owner a good cussing because his gas pumps weren't working. He was with two other guys in a gray van. My deputy pulled in to get a Coke about a minute after you left. The proprietor told him about the disturbance, and he took off after them. He was found shot about twenty minutes later, after radioing in the tag number of the van. He'll live, but it was touch and go for a while. Now my advice to you is to give up your two associates. You need to be the first one out of the gate. Somebody is going to do a lot of hard years over this, and it may as well be them."

"Man, you can't pin this shit on me. I had nothing to do with it."

"Oh yes I can pin it on you, and I will too if you don't get with the program. Let me tell you what's going to happen. The victim was a well-liked young black deputy sheriff, raised right there in Sequoya, the son of the town's most popular black minister. He's also an Iraqi war hero, one who was awarded the Silver Star for bravery and a Purple Heart by being pretty badly wounded while fighting for his country. Get the picture?"

He was beginning to get it. He looked like a deer caught in the onrushing headlights of a ten-ton truck.

"You'll draw a jury that's about three-quarters white," I said. "But that won't help you one bit. In fact, it will do the opposite because there're lots of good white folks eager to prove to the world how much things have changed in East Texas since the old days when blacks had to sit at the back of the bus. The trial won't last long. Your court-appointed lawyer will mount the best defense he can, which won't be very good because all the evidence is stacked against you. The jury will be out a couple of hours just to make it look like there was some real deliberation, which there won't be. Then they'll come back with a guilty verdict. What follows will be the penalty phase of the trial where your attorney will try to show everybody what a poor, misguided, and misunderstood fellow you are. Of course that strategy won't work because our prosecutor can bring in your priors, including that indecency with a child up in Indiana. And you should see our prosecutor. She's beautiful, she's brilliant, and she has the instincts of a hammerhead shark.

"When all is said and done, they'll hang a sentence of fifty years to life on your worthless ass, and at your age that means life. A few days later a couple of the victim's coworkers will carry you down to the Walls Unit at Huntsville for Diagnostic. Or at least I hope they will. For some reason prison runs are a risky business in my part of the state. Seems like every time you turn on the nightly news you hear about some old boy that just got killed trying to escape on the way to the joint."

"What . . ."

Here I gave him a goofy grin and shrugged. "But what the hell, Axel? Shit does happen, you know. If you do make it to Diagnostic they'll give you a whole bunch of tests to help them decide specifically what kind of asshole you are. Since I know some of the shrinks down there who'll be making that determination, I'll feel obliged to call them and put in my two cents worth. Past experience tells me my advice will be of tremendous value to them in concluding that you're the specific kind of asshole who would profit from a little agricultural labor. That means that a few days later you'll find yourself beginning your sojourn with the state of Texas on one of the Brazos Valley cotton farms the prison system keeps for the sole purpose of making guys like you miserable. And you need to take a good, long look at that very first cotton row because it stretches all the way out to the end of your life."

He sat speechless for a few moments, his mouth hanging open. "My God!" he finally said. "What are you trying to do to me? Maybe I done a little burglarin' here and there, but damn! You're trying to send me up for life?"

"Let's not forget the armed robberies, Axel my good man."

"I ain't seen no proof on that."

I leaned a little closer to him and smiled. "I have a lawyer friend who's fond of pointing out that in court you don't have to prove anything. You just have to convince a jury, which is a whole 'nother ball game. Now, as I said, it may be that you weren't the shooter after all. It could have been one of your buddies. I'd buy that because you don't strike me as having the backbone to shoot a cop when he was looking you right in the face. If that's the case, then you're doubly stupid to take the fall. So how about it? Do you want to tell me what happened right now in exchange for some consideration at sentencing time?"

"Hell no!"

I rose and went to the door. "Tag him and bag him, boys," I said to the jailers. "And get me some papers to sign. I'm taking him back to Sequoya."

CHAPTER THIRTY-FOUR

When we got to the airport, Harvey balked on us. "I ain't getting on no damned airplane," he said.

"Why not?" Walter asked.

"I don't fly. It's bullshit."

"You're flying today," I said.

"No I ain't. No freaking way."

I looked at him for a moment, then smiled. "My uncle Julius loved cats," I said.

"Huh?"

"Yeah, he loved cats and always had a half dozen or so around the house. He liked male cats best because they didn't have kittens for him to have to fool with. But tomcats are a pain in the ass. They tear things up, spray the furniture and all. So when they were about half grown Uncle Julius castrated them to settle them down. Know how he managed that?"

He shook his head, his eyes wide with wonder.

"I never saw him do it, but my dad said he stuffed them head-first down a cowboy boot and had at it. See, the boot restrained them and kept them from biting and clawing him. I always wondered about that, so when I was about fifteen I got me a half-grown tomcat and a cowboy boot. That's when I figured it out."

"Figured what out?"

"I figured out that the only way to poke a tomcat headfirst down a cowboy boot is to kill the son of a bitch first. After that, castrating him is no problem."

"I don't get it. What do you mean?"

"I mean that one way or another you're getting on that plane."

We landed a little before four, and I immediately called Judge MacGregor and asked him to appoint an attorney for Harvey. He chose a young lawyer named Sean Wexler who had just gone in with the local state representative, Dud Malone, to handle some of the criminal side of his practice. I also called Liddy Snow to ask her to wait in her office for me. Then I took Harvey straight to the courthouse, jugged him in one of the old holding cells in the basement, and hurried up to Liddy's office after calling in a couple of deputies to take the prisoner out to the jail. I found her working away at her desk and told her what I had.

"How do you prefer to handle this?" she asked.

"I don't want to charge him with the shooting yet. He's not going anywhere because the judge in Cleburne denied bail on the armed robbery since he's from out of state and has no connections with Johnson County. Why don't you get with young Wexler and talk to Harvey this afternoon or early evening. He's already seen the stick, so maybe you ought to be the carrot. Tell him all the nice things you'll do for him if he cops on Toby's deal."

"And what nice things did you have in mind?"

"If he's convicted he'll get fifty to life. How about a plea bargain for thirty plus whatever Cleburne wants to tack on for their business? I get the feeling they would be generous if they knew he was going to be off the streets for a goodly number of years. I mean, if he goes down behind shooting a cop he sure as hell isn't going to get early parole, and we both know it. He'll serve twenty before they even bother to read his application. Maybe talk to the DA over there and get his thoughts."

"I could go for that."

"See how easy it is to work together?"

She gave me a twisted smile and a nod.

"If he cops," I said, "you get to make the announcement. I don't like to talk to the press anyway."

"Is this some of that famous Bo Handel charm I've always heard so much about?"

"Must be, darlin'. Must be."

I didn't hear back from Liddy until I was stretched out on the sofa watching the six o'clock news that evening. "Wexler made a counteroffer," she said.

"Which was?"

"We forget about charging his client with Toby's shooting and the man will cop to a half-dozen burglaries in Caddo, Nacogdoches, and Johnson counties plus three armed robberies, one of them that convenience store here in town that got hit back in November. For all that he's willing to do twenty-five."

"And let him walk on Toby's shooting?"

"Yep."

"Bullshit."

"That is precisely the assessment I gave Mr. Wexler."

"Good for you."

CHAPTER THIRTY-FIVE

After a quiet weekend passed in which I did nothing and enjoyed doing it, I felt rested when Monday morning rolled around. My first order of business was the real estate closing, which had been scheduled at Walter's office at 9:00 A.M. Papers were signed while checks passed hither and thither to the apparent satisfaction of all parties, especially Gabe Jordan. I left my check with Nelda to deposit for me and hurried across to the office, bright eyed, bushy tailed, and ready to start the new week. It was to prove one of the most eventful weeks of my almost three decades in office, and more than once in the following days I was to thank my lucky stars for the rest I'd gotten Saturday and Sunday.

I'd just poured myself a cup of coffee when Maylene informed me that an assistant prison warden I knew well was on the line.

I quickly grabbed the phone. "Remember Neil McGann?" he asked after we'd exchanged greetings.

"How could I forget him?"

"Well, he's convinced me that he has some really valuable information for you. I think you ought to come over here."

The Beto Unit of the Texas prison system is thirteen hundred acres of prime farmland a few miles south of Palestine, a small city of some twenty thousand inhabitants an hour's drive west of Sequoya. The unit's administrative offices are housed in a long, low building made of concrete blocks and covered in front with brick facing.

Neil McGann was the kind of man who could not only survive but actually thrive in such an environment. So sure was he of his prowess and his position in the inmate hierarchy that he didn't even bother to affect a jailhouse walk, that hitching swagger that advertises to the inmate population that a convict is a man to be reckoned with. Instead, he entered the interview room with a smooth, confident gait that could have belonged to a top CEO or a well-heeled banker. At least three inches taller than me, he had much broader shoulders and biceps that were enormous. He was clean shaven and dark haired, with cold blue eyes and fleshy features, and in his prison whites he looked enormous. Yet he was no threat to me since I was the closest thing he had to a friend in the straight world.

Born and raised in Montgomery County down in deep East Texas, Neil came from an insular clan of hard-bitten farm and timber people about whom I'd heard it said more than once, "That bunch would rather fight than fornicate." Right out of high school he'd enlisted in the Marines and put in twelve years. Then, for reasons he never explained, he mustered out eight years short of a pension and drifted down to San Antonio where he joined an outlaw motorcycle club called the Renegades. His force of personality and natural leadership skills quickly came to the surface and within two years he was president of the club's Central Texas chapter. That's when the mayhem began. By the time I met the man, he was the lead suspect in three murders and had been named by both the DEA and the FBI as the cocaine kingpin of the whole San Antonio–Austin area. What brought him to my attention was a class-A misdemeanor assault conviction that grew out of a brawl at a local club. The judge fined him and gave him six months in the slammer.

While he was in my custody I got to know him quite well. Indeed, he fascinated me, and I spent hours talking to him. For one thing, he was well read in philosophy. Not only that, he was quite knowledgeable about literature and classical music. During one of our discussions, I asked him, "Neil, why on earth didn't you take some other course in life? I mean with a mind like yours, why this?"

He gave me a cold smile and said, "I like being a criminal, Bo. It suits me just fine."

He never saw another day of freedom. When he finished his Caddo County bit, warrants were waiting out of Bexar County for murder and drug-trafficking. By the time all the legal dust settled, he'd entered the Texas prison system behind three consecutive life sentences.

While in the Marines, Neil had been married for a short time, a union that had produced a daughter he worshipped. She in turn had moved to New York, married, and given birth to two children, a boy and a girl. When the kids were respectively three and four years old, she moved back to Texas. Neil wanted to see his grandchildren, whom he'd never met. The fly in the ointment was a guard captain who kept him on the no-visitors list for almost a year on one minor and probably imaginary infraction after another. Desperate, Neil wrote to me to ask if I could help him.

I could. A few years earlier, an assistant warden, a fellow known as an up-and-comer in the prison system, had gotten a drunk driving charge in Caddo County. Because his blood alcohol level was only marginally over the legal limit, and because, quite frankly, I saw the value of having a highly placed correctional official indebted to me, I dropped the charges and made certain the record of the incident was buried. By the time Neil McGann wanted to see his grandkids, the former assistant warden was deputy director of the whole prison system. One phone call was all it took.

I'd driven over in my own pickup. It was best for Neil not to be seen talking to a cop, so I left my hat, badge, and sidearm locked up in the toolbox. The warden made an interview room available, and the guards escorted him in without restraints. We shook hands and took seats on opposite sides of the table. "You're looking healthy," I said. "I miss our long talks."

"Me too. You could visit, you know."

"I will after I retire. As it is now, I'm lucky if I get on one of my horses once a month or find time for a trip out to the gun club four or five times a year."

"You got a woman yet?" he asked.

"As a matter of fact, I do. Remember Carla Wallace?"

"That tall, dark-haired deputy of yours?"

I nodded. "That's her."

His face broke into a big smile. "Congratulations, you old devil. I'd be proud to squire her around myself."

"How are the grandkids, Neil?"

"Growing like weeds. And that's what this is all about today. I've felt like I needed to repay you for what you did. You had to spend some political capital, and we both know it."

"You're right," I admitted. "But I never said anything about a quid pro quo."

"So? I pay my debts without being asked."

"If that's the way you feel, what have you got for me?"

He hunched forward and looked me right in the eyes and said, "Bo, I've never snitched or given anybody up in my life, but I'm about to do it now because they tried to have me killed."

"Who did?"

"The Knights of the White Magnolia. They're a small Texas prison gang, a remnant of the old Aryan Brotherhood, which as you probably know has been pretty well broken up by the Feds. They filched the name from a Klan group down in Louisiana after the Civil War."

"You said they tried to have you killed? Why?"

"The excuse was that I meddled in their business when I took up for a kid they were trying to punk out, and it's true that I put him under my protection. But that was just an excuse. The real reason was that I've got a couple of little businesses going here, and they wanted to take them over."

This was a surprise. Upper echelon white career criminals like McGann and Jasper Sparks—the Dixie Mafia types—were generally left alone by the prison gangs for the simple reason that their resources on the outside were too formidable, gang members' family and friends were too vulnerable, and it was too easy for men like them to "reach out and touch someone," as Sparks had once so charmingly put it.

"How did they try to do it?"

"A guy came at me with a shank in one of the corridors when we were alone. But the gods of war were with me that day."

"Yeah?"

He nodded and smiled sardonically. "Before he could get close, he tripped and fell on his shank and expired as a result of his injury."

I smiled right back at him. "And where did this errant shank happen to get him when he took that unfortunate fall?"

"In the carotid artery."

"You're a lucky fellow, Neil," I said.

"That attack was why I asked you to come down here. What kind of intel do you get on that white supremacist group up there in your county?"

"You know about them?"

"Sure. Prison grapevine."

"I've gotten a little info from the Feds," I said carefully. "Why do you ask?"

"What do they say about their connections to the white prison gangs?"

"They say they really aren't connected."

He shook his head and rolled his eyes. "The feds are full of shit on that score. There are lots of connections, but they're personal and not organizational. What's the story on your deputy?"

I quickly told him about Toby's shooting, then decided to lay out the whole case for him. It was hardly top secret, anyway. I told him about the Webern murder and Dual Driggers killing the two meth heads and his subsequent death and Toby's shooting.

"How old did you say he was?"

"Eighty-four. He fought at Normandy."

McGann laughed uproariously. "I'd love to have seen the look on those punks' faces when that old man pulled out his forty-five. I guess they found out that there're some folks in this old world it just won't do to fuck with. How about the other murder? The Webern guy? What was his deal?"

"He was in the Federal Witness Protection Program."

"For sure?"

I nodded.

"And they still got to him?"

"Apparently so."

"That's heavy shit, man. What makes you think they're all connected?"

"The same MO, for one thing. Webern and Dual were both strangled to death. That connects those two. A silver gray minivan was seen outside Dual's house the morning he was killed. It was a silver gray minivan that Toby stopped right before he was shot."

"Sounds like you got it nailed," he said. "Like I told you, there're connections between some of the people in that Caddo County bunch and these White Magnolia assholes. I'm not sure how they pass info back and forth. Family visits probably. But I do know these guys in here like to brag. You know what I mean. What else is there to do? So some skinhead piece of shit gets to talking, maybe with the help of a few pills, and pretty soon he's telling you all the secret, inside information he has."

"You mean you talk to these guys? I mean, considering the attempt they made on your life . . . ?"

He gave me a cold smile. "They've gotten real friendly since their chief enforcer fell on his knife. See, after that there was a rumor going around that their entire leadership was slated for extermination."

"Was it?" I asked.

"Like I said, some people won't do to fool with. But back to business. I don't know anything about your two murders, so I can't help you there. But I keep hearing from a couple of different sources the name of the guy who's supposed to have shot your deputy."

"Who?"

"His name's Leroy Fancher."

CHAPTER THIRTY-SIX

What made McGann's information doubly credible was that his informant quoted Fancher's buddy, Delbert Hahn, as the source of the story. For the first time since Dual Driggers was murdered I was beginning to feel like I had some measure of control over events.

I got back to the courthouse a little before noon and rooted through my office for the file on Fancher that Winthrop had given me. Not finding it, I went into the outer office and looked around. A half dozen or so file folders still lay neatly stacked on Toby's desk because nobody had been able to summon up the heart to refile them since he'd been shot. I knew why. Before he'd regained consciousness, disturbing his workspace would have amounted to a sort of tacit admission that he wasn't expected to return to us. Recalling that I had last seen the Fancher material on the day he was shot, I began to flip through the accumulated folders on his desk.

I never found what I was looking for that morning, but I found something infinitely better when I accidentally knocked one folder off onto the floor. As it landed, it fell open. For a few moments I stood staring at the photo it contained, my hair almost standing on end. Then I bent down and picked it up. I fell back in Toby's chair and indicted myself in the high court of my own mind for not being more thorough. Then I rose to my own defense with the reasonable point that I didn't have time for everything. But self-recrimination could wait. I left the jury of my conscience out for later deliberation and tried to compose my thoughts.

The first thing I did was call Jasper Sparks, but I got no answer. I sat for fifteen minutes fidgeting, unable to get anything done until at last the phone I'd bought to talk to him buzzed. When I switched it on, I heard his voice say, "Sorry about that. I was in a situation where I couldn't talk."

"Didn't anybody wonder why you didn't answer my call?"

"I just told them it was a broad I was trying to give the brush-off. What do you need?"

"Leroy Fancher. Is he out there at the compound?"

"No, he left for Houston this morning."

"Is he gone for good?"

"I don't think so. He didn't take anything with him but an overnight bag. He has some pretty nice clothes and stuff, but he left them here."

"Was he alone?" I asked.

"No, he had some really big asshole with him that I'd never seen before this past week. The guy spent the last few days here at the compound."

"What did he look like?"

"He was about six-four, bearded, longish hair, wore a knitted cap, cheap jeans. Badass demeanor."

"How about Hahn? Did he go with them?"

"No, he's still here. As a matter of fact, he said he was going into Sequoya to have a few beers. Asked me if I wanted to come along, but I begged off."

"When was this?"

"About an hour ago."

"What's his usual watering hole?"

"The Roundup Club, always. He's a big country-and-western man."

I thought for a few moments, then asked, "Do you have any way to get hold of Fancher?"

"Not a chance. He's paranoid as hell about his cell phone number. Won't give it out to anybody, and I know he's got it registered in a phony name. But he's got my number, and I have a feeling that he may be going to call me."

"Why so?"

"About a week ago he asked me if I knew where he could get a passport in a phony name. I told him I knew a guy in Houston who could fix him up."

"Do you?" I asked.

"I sure did at one time, and I bet I could find out quickly enough."

"Just let me know if he calls. And I mean as soon as you can after he gets off the phone."

"I'll do my best, but I may not be able to call right then. Listening ears, you know."

I ended the conversation and called Eva's cell number. "Who are you working with today?" I asked as soon as she answered.

"Otis Tremmel."

"Good. You were here the day Delbert Hahn and Leroy Fancher came in to see me, weren't you?"

"Yeah."

"Would you recognize Hahn if you saw him again?"

"Sure."

"He's supposed to be at the Roundup Club right about now. I want you and Otis to go out there and arrest him and book him for drunk and disorderly."

"Is he?" she asked. "Drunk and disorderly, I mean."

"Probably not. But do it anyway. Tell him we got a disturbance call on him. Take him to the jail and let him have his phone call. Then put him in one of the isolation cells. I'll have a murder warrant on him in a few hours, but I don't want to ring any bells right now."

"Okay. You're the boss."

I laughed softly. "I told you the first day we met that attitude would take you a long ways. Just be casual and make it look like a routine arrest."

I skipped lunch and headed for Tyler. An hour later I was at the intensive care unit at Mother Frances Hospital arguing with a battle-ax of a nurse. The problem was that Toby had been conscious only a day and a half. The doctor's orders specifically stated that no one but family members could visit, and then for only five minutes at a time. The fact that his wife backed me up meant nothing to the rule-addled fool who was running the unit. "No," she said. "Positively not. Doctor's orders."

"Ma'am, he's my chief deputy and my friend, and I wouldn't do anything in this world to harm him. But believe me, if he can ID this photo, it's going to do more to speed his recovery than you can begin to imagine. He doesn't even have to speak. All he has to do is nod. But I'm going in there no matter what you say."

"If you do, I'll have to call security."

I leaned over the counter where my face was only about a foot from hers and riveted her eyes with mine and said, gruffly, "Lady, do I really look like somebody who's going to be intimidated by a bunch of rent-a-cops?"

She stared at me for a few seconds before dropping her eyes and giving me a flouncy shrug. "Perhaps not, but I can't give you permission. If you go in there I'll have to make a note of it on the record."

"You do that," I said. "By all means, let's keep that record."

Latoya came in with me. Toby looked better than I expected. He'd lost weight and appeared shaky and weak, but his eyes were bright and he smiled when he saw me.

"Don't try to talk," I said. "Just look at this."

I drew the photo out of my coat and held it before his eyes. He gazed at it for a moment, then looked up and nodded. "That's him," he whispered.

"We're going to get the bastard," I said. I gave his hand a quick squeeze and was on my way.

I was in the hospital parking lot when Eva called. "We nailed Hahn," she said. "But guess what?"

"I have no idea."

"He fought us. He was pissed off about something, and got real obnoxious. Called me a spic cunt and accused me of being an agent of ZOG."

"You didn't get hurt, did you?"

"Are you kidding?" she asked with a laugh. "With Otis and that slapjack of his to back me up? However, we were forced to fuss at him severely."

"Did this fussing involve any broken bones or require stitches or anything like that once you got done?"

"No, but he is a little bunged up. Between that and his intoxicated state, we judged that he was incapable of making his statutory phone call before morning."

"Excellent. Now we've got him for resisting arrest, foul and abusive language, and assault on a peace officer."

On the way home I considered the possibility of putting out a statewide bulletin on Fancher, but decided to wait a couple of days. Any Ranger confronting him would know how to handle the situation, and so would the Feds and the highway patrol. But some impulsive small-town deputy or a precinct constable might not take the "armed and extremely dangerous" part of the alert seriously enough. I was mindful that the man had already demonstrated his willingness to kill an officer. I saw no reason to give him a second opportunity unless it was absolutely necessary.

I forced myself to simmer down and checked back in at the office. Finding everything quiet, I decided to go home early. Carla stopped by a little after six with a take-out pizza. We each had a drink, a couple of slices of pizza along with a couple of beers, and . . .

We drifted off to sleep snuggled comfortably together.

CHAPTER THIRTY-SEVEN

As usual, Carla was gone when I woke up. I ate a slice of toast and a couple of pieces of fruit for breakfast and headed off to the office. I was calmer than I'd expected to be, but I'd decided that if I hadn't heard from Sparks by late afternoon, I would go ahead and put the bulletin out on Fancher.

I put the matter as far out of my mind as I could and applied myself to my paperwork. Then, a little after nine, Maylene buzzed to tell me that Reverend Dawkins was in the outer office demanding to see me. "Send him in," I said. "I need some comic relief today."

A moment later we were shaking hands, and I motioned for him to sit. "It's my understanding that you have a suspect in the Parsons shooting," he said.

"That's right."

"Tell me about him."

"I'm not in the habit of discussing evidence with anyone who's not in law enforcement or in the DA's office."

He started to speak, but I cut him off. I'd decided to play the farce on out. If the news got abroad that we had a suspect, I wanted that suspect's name to be Axel Harvey and not Leroy Fancher. "However," I said, "in this case I'll do you the courtesy of telling you that he fits the description of one of the men we believe was involved in the shooting. We also have proof that he stayed at a local motel the night before Toby was attacked."

"And you expect to get a conviction on that?"

I sighed and shook my head in exasperation. "Reverend, there are really two types of evidence, though they overlap. One kind is the sort you use in court. The other is the kind you sometimes can't use in court, but which is valuable in actually leading you to the perpetrator. That kind brings you to an arrest, and after you have the perp in your clutches you hammer and grill him until he confesses and cuts a deal. The evidence we have on this guy overlaps. It may not be enough to give us a conviction at this point, but it is enough that we are fairly sure he was involved."

"Is this suspect affiliated with the Aryan League?"

"There's no indication that he is. He seems to be a man with no political motivations of any kind, a low-order career criminal who drifts around the country living off residential burglaries and the occasional convenience store robbery."

"Well then, there you have it," he said with what seemed like profound satisfaction.

"Have what?"

"You're not looking in the right place. This was obviously a racially motivated crime."

I almost laughed. "So where should I look?"

"The Aryan League."

I gave him a sage nod. "Let me tell you a little story. Back years ago I happened to be down on the square late one evening after everything was closed, and I saw one of our local alcoholics, Pappy Clyde, down on his hands and knees under a streetlight. It was obvious that he was drunker than Cooter Brown, and it was equally obvious that he was searching for something. I said, 'What you looking for, Pappy?' 'My keys,' he replied. 'Did you drop them here?' I asked. 'Hell, no,' he replied. 'I dropped them over there by the door to the café.' I asked him why he didn't look for them over there where he'd actually dropped them, and you know what he said?"

Dawkins shook his head, obviously puzzled.

"He replied, 'Because there ain't no damned light over there by the door.'"

He even rewarded me with a little polite laughter. "A funny story, but I don't see how it's pertinent to our discussion."

"It's pertinent because you want me to look for Toby's assailant where you want him to be found. I want to look for him where he actually is."

He started to speak, but I raised my hand to silence him. Then I pointed to my bulging in basket. "Peace, Reverend. Have mercy. I've been working night and day on this case in addition to a murder. I'm so far behind on this paperwork that I feel like screaming. We're not going to have a meeting of the minds on this, so let's just let it go at that."

He gave in with good grace, rose to his feet and I did the same. We leaned across the desk and shook hands. "My best wishes to you, Sheriff," he said.

"The same to you, Reverend."

The rest of the morning passed in relative quiet. Then a few minutes before noon Nelda Minton knocked on my door. "Come on in," I said. "What's up?"

"You need to watch the midday news out of Lufkin," she said.

"How come?"

"You'll see."

I switched on the portable TV I keep in the office and poured us each a cup of coffee, then we settled down in front of the screen. It was the fifth story, right after the national headlines, and I almost laughed. Reverend Dawkins was attracting more media attention, which, of course, was his objective. Once more he was bloviating from the steps of the courthouse, and once more his gassy rhetoric was aimed at me. When it was over, she turned down the volume and turned to me. "Anything to say?"

"He was here this morning, so this doesn't surprise me."

"He came by your office?"

I nodded.

"What did he want?"

"He came by to tell me where to look for Toby's assailant."

"Then what was this broadcast all about?"

"You heard him just like I did. He's claiming that one of my oldest friends is connected with the Aryan League."

"Who on earth does he mean?" she asked.

"It would have to be Lyndon Till. I don't know anybody else out there."

"But the two of you aren't friends, are you? I seem to recall Walter telling me that you don't even like the man."

"I don't," I said. "The first thing I did when I came back home to take over the family business after my dad died was fire him. Do you happen to remember Coy Presnell?"

She nodded. "Sure. His family belonged to our church. Daddy preached his funeral."

I told her the whole story. When I finished, she asked, "But what's Till got to do with the Aryan League?"

"They hired him to man the gate. He sits in a little booth and screens visitors."

"And that's his only connection?"

"I'm pretty sure it is."

"Bo, you've got to defend yourself this time. This isn't like his other charges. You and Till do have a past, and you need to explain it."

"No," I said firmly, shaking my head. "If the question comes up in the next election campaign, I'll explain myself to the voters of this county. Everybody else can go straight to hell."

"But why?"

I laughed and shook my head ruefully. "I try to tell myself it's on account of certain personal principles I won't violate. My wife had a little different perspective on the matter. If she was still alive she'd tell you it's because I'm a bonehead."

"And she'd be right on the money," she said hotly. "I'm going to the press myself and straighten this business out."

"Nelda, as a personal favor to me, I'm going to ask you not to do that."

"But why, Bo? If you won't defend yourself then at least let your friends defend you."

"You already have, and I appreciate it more than you can know. But there are some things going on that I can't tell you about, and the truth is that this situation doesn't need any more publicity."

She gazed at me intently for a moment before nodding slowly. "I should have known."

"Just keep it to yourself. Don't even tell Walter." I glanced at my watch. "Say, have you eaten yet?" I asked.

"No."

"I was thinking about barbecue. Let's have lunch at Seabrook's."

"Sure. Let's go."

I'd been back at the office for about an hour when Sparks finally called. "Just heard from Fancher," he said. "I was right about the passport. He'd been awfully interested when we talked about bogus documents."

"Are you supposed to call him back or what?" I asked.

"No, he still won't give up his cell number, but you can feel free to get the Rangers or the Feds to pull my phone records and get it if you want to. Then you can pinpoint him with GPS."

"I don't like that idea," I said. "He might accidentally leave his phone in a café or bar or something. It would be much better if you could set him up for us. You know, have him some place at some specific time, maybe to meet your guy. I think that's a better bet. Would you be willing to do that?"

"I thought you'd probably want me to do that. I told him I'd talk to my guy, but that I probably couldn't get hold of him until later this evening."

"When are you supposed to hear from Fancher again?"

"Tomorrow morning. I think he's shacked up at some gal's place. He's eager but not desperate. And by the way, he did say that he wants to leave the country. What's that all about?"

I thought about deals with the devil, then made a snap decision to trust the man. "He's been running on a short fuse. I've got him on two murders if I can get my hands on him."

"Let me talk to my friend in Houston and then get back with you as soon as Fancher calls me tomorrow."

I had one more thing left to do. First I called Liddy Snow and told her we needed to take the deal Sean Wexler had proposed for Axel Harvey. She was puzzled but agreed when I told her it was the best move we could make. "Is this one of those instances where I don't want to know what you're doing?" she asked.

"Could be," I replied.

I called Wexler and told him we were willing to clear Harvey on the shooting if he would cop to all his East Texas business along with the Johnson County robbery. "Think he's still interested?" I asked.

"I don't know," he said. "What changed your mind?"

"The DA and I don't see eye to eye on this one," I said, prevaricating smoothly. "Toby is conscious and on the mend, and she's more interested in clearing a bunch of unsolved cases than she is in trying one difficult case. However, you need to be aware that this is a one-time offer. The train is leaving the station this afternoon, and your client just has this one chance to get aboard."

"Let me talk to him," he said.

"Meet me at the jail in thirty minutes."

I read Harvey the riot act. "I'm not hot on this deal, anyway. It's the DA's idea, so if you let me think for one moment that you're lying you go back to your cell and I start digging for more evidence on the shooting. And understand up front that you have to eat the Johnson County armed robbery. If I'm going to do this, I have to have something to give the sheriff out there."

Harvey looked at his attorney. "What do you think?"

"Remind me how many burglaries we're talking about?"

"Five."

"And two armed robberies," I said.

"Twenty-five years is a good offer," Wexler said with a nod. "I think we *might* beat the shooting charge, and I'd love to try the case. But I'm obligated to give you the best advice I can and disregard my own personal desires. If we try it and don't beat it, you'll get at least fifty years. Maybe life. Then if they can find enough evidence to convict you on a couple of these burglaries and even one of the armed robberies, they'll stack at least fifteen more years on top of that. So you'll be looking at sixty-five or seventy years instead of twenty-five. And you'll get convicted on some of this shit, believe me. It's unavoidable. So if we go to trial on the shooting, you'd be risking fifty years to maybe get five knocked off the top."

"Where do I sign?"

Wexler wanted the agreement in writing before the confessions started. I called Liddy. She drew up the plea bargain and delivered it to the jail herself. We brought in a stenographer and a video recorder, and Harvey began babbling like there'd be no tomorrow.

When I got home that evening I called the Johnson County sheriff and told him we had a confession on his armed robbery plus two burglaries in Cleburne for which Harvey hadn't even been suspected.

"He decided to clear the slate, huh?" he asked.

"That's right. Will your DA go for twenty-five for the whole ball of wax?"

"Sure," he said.

"Fine. I'll have his confession faxed to you some time tonight."

"I don't know what you did, but I'm all for it."

CHAPTER THIRTY-EIGHT

The next morning I got to the office at eight and forced myself to quell my anxiety and put in two hours trying to dig out from under a morass of paperwork before my cell phone buzzed. Jasper Sparks's name came up on the screen, and I switched the thing on. "Tell me something good," I said.

"I've got it all arranged if you can be at a place called the Climax Club in Houston at eight this evening."

"I can be there or bust trying. What kind of place is it?"

"It's a black nightclub in the Fifth Ward. Are you familiar with the Fifth Ward?"

"Sure. It's the kind of neighborhood our daddies warned us to stay out of."

I heard a soft laugh. "You got that right. Fancher is going to be there meeting with the owner, who is an old associate of mine named Omar Turpin. The good deal about this is that everybody in the business knows that Omar used to be the man to see about bogus papers of every kind. That means if Fancher should happen to ask around he'll hear all the right things."

"So Omar is going straight now?"

"Very much so. He took a couple of falls, after which he decided that a man with his brains and talent could do better on the right side of the law."

"If he's an ex-con how does he rate a liquor license?" I asked.

"The whole thing is in his daughter's name. The cops know he's the real owner, but they don't hassle him. Don't worry about Omar. He's solid. Trust me on this."

"I suppose I have to," I said. "Is Fancher willing to go in there blind on the strength of your assurance?"

"Being Jasper Sparks buys me a lot of credibility with guys like him. Besides, he doesn't have any choice if he wants that passport. I told him that Omar would be there and meet him at eight on the dot, and that he likes punctuality. I also told him that Omar is jumpy about the law, and if he's late he might not do business. So if he's going to be there, he'll be there at eight. As for the rest of it, that's your worry."

"What's the place like?" I asked.

"A big, tall-ceilinged joint. It's got a dance floor in the center with tables and booths along the walls. The office is through a door that opens behind the bar, and that's where they're going to meet."

"Where are you?" I asked.

"In Nacogdoches running some errands."

"Try to stay where we can talk for the next few hours."

"Sure. I'll eat lunch and then take in a movie. Just call if you need me."

"Okay. I may call or I may not," I said.

"No problem. There's a film showing that I want to see anyway."

I looked at my watch. It was a few minutes after ten. The raid was doable, but it meant that I had a dozen details to take care of in preparation. First I called Liddy and told her to see to it that Hahn was held for the full seventy-two hours allowed by the law even if he posted bail on the drunk and assault beefs.

"I assume there will be charges forthcoming?" she asked.

"You bet there will. Carla is going to interrogate him this afternoon. Be sure to stay available by phone."

"Until when?"

"You should hear from me by midnight. If all goes well, you'll like what you hear. I promise."

"Where are you going to be?" she asked.

"I'm off to Houston to catch a bad guy."

"Who?"

"Leroy Fancher. And yes, he's hooked up with the Aryan League. He and Hahn have both been living out there."

"Any of our federal friends going along?" she asked.

"No, no, and hell no. Not this time. And don't say anything to anybody."

"Okay. You have my cell number, don't you?"

"Sure."

I switched off and called Don Thornton and told him what I had. "You want a piece of it?" I asked once I'd briefed him.

"You bet I do."

"So how do you think we need to go about this?"

"A multiagency task force, as they say on the crime shows. We'll have to alert the Harris County Sheriff's Department Fugitive Squad. I know the guy who heads it up. And I'd like to call the Captain of Ranger Company A down there and give him the courtesy of telling him what we're up to since it's his bailiwick. I expect he'll assign one of his Rangers."

"Good deal."

"I'm assuming you don't want to call on any federal resources that might be available?"

"You got it."

He laughed softly. "I'll call you back once I get it set up."

I forced myself to slow down and get a cup of coffee and a couple of Maylene's homemade cookies. My next call was to Carla to wheedle her into coming down to interview Hahn. She was a highly competent interrogator, and I knew if anybody could get him talking she could. I told her in detail what I had and what I needed while she took copious notes in shorthand. Next I called Eva and told her to drop what she was doing and report to my office. After that I went upstairs to Judge MacGregor to get my warrants.

When I got back I found Eva waiting.

"It's asking you to go above and beyond," I told her. "It'll mean working a double shift, but are you willing to go to Houston tonight to arrest the bad guy?"

"Sure. What bad guy? The one who shot Toby?"

"That's the one."

"Then I'm definitely in," she said.

I called across the street to the Texan Café and ordered hamburgers for both of us for lunch. After we'd eaten, we settled down to wait for Thornton's call. It wasn't long in coming. When I answered the phone on the first ring I could hear him on the other end of the line. "We're set," he said. "A young Ranger named J. T. Hoskins will meet us at the sheriff's department substation. And we'll have three officers from the sheriff's fugitive squad, including Hiram Cray, the commander. Ever met Hiram?"

"I don't believe so."

"Black guy. Ex-Marine. Knows his business and doesn't get excited. Who are you bringing?"

"My new deputy, Eva Mendoza. She's ex-Houston PD. I called the Sequoya police to see if Leon wanted to go, but he's out of town, so I picked Otis Tremmel from my own force. We'll take the department's Suburban. I still need to load our flak jackets and stuff. When do you think we should kick off?"

"Let's meet at the courthouse a little before three and leave from there."

"Good deal. I'll see you then."

CHAPTER THIRTY-NINE

Five hours later, we'd just reached the northern outskirts of Houston when my cell phone buzzed. It was Carla. "How did it go?" I asked.

"It was pretty funny, really."

"Did he ask for a lawyer?

"No, he got very interested when I told him we had a positive ID on his buddy, but he got fawningly eager to talk once I mentioned capital murder. The thought of the needle had him spewing like a Yellowstone geyser."

"I don't doubt it. You can be very intimidating. In fact, you're the best interrogator I ever had on the force."

"I don't know about that, but it's worse than you thought. Or better, I guess, depending on how you look at it. You were right about him and Fancher robbing Buck Kaiser up there at Texarkana. But there's more. A lot more. Listen to this . . ."

When she finished speaking my heart was pounding with excitement. I'd never before had so many things fall into place in so short a period of time. My business just doesn't work that way.

"Good show," I said.

"One other thing. I found out how they knew Webern was living in Sequoya. One of the high-level members of the cartel has family here in town. He was visiting and saw him at one of the clubs."

"So you buy that?"

"I believe that Hahn bought it. It's what Fancher told him, and he claims Fancher believed it."

"Well, I guess even stranger things have happened."

"Bo, you need to find out who the guy and his relatives are."

"Yes, I sure as hell do," I said. "But even if we never know, you outdid yourself, and I'm deeply obligated to you."

"Indeed I did, and indeed you are. And now I'm going home and going to bed."

"Did Hahn sign anything?"

"He signed everything he could get his hands on. Full confessions all around."

"You are a wonder," I said. "An absolute wonder. Truly a girl for all seasons."

This brought a long pause. "Why am I very suspicious all of a sudden?" she asked.

"Well . . ."

"Out with it."

"I might need you tomorrow or the next day."

"What for?"

"A little horseback riding if things break the way I expect them to. A very important detail."

"Why not," she said with a sigh. "Have you nailed Fancher yet?"

"We're just about to make our move. If he shows up we should have him within a couple of hours."

"Be careful, Bo."

"I always am."

We found Hiram Cray and three other deputies from the Fugitive Squad waiting for us at the sheriff's number three substation.

Cray was big and beefy and good-natured with an easy, relaxed manner about him. Also present was Ranger Hoskins. He was of medium build with intense eyes and iron-hard handshake. We had an hour to kill, which we spent getting familiar with one another. A few minutes before eight we piled into three vehicles— our Suburban and two Houston patrol cars. Eva and Hoskins were to cover the rear. Cray and one deputy were to take one side of the building, the other deputies the opposite side. Thornton and I would go in the front with the last Houston deputy covering the entry behind us. I had no illusions, though, that it was going to be an easy takedown. The first casualty in any offensive is usually the plan of battle.

My grandmother used to say, "The Devil never rests and sin knows no Sabbath," an adage that popped into my mind when I saw the Climax Club. At best, the place could only be described as a dive, one no different from dozens of other old roadhouse honky-tonks I've known back home in East Texas. It squatted, big and sagging, sheathed in paintless clapboard and roofed in rusted tin at the dead end of Nolte Street in the toughest part of Houston's Fifth Ward. If you've been around at all you've probably seen a few streets like Nolte. Every town of any size in the country has at least one. It's always a narrow, ill-lighted lane where dim figures move in the shadows and turn their faces away at the approach of your footsteps and where the backfire of a car's exhaust brings eyes that are more feral than human to peer for a quick moment around the doorjambs of dilapidated rooming houses and cheap apartments before the doors are quietly but firmly shut. A street where the blinds are always drawn and the occasional night-scream is heard, but where the cops, when they bother to come at all, come in force. A street where even the kids are as wise as Solomon, but where nobody ever knows anything.

We let the two patrol cars get ahead. Once the three teams had radioed that they were in place, I pulled the Suburban into the front parking lot and we climbed out. The asphalt beneath our feet was littered and potholed, but the cars parked there included several late-model Mercedes and Lexus sedans, and one lone Corvette that still sported its dealer plates. A dive this might be, but it nevertheless attracted some patrons who were in the chips.

Just as we reached the entry we suffered the worst possible luck. The door opened and our quarry took one step out, the door still ajar behind him. He saw me and froze for a moment. Before we could react, he darted back into the building. We ran to the entry and went carefully through the doorway to find ourselves in a sort of anteroom. On its other side hung a pair of swinging doors with glass ovals set in their centers. Through the glass I could see the fugitive threading his way quickly across the dance room ahead.

"Come on, Bob," I yelled and shouldered the double doors open.

Inside, the Climax Club was a great dark cavern of a place, with a ceiling at least twenty feet tall. The bar was in the left rear corner, and to the right of the bar hung another pair of swinging double doors that no doubt led to the back of the building. What little illumination the room had came mostly from fluorescent beer signs that hung on the walls and ceiling. The dance floor was crowded and the jukebox wailed.

My mind registered the fact that about a third of the patrons were white. It also took note that they appeared to be the sort of whites who would be comfortable coming to a black nightclub in the worst part of the toughest ward in Houston. Despite the city's antismoking ordinance, the air was thick with tobacco smoke, and I caught a faint overlay of marijuana.

I first sensed, then heard, a commotion at the back of the room. A door slammed somewhere in the rear and a single shot rang out behind the building. The effect on the crowd was galvanic. These were people adequately familiar with the sound of gunfire not to mistake it for an auto backfire. About half of them reflexively hit the deck while women screamed. Most of the ones who hadn't gone to the floor went into nervous fits instead. They seemed to be moving at light speed in every direction at once with nobody getting anywhere.

Suddenly, the door behind the bar burst open, and a huge white man I'd never seen before emerged like a ten-ton Peterbilt roaring out of a tunnel. He brushed the bartender aside like an empty paper sack, vaulted over the bar, and stood glaring at us for a couple of seconds. He was enormous and tough looking and wild eyed in the dim light of the club. With a full beard and longish hair, he wore dark jeans and a heavy sweater that looked like navy issue. The sweater alone looked big enough to house an ox.

After a moment's appraisal of his situation, he bellowed like a wounded bull and thundered toward us. His objective was the front door, and Thornton and I were between him and it. In his right hand he held a big revolver that was pointed in my general direction.

I had no choice and little time. I threw a quick shot at him and saw him stop and bend double as the bullet hit him in the lower abdomen. Then he fell back on his butt and grimaced in pain, but he wasn't out for the count. As I took a couple of steps in his direction, his revolver was starting to rise once again. This time I held my sights carefully on his upper torso and gently squeezed the trigger. Just as I did I realized that the edge of a flak jacket could be seen protruding above the neck of his sweater, which explained why my first shot hadn't made a more lasting impression. No matter.

Thornton's Colt roared at the same time mine did. Both bullets hit the man's Kevlar vest in the center of his chest and rocked him to the core. He fell backward, the revolver flying out of his hand. While I walked past him to secure the gun, I kept my .45 pointed at his head. By that time Thornton was on his other side with his gun's muzzle three feet from the man's temple, its hammer cocked. I felt confident that if there was any fight left in him, between the two of us we could purge him of it in short order. Like Delta Airlines, we were ready whenever he was.

His weapon turned out to be a Ruger .357 magnum. I stuffed it into my belt, and the two of us rolled him over on his belly. When we did, he screamed in agony and I didn't give a damn. We cuffed him and Thornton motioned for the Houston officer who had come in behind us to stand guard. Our three shots had a marked effect on the crowd. Patrons who had been hyperkinetic a moment before now stood frozen in terror as we threaded our way toward the rear. We stopped at the back door and I pulled out my cell phone. It had occurred to me that it might be prudent to find out what the situation was outside before we crashed through the door. Thornton was as pumped as I was, and I suspected the officers outside were as well. We were both too old to suffer the disgrace of falling victim to friendly fire.

I was just about to punch in Eva's number when my own phone buzzed. It was her. "What's the situation?" I asked.

"We got him. Come join the party."

I pushed the door open and we stepped carefully out into the dimly lit rear of the building. The man we'd come for was slumped against the back wall of the club. We all stood for a few seconds, staring down at him, saying nothing. My hands were beginning to shake from the adrenaline rush, and we were all breathing hard.

Eva was trembling too. Ranger Hoskins lit a cigarette with unsteady hands, and offered her the pack. "I quit," she said as she took one. He held his lighter for her and between the two of them they managed to get the thing going. "This woman is one hell of a shot," Hoskins said. "She got him in the upper leg."

"I really can't take much credit for that," Eva replied. "I

recognized him from the day he came to the office. I also saw that he was armed the second he came through the door. I just aimed low and hoped for the best. If I'd missed, the next one would have gone in his chest. Provided, of course, he hadn't gotten me by then."

I squatted down and shined my light on the man's wounded thigh only to find that it was barely bleeding. He halfway smiled as he gazed at me. He knew that I knew. He knew something else too: He knew it was the end of the line for him.

"Lamar DeLoach," I said, "you're under arrest for the murder of Dual Driggers."

"Who?" Eva asked.

"Lamar DeLoach."

"But DeLoach is dead. This is Leroy Fancher."

"No, he's not," I said. "There is no Leroy Fancher. That's DeLoach right there in front of you." I poked the man with my flashlight. "Did you understand what I said?"

He gave me a faint nod. I quickly recited the Miranda warning and asked him if he understood his rights. He nodded once again.

Hoskins searched him very carefully, after which I cuffed his hands in front of him to make life easier for the paramedics when they arrived.

"What kind of weapon did he have?" I asked.

"A Browning Hi Power."

"That's the same type of gun the Bureau's ballistics wizards say killed Crystal Henderson."

"That's right," Eva said. "I'd forgotten."

The man was silent. "What's the matter, DeLoach?" I asked. "That bullet take all the fight out of you?"

"Hurts like the devil," he said ruefully.

Just then the big black deputy, Hiram Cray, came up and knelt down beside me and peered carefully at our prisoner. "Lamar, what the hell you doing in this part of town?"

"You know him?" I asked.

"Sure I do. I thought you said the bird we were after was named Fancher."

"I did, but that's an alias he used. How do you know him?"

"I worked a case on him about five years ago. He caught a brother fooling around with his old lady and beat him half to death with a four iron."

"The guy he caught in bed with his girlfriend was black?"

"Sure was."

"That explains a lot," I said.

"How's that?" Cray asked.

"He's been running with some white supremacist, neo-Nazi types here lately."

"Well I'll be . . ." He peered at DeLoach for a moment. "What's that all about, Lamar? I know you don't like black folks, but I can't see you goose-stepping around nobody's back-yard, either."

"Go to hell," DeLoach said without rancor. "Both of you."

"Who's the guy I shot inside the club?" I asked him. "A buddy of yours or just some random thug who happened to be in the wrong place at the wrong time?"

"Why don't you ask him?" DeLoach said.

I turned to Cray. "I assume there's an ambulance on the way," I said.

"Two of 'em," he replied. "The one inside was wearing a flak vest under his sweater, but he's in bad shape anyway. Looks like he's got some broke ribs and maybe a ruptured gizzard or what-ever."

"Good," I said.

Cray laughed. "Man, you on a rip tonight, Sheriff."

"Any bastard who points a three fifty-seven at me gets on my permanent shit list. We'll need to run his prints and find out who the hell he is."

"I'm on it. He's got my curiosity up."

"Why were you coming out the front door?" I asked De-Loach. "Did you get squirrely and decide to leave?"

"I said go to hell."

"You may as well tell us since you're not admitting to a crime in doing so."

He seemed to ponder this for a few seconds, then he laughed. "I went out to get my passport photo. I'd forgotten and left it in the car. Isn't that a hoot?"

"You won't be needing a passport," I said. "The death house is here in Texas, and that's the only place you're headed."

He stopped smiling and looked up at me with those cold dead eyes that nothing ever touched and said, "A lot can happen between here and there, now can't it?"

CHAPTER FORTY

We followed the ambulances to the hospital where we were met by two other Houston deputies. Hoskins and Cray stayed in the examining room to guard DeLoach while three Houston deputies loomed over the bearded giant in another. The rest of us hung around in the corridor outside. After about a half hour, Eva was able to extract some information from the charge nurse, who was also Hispanic. The two of them had a lengthy, intense exchange in Spanish, then Eva come over to where Thornton and I sat.

"What's the verdict?" I asked.

"The bullet went all the way through. No arteries severed, or major veins either. Minimal blood loss. He's in no danger, and she says he can be moved if the doctor will okay it."

I looked at Thornton. "What do you think, Bob?" I asked.

"If they'll release the son of a bitch, let's take him home."

A couple of minutes later I caught the ER doctor coming out of the room where DeLoach lay. He was an impatient-looking young guy about my son's age. I pulled him aside and said, "Unless his life is in danger, I want to take him back to Sequoya tonight."

His eyes widened and his mouth tightened and I could tell he was on the verge of objecting.

"Look," I said, "we've got this man rock solid for two contract killings and the attempted murder of my chief deputy. He's already been to prison for beating a guy half to death over nothing. On top of that, there's a good chance that he killed his ex-girlfriend a few months back just because she was annoying him. He's an ex–Navy SEAL who will do *anything* to escape. You do not want him in your hospital."

I could see he was wavering. "Well—" he began.

"Believe it. This guy is a John Dillinger–grade badass without Dillinger's style or sense of humor. If you keep him here, even under police guard, you're apt to come to work some evening and find him long gone and a couple of your people dead. Are you ready to take that on yourself? This man should be locked down behind iron."

He nodded in resignation. "He'll need a round of antibiotics, which we can give you at the hospital pharmacy here before you leave. Also some painkillers. And he'll need to be examined by a physician in a day or so. If you'll agree to all that, then—"

I cut him off. "Done."

"Okay. I'll sign a release order right now. They should be about finished cleaning the wound and applying the bandage. There's really no medical reason to keep him here, though I would hold him overnight if he were a regular citizen."

"If he were a regular citizen I would encourage you to. My female deputy was a trained paramedic before she went into law enforcement. She can see to it that he doesn't bleed to death."

"There's no danger of that," he said. "Sometimes in these shootings it's the aftershock that causes problems. His blood pressure is elevated, and he has several other symptoms that make me think he's been using cocaine lately. Add all that to the stress of tonight's physical trauma and his heart could be in some danger."

"No need to worry about that. This guy doesn't have a heart."

As soon as he went off to post his orders, I called Liddy Snow. She answered on the first ring.

"Wake up," I said. "It's time for you to strut and fret your hour upon the stage."

"What?"

"Are you at home?"

"No, I've been here at the office chewing my nails ever since you left this afternoon."

"Good. Any reporters around?"

"I don't think so, but I bet I could get them around. CNN is back in town."

"Then it's time for you to have a little late-night press conference. Just be sure to call Sheila first. Okay?"

"Okay."

"Good. I'll go real slow so you can get it all down and—"

"No need. I've got a recording system that I can attach to my cell phone, so with your permission I'll just . . ."

I should have known. Another Shakespearian quote popped into my mind, this one about overweening ambition. But I pushed it aside and began to dictate. "Tonight officers of the Caddo County Sheriff's Department, the Texas Rangers, and the Harris County Sheriff's Fugitive Squad raided a nightclub in Houston's Fifth Ward and apprehended a suspect wanted here locally for the murders of Aaron Webern and Dual Driggers, and who is the prime suspect in the attempted murder of Chief Deputy Tobias Parsons. The suspect's name is Lamar DeLoach, and he has a prior criminal rec—"

"Wait a minute! I thought you were after a guy named Fancher."

"Liddy, Fancher *is* DeLoach, who was mistakenly thought to have died in a shootout with West Virginia State Police two years ago. I'm sure as soon as those folks up there find out he's alive they'll issue a warrant on him for the murder of a West Virginia state trooper."

"Mistakenly thought? But how . . . ?"

"The first day Eva worked for me she got the FBI file on De-Loach. It showed he'd been killed in a standoff in a farmhouse out in the country. Flash canisters set the house afire. When the ashes were sifted, a badly burned body was found, which was assumed to be DeLoach since he was thought to be the only person in the house. Because I thought he was dead, I never bothered to look at the file and I never saw his picture. If I had, I would have recognized him the day he came to my office with Hahn. It was a mistake on my part."

"Okay, how about the press release?"

"DeLoach, who has a previous criminal record including one stretch in the Texas prison system for felony assault, tried to flee his arrest this evening. He was wounded by Caddo County Deputy Eva Mendoza. An accomplice was wounded by me and Texas Ranger Bob Thornton. Be sure to give due credit to the Harris County folks. And you can also tell them that Judge MacGregor signed our warrants this afternoon, and that the man will be formally charged with all three crimes tomorrow morning."

"When are you bringing him home?" she asked.

"Shortly. It was a minor flesh wound, a bullet through the meaty part of his thigh. The hospital is releasing him, and we should be able to leave here in about a half hour."

"I'll see if I can have some cameras waiting when you get here."

"Good. Have 'em waiting out at the jail. You be there too and I'll let you do most of the talking."

"But I can't figure out why you're going for such a big media splash. It seems very much unlike you."

"I'll tell you when I see you."

———

Less than thirty minutes later we were in the department Suburban. I had DeLoach firmly chained fore and aft and in the center of the rear seat between Thornton and myself. I was mindful of his SEALs training, and had no doubt that he could cause us some trouble even wounded and manacled.

"You've got a choice," I told him. "You can either behave or we'll drag you out of this truck and beat on you until you can't misbehave anymore."

"I won't cause you any problems. I just want to sit here and enjoy this shot of Demerol the doctor gave me."

Eva was the youngest with the best reflexes, so I told her to get behind the wheel. "I normally don't like fast driving," I said. "But we've got some folks waiting for us at the jail, and I want to get home in time to get a little sleep tonight. Let the hammer down on this thing, and let's make some time. Turn on the flashers now and use the siren when you need to . . ."

We were almost to Livingston on U.S. 59 when my cell phone buzzed once again. It was Hiram Cray and he had some very interesting information about the search of DeLoach's car.

"How much?" I asked.

"A little better than seventy thousand dollars. In the trunk, locked up in a heavy steel box. Would have been kinda bulky to haul it around with him, anyway, so he didn't have much choice."

"That's a good point."

"Where in the hell did it come from?" he asked.

"He hijacked his own buddies for some fully automatic AK-forty-sevens and sold them, along with a moving van that belonged to a friend of mine."

"No joke?"

"I'll call in a few days and give you the whole story on this guy."

"Please do."

CHAPTER FORTY-ONE

Reverend Dawkins's posturing had unintended consequences. The previous day's "revelation" about Lyndon Till had brought the outside press back to town. The CNN team was in town putting the finishing touches on their documentary, and one of the Houston stations had covered his press conference. When we arrived at the jail there were about a dozen reporters waiting, along with a camera crew from the local network affiliate in Lufkin, including Emma Waters, the station's pretty blond coanchor. Except for Dan Ryder, a habitual smart-ass who served as the wire service stringer in central East Texas, the rest, including my niece Sheila, were from local dailies.

Sequoya actually had a perp walk. As Thornton and I hustled DeLoach into the building, video cameras recorded and flashes flashed. Once I had turned him over to two husky, no-nonsense jailors with instructions to house him in solitary confinement, I came back outside to face the music. Thornton ducked out the back door to avoid the press, just as he always did.

Liddy was magnificent. She adroitly fed them the information I'd given her over the phone. I let her field most of the questions, but several were addressed to me directly, including a couple from Ryder. "So you shot another man tonight, Sheriff. How many does that make?"

I answered this silly inquiry with a good-natured laugh. "You don't need to worry, Dan. None of them were reporters."

This brought a titter from the assembly. Emma Waters caught my attention. "Sheriff Handel, it's been rumored that both men who have been arrested in this matter are affiliated with the Aryan League. Is this true?"

This was the moment I'd been waiting for. "Yes, that is correct. They have both been living at the League's compound off and on for several months."

"Then can we assume that they are sympathetic to its political aims?"

"Most assuredly they are."

"Were the two murders with which DeLoch is to be charged related to the League's activities in any way?" she asked.

"So far as we know they were not," I said. "It seems as though both men were freelancing."

"Was DeLoach involved in the Parsons shooting by any chance?" Ryder asked.

"Yes. Chief Deputy Parsons made a positive photo ID of the man yesterday, and we have other evidence as well."

Ryder persisted. "Considering that Deputy Parsons is black, isn't it reasonable to assume that the Aryan League was involved in his shooting as Reverend Dawkins claimed and—"

I cut him off. "No, it's not reasonable at all because it's contrary to the facts. It's true that Lamar DeLoach is a virulent racist, and no doubt his personal hatred of blacks was a contributing factor in his actions. But the shooting was not a policy decision made in some sort of lodge meeting out there. It was an impulsive act on the part of one man, and you'll get all the details in a couple of days."

"Is there any sort of legal or police action planned against the Aryan League?" Emma Waters asked.

"Not by the Caddo County Sheriff's Department," I said innocently. "As for what the various federal agencies might have on their agendas, I couldn't say."

This brought a blizzard of excited questions.

I waved them off and said, "One last thing. This is the second time in four months that Ranger Bob Thornton and I have gone into a shooting scrape together, and if it ever happens again I want him there with me. He is a friend and a man of great courage. We should all appreciate him even though he refuses to come out here and take his share of the laurels."

There were more questions, but I'd had enough. "That's all," I said loudly and took Liddy by the arm and steered her inside the jail lobby.

"What?" she asked once the door was safely closed behind us.

"Have you figured out my reason for the press conference?"

"I think so. You did it to force Winthrop's hand."

"To force Washington's hand. Winthrop wanted to do the raid last week, but the AG's people ordered him to hold off. The truth is that I've done him a favor. But we should be aware that the Feds have been uncharacteristically cooperative on this venture. I think we need to throw them a bone."

"What do you have in mind?"

I quickly told her.

She took a deep breath and nodded. "I don't like it, but I won't object."

"Remember what Mr. Rayburn said? You've got to go along to get along."

She smiled. She had a very nice smile when she bothered to use it, which wasn't very often. "Why do I suspect I'm going to hear that a lot in the months and years to come?"

"Maybe you're psychic."

CHAPTER FORTY-TWO

I got into bed a little before 3:00 A.M. and managed to log nearly five hours sleep before the phone rang. I glanced at my watch to see that it was two minutes after eight. The caller was Winthrop. "When can we meet?" he asked.

"Who?"

"Me, you, Thornton, Miss Dee, the DEA people, and the assistant federal prosecutor who's handling this case."

"What's up?"

"The raid is on for today. Does that surprise you?"

"I kinda thought it might be today or tomorrow. Folks up north upset?"

"Actually, the assistant AG that's running this whole white supremacist investigation is a pragmatist. You made an end run around him, and that's water under the bridge to him. To tell the truth, I think he admired your gall in doing it. Some of those other guys would have got their shorts all in a twist and forced me to exclude you from the bust even though we don't currently have enough assets on the ground."

"That's what it's all about, isn't it?" I asked. "Assets on the ground, I mean."

"That and politics."

"What say we meet at ten o'clock at the new jail?"

"Perfect," he said. "I've already briefed Thornton by phone. He can get a helicopter from the Department of Public Safety."

"Good deal. See you at ten."

I made a quick call to Carla and give her some detailed instructions. Then I called Liddy. After we spoke, I put on the coffeepot and scrambled myself a couple of eggs.

Once I'd eaten, I remembered a promise I'd made and almost forgotten in the mad rush of the last few days. After digging Inspector Bierman's number out of my wallet, I gave the man a call. It was early afternoon in the small village in the foothills of the Bavarian Alps where he and his family lived. He was happy to hear my news. "Thank you," he said softly. "This will put my wife's mind at ease."

After promising to keep him informed about the progress of the prosecution, we hung up.

On the way across town my phone buzzed. Once again the caller was Hiram Cray of the Houston sheriff's office. "We didn't even have to run the prints on the guy you shot," he said. "He told us his name."

"Which is?"

"Derick Malloy. He's got quite a sheet too."

"What's on it?"

"Well, he did one jolt in Pennsylvania for armed robbery and one in Maryland for extortion. He and a couple of his buddies were running some kind of half-assed protection racket that blew up in their faces. And there's a murder warrant on him from Maryland."

"What are you going to do with him?"

"Beats me. There's a good reason why he talked. He claims to be a DEA snitch who was working DeLoach for some contacts with some East Coast drug bunch. He also says the Feds have promised him all sorts of slack for his services. He's asking for a lawyer and he wants to see somebody from the DEA."

"So are you going give him the red-carpet treatment?" I asked.

"Yeah. We'll get him a public defender and call the Feds. We've got no other choice. If they don't bust him loose from us, first we'll file charges here in Houston on last night's business, then we'll ship him up to Baltimore. It's our policy to do the most-est with the leastist. That means we let Maryland have first shot at him since their business is a capital offense. Our assistant DA is going to try to get him to plead out on last night's felony assault in hopes of having some nice hard time already waiting for him here in Texas just in case by some miracle he should happen to shake loose from the Maryland beef. That is all contingent on the Feds not spiriting him out of our hands, of course. As they have been known to do in the past."

"If you ship him up to Baltimore, do it with my blessings. I don't like him."

He laughed. "We will, and it was a pleasure working with you."

"Likewise," I said. I thanked him and hung up.

CHAPTER FORTY-THREE

I was the last to arrive at the meeting, which was held in the conference room at the new jail. A long mahogany table and about a dozen chairs took up most of the space. Winthrop and Hotchkiss were both there, sitting between Ranger Bob Thornton and DA Liddy Snow. So were a young black man and a young white woman in FBI windbreakers, along with a fortyish fellow in a gray suit, none of whom I'd ever seen before. At the head of the table opposite the door sat a tall individual with short, brush-cut hair. He had big hands, a wide, almost lipless mouth of the sort that wouldn't smile very often, and a long, hard face that held an expression that said its owner was used to giving orders and seeing people jump. I made him for a college basketball player about fifteen years and twenty-five pounds down the road from his hoop-shooting days. He was also seething. Miss April Dee of the ATF sat at his immediate left, and she was seething too. Superb. Maybe they could get together and spawn a whole litter of little seethers.

I had no more than shut the door when he spoke, and when he did his voice was an authoritative bark. "I'm Ben Chambless, DEA."

"You're also in my chair," I said calmly.

"Huh?"

I pointed to an empty place at the side of the table. "You sit over there," I said. "I get the Papa Bear place."

"Are you actually going to make an issue out of a chair?" he asked.

"Haven't you ever studied hierarchical psychology?" I asked, conjuring up a nonexistent discipline. "The person who sits at the head of the table is the *capo tutti capi*. The tush hog, as we say here in East Texas. That's why I always get the place of honor on my own ground. Now move."

Chambless moved slowly and reluctantly, but now there was a little wariness in his eyes. Once seated, he said, "I hope you realize you ruined an important DEA investigation."

"We'll get to that in a minute," I said. "First, the introductions. You've already told us who you are, so maybe if the gentleman next to you would be so kind?"

"Patrick O'Dyer," said the man in the suit. "Assistant U.S. attorney for the Eastern District of Texas."

They went around the table, with the two new Bureau agents identifying themselves as Lloyd Cole and Lynette Styles.

"And I'm Sheriff Bo Handel of Caddo County," I said when it was my turn. "Pleased you could all be here." I turned to Chambless. "Now let's hear your beef."

"Last night's raid. The guy you shot—"

"Derick Malloy, you mean," I said.

His eyes widened a little in surprise and he gave me a grudging nod. "He was a DEA undercover operative working Leroy Fancher for his contacts to some heavy-duty East Coast drug importers. You blew it for us."

"First, you need to understand that I didn't know about your investigation. Second, you need to understand that it wouldn't have made me one damned bit of difference if I had. We have the man you call Leroy Fancher solid for two murders right here in this county. That's what matters to me."

"This was a major operation."

"Not anymore it's not," I said, then decided to twist the knife a little further. "But I would like to know if Malloy was an agent or a snitch. I hope he was the latter because he was pointing a three fifty-seven at me when I shot him. I'd sure hate to think one of your agents would do that."

The look he gave me would have curdled milk. "He was an informant, of course."

"Then I can assume his rap sheet was for real and not a red herring stuck in the federal data bank to bolster his story in case there were some crooked cops involved?"

Chambless opened his mouth, then snapped it shut and gave me the evil eye.

O'Dyer spoke. "It's authentic."

"Including the murder warrant out of Maryland?"

He nodded.

I looked around the table. "Anyone else have anything to add?"

They all shook their heads. I turned back to Chambless. "We need to clear up a few points. For one thing, you weren't working Leroy Fancher for his drug contacts, and you know it. That's because Fancher's sheet doesn't list any. But the sheet he has under his real name does, that name being Lamar DeLoach. And that brings up the question of how you found out who he is."

Chambless appeared very uncertain of himself all of a sudden. He looked at O'Dyer, who nodded.

"Well?" I asked.

Chambless took a deep breath, then spoke. "DeLoach was picked up on a drug beef up in Paris, Texas, about two months ago. The cop who ran his prints saw his value to us because of his reputed contacts with the drug cartel. He called us, we got involved, and managed to get the charge dropped back to a misdemeanor so he could stay on the street."

"And how did Malloy come into the picture?"

"He attracted our attention with some of his criminal activi-

ties, and he was willing to work for us in return for a little consideration."

"Witness protection?"

"That's what he thought, anyway."

"Or not," I said.

"Oh? You think you know something that I don't?"

I was tempted to tell him that I was pretty sure I knew a lot of
things that he didn't, but I let it pass. Instead I said, "Let me tell
you what I think really happened. DeLoach is bound to have
been living in fear the last couple of years that some minor bust
would lead to his exposure through his prints being run nation-
ally . . ."

"But a lot of these small-town forces don't automatically run
prints," he said.

"That's right, but DeLoach is no fool, and you all but told
him they'd been run when the charge was reduced to a misdemeanor. You know why? Because that just doesn't happen in
places like Paris, Texas. What did they catch him with?"

"Cocaine."

"How much?"

"A quarter ounce. A relatively small amount."

I threw up my hands. "There you have it. That's a long-term
offense in this state. These rural juries routinely hand out twenty
years for that amount of coke, then go home and sleep soundly,
content that they've done the Lord's work. Which meant the
prosecutor had no real reason to cut him any slack, and you can
bet DeLoach was savvy enough to know that. The whole thing
spelled federal intervention. So after that rather obvious little
charade, he was almost certainly expecting somebody to pop
out of nowhere and get real friendly with him. When Malloy
showed up, he no doubt made him for a fellow criminal in about
three seconds. I bet DeLoach outed him to his face, which led to
the two of them having themselves a nice little sit-down somewhere, maybe over a few beers. After that, they were working

together, feeding you a little of what you wanted to hear until they could get in a position to jump the country."

"That's all speculation on your part," he said.

"Not when you factor in the seventy thousand dollars De-Loach had in the trunk of his car when we nailed him last night."

"What!?" he yelled.

"I'm pretty sure you heard me just fine," I said.

"But where in the hell did he get that kind of money?"

"From selling the AK-forty-sevens he stole from his own buddies out at the Aryan League. Plus whatever he got for the rig that was hauling them."

"You mean he's the one who—" Winthrop began.

"That's exactly what I mean," I said. "He and Hahn hijacked that truck. While we were on our way to Houston yesterday, my best interrogator was grilling Hahn, and he flipped completely. He was already pissed at DeLoach for disappearing with his half of the take from the hijacking. Since DeLoach didn't mind screwing Hahn, who was a guy he'd been running with for a year or longer and who could rat him out for two murders, it doesn't seem likely that he would have drawn the line at Malloy. I think he was planning to vanish and leave Malloy's body floating in some bar ditch somewhere down near the coast. That's why he was at the Climax Club trying to make arrangements to buy a bogus passport."

"A passport?" Chambless asked. "How in the name of God would you know about something like that? Hahn?"

I shook my head. "A confidential informant set him up for me. I've been sharing this guy with a couple of pretty good lawmen, but I'm his main contact. He's the same man who arranged the meeting at the Climax Club that we raided last night. Only we didn't know about Malloy, and the damnedest thing happened. DeLoach had forgotten and left the photo he wanted to use for his passport in his car. He happened to be on his way to get it when we approached the door. If that hadn't happened, the whole thing would have gone a lot more smoothly."

"But why was he trying to find a passport at some black dive in Houston?"

"Because Omar Turpin, the guy who runs the place, used to be a big-time hood with all sorts of scams and rackets going. One of them was bogus papers of all kinds. He had a couple of forgers who could cobble up anything you needed, and it would pass muster. DeLoach was trying to leave the country, no doubt to some place where we don't have an extradition treaty in effect. He called our informant about getting a passport. Our man thought of Turpin because back in the early seventies they'd been pretty thick." I stopped and let this sink in.

Chambliss thought for a moment, then said, "I don't understand why DeLoach would think your informant would know about where he could get a forged passport."

Winthrop spoke. "If you were familiar with our informant you would. And just for the record, I think Sheriff Handel is right on the money with his scenario."

I looked across at Miss Dee. "And what does *your* snitch have to say about all this?" I asked.

"What?" she asked, clearly surprised.

"The man the ATF has undercover out there. You let that cat out of the bag when you mentioned Kaiser Trucking the first day we met. You see, there's no way that truck could have been seen from the road. Had to be somebody inside that told you about it."

She was seething once again. "I'm not at liberty to discuss that."

"I didn't think you would be," I said.

There was a momentary clash of the titans when Liddy Snow smiled across the table at her and asked, "Ever read *The Man Who Was Thursday*?"

"What?"

"G. K. Chesterton. It's a great book about a guy Scotland

Yard gets to infiltrate an anarchist group in Victorian London. There are seven in the group, each with a code name for one of the days of the week. He becomes Thursday. Turns out that all of them were Scotland Yard plants except Sunday, who was the ringleader. But they almost carry the plot through and blow up Parliament because each is afraid to out himself in front of the others. This situation brought it to mind, and I can't help but wonder if you're really sure any of those people out there are bona fide white supremacists."

"Of course we are," Miss Dee spat.

"All of which begs the immediate issue," O'Dyer said with a little cough, "which is that the raid on the Aryan League compound is on for four this afternoon. That is what this meeting has been called to coordinate."

"Then let's get all our cards on the table," I said. "We've seen here this morning the disadvantages of not letting the left hand know what the right hand is doing."

"Sounds good to me," Winthrop said. "The AG's office has given my agency command of this operation, but I don't like to run over people. So let's just say that I am the chief coordinator. The DEA will get the drug charges, and the ATF will handle the firearms beefs. The Bureau will be in charge of making the conspiracy cases that come out of today's activities, and believe me, they will come. Sheriff Handel and his people have been of enormous assistance. He's run our informant and developed other sources of valuable intel. I would like to know what he wants in return for his efforts."

"You already know what I want," I said. "No slack for De-Loach on the murder charges. No spiriting him out of state hands by you Feds for *any* reason. Let me have that and you'll have full cooperation of my department and the local DA's office."

"I think you nixed any possible deals for DeLoach, Sheriff," O'Dyer said with a cold smile. "Your press conference was aired all over the country on CNN this morning."

"That is what it was meant to do," I said.

"So how about the Rangers and the state people?" Winthrop asked, turning to Thornton.

It was Thornton's turn to speak. "We'll coordinate with the Texas AG's office and the local DA on any charges beyond what you Feds file. It wouldn't surprise me a bit to find some state warrants on some of these guys. We might clear some cases out of this. On a personal note, I'm happy to have the Driggers murder cleared since I've been working it alongside Bo from the beginning."

"Good deal," O'Dyer said. "Now on to the raid. What do we have planned?"

Winthrop fielded the question. "The way it unfolds will depend to some extent on the state's contribution." Winthrop turned once again to Bob Thornton. "What can we count on there?"

"We've got four highway patrol cruisers set to converge in pairs and cover the side roads in case any of these birds try to flee the compound that way. That's two troopers to a car, and these boys will stay alert. And we have the DPS helicopter I told you about this morning. It'll hold five besides the pilot. I'm thinking of me and the Ranger from Nacogdoches County along with three of your folks. The copter is equipped with bullhorns and a PA system. We can pull an *Apocalypse Now* number on them as we come in if you want. Tell everybody to come out empty-handed and so forth."

"Sounds good," Winthrop said. "Cole and Styles and one other agent can go in the copter."

"I like to fly," Chambless said.

"Fine. You are now the third agent. The three of you will need to go with Thornton when we break up here."

"We've also got a twenty-passenger bus coming from the Beto Unit of the prison system," Thornton said. "It's fixed up where we can chain 'em together. I figure it ought to be big enough to haul this bunch of clowns into the jailhouse."

"That's great, Bob," I said. "I was starting to worry a little about how we were going to get them all back to town."

"How about the front?" O'Dyer asked.

"Three vehicles," Winthrop said. "A Suburban from Caddo County with the sheriff, two deputies, and a couple more agents. Two federal vans with our people and the ATF and DEA guys. Straight in through the front gate. If it's closed, we crash it."

"What about the guard at the gate?" Thornton asked.

"Forget about him," I said. "He's neutralized."

"Sounds like you got him in your pocket," O'Dyer said.

"I've known him all my life. He's a racist peckerwood, but he's all talk. He heard some rumbles about the guns, and came to me a while back. I also want him to get a walk on this. No arrest since he hasn't done anything."

"Sure," O'Dyer said.

"One thing that concerns me is the back of the property," Winthrop said. "The front and sides are bounded by roads, and that's easy enough to cover. But the rear backs up against a pretty dense stand of woods. If some of these bozos were to get back there we could lose them."

"That's no problem," I said

"How so?" he asked.

"Horses."

"Shit!" Chambless exclaimed. "What are you trying to do? Play Walt Longmire?"

"Not at all. Look at the map. There are about two hundred yards of fence back there to cover, with the tree line about thirty yards beyond the fence. I'm putting a couple of my deputies back there just inside the woods on horses. If anybody gets through or across the fence they can run them down in no time at all."

"But why horses?" Chambless asked.

"Because a horse can run faster than a man. Why have people on foot when they can have the advantage of being mounted?"

"You already have the horses?" O'Dyer asked.

"Yeah," I said. "Dogs are available too, if we should need them. Trailing hounds. There's thousands and thousands of acres of timber land in this county, especially in the northwest along the Angelina River. About two or three times a year some damn fool nature lover gets lost, and the only practical way to go after them is with horses and hounds. We've even had a few fugitives to get loose out in the woods over the years."

"Sounds good to me," Winthrop said. "How soon can you get them moving?"

"The horses are being loaded into my trailer right about now," I said. "They're going to go around to the far side of that stand of woods and come through the trees. They'll be in place well before we hit the compound. All I have to do is call them and tell them when."

"Who do you have assigned to the horses?" Winthrop asked.

"A former deputy of mine named Carla Wallace. She still holds a Texas law enforcement commission and fills in part time on occasion. And a new deputy I recently hired fresh from a decade with the Houston PD. Her name is Eva Mendoza. You've met her at my office."

"Two women?" Chambless asked.

"Two Valkyries is a more accurate description," I said. "Both these girls were barrel racers in their teens, which means they can ride better than most men. Plus, neither one of them is anybody I'd want to go up against in a gunfight. They'll have riot guns, and they can handle anything that comes over that fence. Count on it."

"Good enough," Winthrop said.

There were more details to iron out, especially the problem of coordinating the helicopter's arrival with our entry through the front gate. But I left such matters to those better qualified to deal with them. The meeting broke up after another half hour. As the others were leaving Winthrop pulled me over to one side. "I talked to the people in Washington about Spencer's house," he said.

"And?"

"They were reasonable about it. Particularly after I pointed out the possible political repercussions of throwing an old man and an old woman out of their home."

"Whatever works."

"Spencer isn't even going to be arrested and charged. They're willing to take Sparks's assessment that the old man had nothing to do with the guns."

I shook my head. "I didn't ask you to go that far. In fact, it sounds very un-Washington-like to me."

He smiled and shrugged. "A new administration, a new way of doing things. Besides, there's been some rethinking done."

"Yeah?

He nodded and his voice grew hard. "The press release is going to be worded in such a way that the natural conclusion will be that Spencer himself asked us to clean out this squirrel cage after things got out of hand."

I shook my head in wonder. "That's cold. Creative, but cold."

"Do you care?"

"Hell no."

"It should undermine any future influence he might have on the white supremacist movement by ensuring that he'll be seen as a turncoat. Hell, it's better than arresting him. His great dream of union is over."

"It never was much of a dream anyway, now was it?" I asked. "Uniting what? Thirty thousand political marginals? That's about as meaningful as uniting all the bag ladies of New York."

"The German Workers' Party only had about two dozen members when Hitler joined it. No one knows what the future might have held for this bunch."

"If anything like that ever happens in this country I'll be long gone, and you younger folks can worry about it." I stuck out my hand. "I appreciate your effort. You did the right thing."

"I know. There was also his wife to consider. By our intel, she neither shares nor cares about his political opinions."

"I'm not surprised," I said. "Are you riding with me?"

"I thought I would."

"Then let's check our gear and then have a light lunch. We've got some time to kill."

CHAPTER FORTY-FOUR

I drove the Suburban with Winthrop in the front beside me co-ordinating by radio with the helicopter. The two federal vans loaded with agents and three of my deputies were behind us and the prison bus was behind them bringing up the rear. I stopped a quarter mile down the road from the gate and waited for the signal, which came when the copter was about two minutes out. I gunned the vehicle and swung up in front of the gate house. Lyndon Till stepped out, his eyes full of alarm.

"Open up and haul ass for home, Lyndon," I said. "It's all over for this bunch."

Once again I got that fishing-cork nod, and this time it was full of unvarnished enthusiasm. He threw the switch and the gate swung open. As I sped by I could see him scurrying out the back door and toward his pickup faster than I ever thought a man his age and bulk could move.

"So that's your local redneck?" Winthrop asked.

I nodded. "That's him."

"Looks like he's deserting the cause."

"The man is glad to be shut of this place."

The road led through that same small stand of woods and on past Spencer's house to a wide expanse of grassy field directly behind it. The buildings and mobile homes were some hundred or so yards away, strung out on the far side of the clearing. Besides the residential trailers, there was one twelve by forty that served as an office. To the east side sat two metal buildings and a large barnlike structure that was roofed and sided in corrugated iron.

As I pulled up and stopped I heard the copter's blades and Thornton's voice booming out over the PA system telling everybody to come out with their hands in the air. *"This is a raid. Use your heads and come on out with your hands in the air. I repeat: this is a raid, and we have state and federal warrants. The grounds are fully covered and you are surrounded. You have no choice but to come out peacefully. I repeat: this is a raid. Come out with your hands in the air."*

Faces appeared gaping at windows. A few heads began to poke out of the various trailers in the distance. Then doors opened reluctantly and men and women began to step hesitantly out, their hands above their heads. They were all reasonably respectable looking, the men in jeans and most with either goatees or neatly trimmed full-face beards, the women in jeans and sweaters.

The copter touched down and Thornton and Chambless and the other agents poured out in flak gear, holding M-16s or riot guns at port arms. Thornton carried the old Remington semiauto .308 with its Lyman receiver peep sight that he'd used as his duty rifle ever since I'd known him.

The officers in the vans behind us spread out and began to make their way carefully toward the trailers, with one heading for Spencer's house. Billy Don Smith and two of my other deputies jogged past us, along with agents from the ATF and the DEA. They fanned out on both sides of the clearing, following the tree lines for cover. Styles and Cole broke away from Thornton and Chambless and disappeared into the woods on the east side of the clearing.

"What the hell are they doing?" I asked Winthrop.

"Aerial photos show one travel trailer up behind that tin barn. They're detailed to check it out."

The office trailer sat at the left side of the clearing. Suddenly the door burst open and a large, bald man lunged out with what looked like an AK-47. Then the fool raised the rifle, pointed it our way and squeezed the trigger. The weapon popped four times, and bullets whizzed over our heads. He was a good seventy yards distant, but Thornton took him down with one shot, his Remington barking as soon as the stock hit his shoulder. The man fell to the ground clutching his belly. Women screamed while men ducked and cowered.

I grabbed my cell phone and dialed the office and told the dispatcher what I needed. "Get two ambulances out here as quickly as you can," I said. "First call the Sequoya Fire Department and have them send their rescue unit along with the paramedics. Then get one from Nacogdoches."

Winthrop's radio squawked. He hefted it to his face and said, "What have you got down there?"

"One subject headed for the rear of the property and two others made a break for the road on the west side."

"Alert the Highway Patrol," I said. "They'll get the two headed west." I quickly called Carla and told her the action was coming their way.

Winthrop and I were only a few yards behind the house. I looked over my shoulder to see Dr. Spencer standing on his patio observing the proceedings. The agent who had been detailed to cover his house was at a loss as to what to do. I hurried up to where he stood and said, "We aren't here to arrest you. Go inside and get your wife and take her to the front side of the house. Stay away from the windows. There could be more gunplay."

He hesitated, for a few seconds, his face full of surprise.

"Your wife could be in danger," I said. "Go take care of her, and do what this young man says."

He nodded sadly and turned back toward the doorway with the young agent following. I looked back toward the clearing and spotted Winthrop waving at me. I made my way back to where he stood. Agents had a dozen or so people in handcuffs and were dutifully marching them across the clearing and toward the main road where the bus waited. "What's the problem?" I asked.

"Two guys won't come out of the office. They say they have weapons."

"Any hostages?"

"No. Just two scared assholes."

"What do you want to do?" I asked.

"I'm not interested in dickering with these jerks all afternoon."

"Me either," I said. "Why don't we send a couple of guys around back through the trees to the rear of that trailer to lob in tear gas canisters? Then let's get on the bullhorn right before the tear gas goes in and tell 'em what's about to happen. Maybe they'll surrender when the gas drives them out."

"I was thinking the same thing," he said. "But just in case let's have Thornton and at least one other good rifle shot ready."

"I'll take second rifle," I said.

He told one of the federal agents to give me his M-16 and then radioed for one van to be brought up. Thornton trotted back toward us from where he'd been examining the man he shot. "How is he?" I asked.

"Gut shot. It looks like I missed his aorta and his spine. I think he'll be okay."

"We've got an ambulance on the way," I said.

Winthrop and Thornton and I got in. The driver made a long, curving sweep and stopped about twenty yards away from the trailer. We got out of the side of the van opposite the trailer and used the vehicle for cover. Then came a wait of about five minutes while the two men with tear gas guns worked their way around to the rear. When they radioed Winthrop that they were in place, he took his bullhorn and said, *"We've got tear gas coming in. You are surrounded and covered by officers armed with fully automatic rifles. Throw down your weapons and come out with your hands above your heads. Any show of resistance and we will open fire."*

Thornton and I were both ready, our rifles at our shoulders. A few seconds later we heard two muted gunshots, followed by the sound of breaking glass. Next came the coughing and snorting and yelling. Finally the front door opened and a pair of empty hands emerged.

"Don't shoot!" we heard the man say. "For God's sake, don't shoot!"

"Come down the steps and hit the ground facedown," Winthrop said over the bullhorn.

A tall man clad in jeans and a red checked flannel shirt stumbled across the small porch and down the steps and went down on his knees before stretching out on the grass.

"Where's your buddy?" Winthrop asked.

"He says he's not coming out."

"Yes I am! Yes I am!" a high-pitched voice screeched as the second man stumbled through the doorway. He appeared to be a clone of the first except that his shirt was green checks. Temporarily blinded by the gas, he managed to get down the steps without falling, but he got tangled in his cohort's legs and fell face-first onto the ground. We quickly swarmed the pair and got them both cuffed, searched, and on their feet. Winthrop motioned for two of the agents to search the trailer. It didn't take long. One young ATF officer stepped out onto the porch holding up a pump-action .22 rifle. "This is their weapon," he said disgustedly.

"Don't scoff," I said. "That damned thing will kill a man just as dead as a bazooka if it hits him in the right place."

The two culprits were still coughing and tears were pouring

from their reddened eyes as we started walking them toward the bus. Suddenly Winthrop's radio came alive and I could hear April Dee's voice over its speaker. "Agent Winthrop, we need you down here at the tin barn," she said.

"What's going on?"

"Looks like we've got a hostage situation. Three of these people got the drop on Agent Styles and took her sidearm. She's inside with them."

"Does anybody know who they are?" I asked as we started down toward the shed. Winthrop relayed my question to her.

"Two are unidentified, but one of the perps out here saw them go in. He couldn't tell who the other two are, but he says the third is a guy named Jasper Sparks."

CHAPTER FORTY-FIVE

We jumped into one of the vans and drove down to the barn, stopping about fifty feet away from the front door. We piled out on the side opposite the building and hunkered down behind the vehicle. The world around us was sunny and silent except for a faint breeze rustling the leafless branches of the trees. The barn looked sedate and innocuous, just a well-built tin building like thousands all across East Texas. I shivered a little. Something I have learned in my years as sheriff is that the most prosaic and innocent of scenes can mask the worst and bloodiest of atrocities.

"Does anybody have any experience in hostage negotiation?" Winthrop asked.

No one spoke for a few moments. Then Chambless said, "I've had a lot of training, but I've only handled one actual hostage situation."

"How did it end?"

"Good enough, I guess. I managed to talk them into giving up."

"That makes you the most experienced man here," Winthrop said. "The ball is in your court."

Chambless nodded, a worried frown on his face. "Then the first thing we have to do is establish communication."

Winthrop hailed Styles twice over the radio, then pulled out his cell phone and punched in her number. He handed the phone to Chambless and said, "I hope to God somebody answers."

A few moments later we heard a one-sided conversation as Chambless said, "And your name is? Good, Mr. Graves. Who am I? Well, sir, I'm Ben Chambless with the DEA. You can call me Ben if you want to. We're going to have to talk on the radio. This cell phone is almost out of power. That's right, Agent Styles's radio. Just make sure it's on and push the red button when you want to speak."

He switched off the phone and drew a relieved breath. I was impressed. His demeanor was calm, pliable, nonconfrontational. Not at all what I would have expected from him. "I'm putting him on radio so we can all hear," he said, looking first at Winthrop and then at me. "I welcome your suggestions, but please don't say anything while I'm speaking over this thing. We don't want to confuse the man."

A moment later a voice came through the radio, and I could tell the speaker was stressed, near hysteria. "Graves here. Are you a white man, Ben?"

"Yes, I certainly am," Chambless replied.

"You're not a Jew, are you?"

"No, I'm a Methodist."

"Good, because I won't deal with no Jews or coloreds."

"I'm English and Irish with a little German thrown in. But this isn't about me. It's about you. Now I need to know if anyone has been hurt in there."

"No, we're all fine. I've got this woman agent of yours. She says her name is Styles. You need to keep that in mind."

"We're aware of that. Is she okay?"

"I told you she was, didn't I?"

"I'm sorry. I didn't understand you. Would you let me come in and see for myself?"

"No. Don't you believe me?"

"That's not the problem," Chambless said smoothly. "I'm not

the head man out here. We have to convince the senior agent who's running the show. Now, you need to understand that I want to resolve this peacefully, but you also have to understand that I have some constraints I'm working under. If the hostage is harmed in any way, the negotiations will be over. That's not me saying that, it's the man who's in command. So I really want to impress upon you that no matter how badly I want this to end well, if the hostage is hurt in any way the whole thing will be taken out of my hands. Do you understand that?"

"Yeah, I got it. Do you think I'm stupid, Ben?"

"No, Mr. Graves, I think you're pretty smart. That's why I have every confidence that we can bring this to a satisfactory conclusion. Right now this is only a case of unlawful confinement. We want to make sure it doesn't go beyond that."

"If you try to storm the building I'll kill her first thing," Graves said, his voice edging near hysteria once again.

"That's not going to happen as long as she's safe and unharmed."

Graves muttered something unintelligible into the radio, then said, "Let me think for a minute."

"Take your time," Chambless said and turned to Winthrop. "We need to know more about this guy. Do you have a file on him?"

"No, he's new here."

Miss Dee spoke up. "Our informant might know him."

"Where is he?" Winthrop asked.

"On the bus. We arrested him to maintain his cover."

"That's a secondary consideration now," Winthrop said. "Get his ass back down here. And bring that other van up. We need more working room."

Chambless keyed the radio and said, "Are you there, Mr. Graves?"

"Yeah, I'm here."

"We're bringing another van around to work with. It has the

gadget we need to plug the radio into the charger on its dashboard. Do you understand?"

"Not a fucking thing I can do about it, is there?"

"We need to maintain communications," Chambless said, once again avoiding answering his question. "This radio shows a weak charge."

"You're having a lot of battery problems today, aren't you, Ben?"

"We'll get it taken care of. I'm here to listen. I need to hear what you have to say."

The van drew up immediately behind the first one. Soon April Dee was back with her informant. "This is Agent Jackson Knapp of the ATF," she said.

I had to laugh. The man had completely fooled me.

"Hello, Sheriff," he said with a twisted smile.

I introduced him to Winthrop and Chambless.

"We need your help here," Winthrop said. "The guy running things in there is somebody called Graves. What do you know about him?"

"His full name's Layton Graves," Knapp said. "He's a hardcore speed freak. What more is there to know?"

"Damn!" Chambless said.

"Is he speeding today?" I asked.

"Layton only has two operating modes," Knapp said. "He's either cranked to the gills or he's crashed and asleep. Sometimes he stays up four or five days at a time on that crap."

"Are you still there, Ben?" Graves suddenly screamed over the radio.

"I'm here," Chambless said soothingly. "I'm not going anywhere."

"I want a car. I want a car, and I want you people to get way back out of the way. We're taking Miss Priss, and we're getting the hell out of here."

"That may take some time," Chambless said. "We would have

to clear something like that with Washington first. Let me see what I can do."

"You better do something quick! I'm giving you an hour."

"Let's just both stay calm and I'll get started and see what I can do."

Winthrop turned to Knapp. "Graves has a buddy in there with him. Who do you think it might be?"

"A buddy?" Knapp asked. "Agent Dee said there're three men in there, and that one of them is Jasper Sparks. That worries me."

"Don't let it," Winthrop said. "He's a Bureau informant."

She stared at him a moment in disbelief. "If he's an informant, what's he doing in that shed?"

"I don't know," Winthrop said. "He could be a hostage too."

"Maybe he turned right here at the end," Knapp said. "Nobody ever knows what a psychopath is going to do."

"You sound like you're familiar with him," I said to Knapp.

Knapp nodded. "We both are. I got the file on him after I met him. He's one freaky dude, let me tell you."

"A mutual admiration society," I said.

"What?"

"He said the same thing about you. Any idea who the other man might be?" I asked.

"Probably a guy named Jay Wilson," Knapp said. "He and Graves are running buddies."

"Is he a speed freak too?" Chambless asked.

"He likes the stuff, but he's not nearly as bad as Graves."

"How old are these birds?" I asked.

"Late twenties," Knapp said. "No real criminal record on either one."

"Damn!" I said with a grimace. "That's one reason why this happened."

"What makes you think so?" Knapp asked.

Chambless answered for me. "Neither of them has ever been in the system, so they've got no perspective. The bust happens, and the first thing they do is visualize a lifetime in prison stretching ahead of them just for being here. Add in the effects of the speed, and one of them loses it. Most probably Graves, if he's as crazy as you say. So instead of going along peacefully and getting a lawyer and negotiating, here we are. Right, Sheriff?"

I nodded. "Exactly. The two most dangerous types of criminal a lawman can deal with is a greenhorn felon facing the joint for the first time and scared half to death, and the old-timer who's gone on a spree and racked up so many charges he's got nothing to lose."

"Are you people just fucking around out there?" Graves screamed over the radio. "You better be talking to Washington!"

"We're trying to find a fully charged cell phone," Chambless said. "We'll get through to them in a couple of minutes."

"You better get moving or I'm gonna kill this bitch!"

"Do you need anything?" Chambless asked calmly. "Maybe water or some soft drinks or something?"

"We need that fucking car. That's what we need, and that's all we need."

"We're working on it," Chambless said.

"If it came down to it," Winthrop said, turning to me, "and we brought a car up here to entice them outside, do you think you and Thornton could take them out with rifles?"

I shook my head. "Graves is not going to let you park the car any distance at all away from the door. He's going to want you to run it right up against the side of the building in front of the door, and that would give us too small a window of time. Even if one of us could get a shot, he's probably going to have his pistol right up against her head with the safety off. Too much risk of him pulling the trigger by reflex even if we get a brain shot."

"I worry about the time limit he set," Winthrop said.

"I don't intend to mention that," Chambless said. "Standard procedure in hostage negotiation is not to refer back to any time limits the hostage-taker has mentioned. You try to distract him with conversation when the deadline is coming up and hope that it passes without his noticing."

"I don't think that's going to work with this guy," I said. "He's too cranked up."

"What's going on out there, Ben?" Graves screamed over the radio.

"I'm just dealing with Washington. The individual I spoke to has to go up a couple of levels. He doesn't have the authority to okay a car for you."

"Somebody with some kind of goddamned authority better do something quick. The clock is ticking away on this deal."

"What's that building used for?" Winthrop asked Knapp.

"It's where they keep the tractor and a bunch of tools."

"Is the tractor in there now?"

Knapp shook his head. "It's in the back pasture. They were digging some post holes with the auger."

"How many doors?" I asked.

"One back door, and the big one on the side where they drive the tractor in. The floor's concrete, and the other doors are always kept locked from the inside."

"Windows?" Winthrop asked.

"None. It's wired for electricity. It's got a couple of three-hundred-watt bulbs overhead, and a long, double fluorescent fixture over the workbench."

"No way to get in quick enough to have the element of surprise, then?" Chambless asked.

"No," Knapp said. "Those doors are way too secure. Iron bars and chains."

Winthrop looked off into the distance and seemed lost in thought for a few seconds. "There's no way in hell we give these guys a car," he said. "As long as this situation is contained here at the compound the public isn't in danger."

"That was never an option as far as I was concerned," Thornton said.

Winthrop shook his head sadly. "With a guy like that you wonder if you're talking to the man or the drug," he said.

"It's the drug," I said.

"Then I'll just have to get through to the man," Chambless said grimly and raised the radio once more to speak. "Mr. Graves, are you there?"

"Hell yes, I'm here. Have you heard from Washington?"

"Not yet. We're still waiting."

"Somebody better hurry up and get their asses moving!"

"Mr. Graves, according to our information neither you nor Mr. Wilson have any prior convictions."

"I got some juvenile beefs on my record."

"Those don't matter," Chambless said. "What matters is that without any prior adult convictions, as things stand now you aren't jammed up bad at all. We need to end this peacefully. If it goes any further you will really be in over your heads."

"Can you guarantee no charges will be filed against me?" Graves asked.

"I can guarantee that if you come out peacefully and no one is harmed I will personally go to bat for you with the federal prosecutors. I give you my word on that, and I promise you I will do my best."

"There's still the state," Graves said. "I saw the sheriff out there."

Chambless looked at me questioningly.

"I think he's a little calmer, don't you?" I said.

"Yeah."

"Tell him I can guarantee no state charges will be filed at all."

"Can you really come through on that?" Winthrop asked.

"Yes I can."

Chambless raised the walkie-talkie once again. "Sheriff Handel guarantees that no state charges will be filed if you come out and end this thing."

"I'm not sure I trust . . ." Graves began, then broke off. A moment later we heard him scream, "Dammit, I'm going to kick some ass!" and the radio went dead. Suddenly, we heard yelling through the walls of the building. We stood, hardly breathing. The speaker sounded like Graves, and he was ranting and raving. We heard him scream, "Fucking snitch!" A second later came the sound of two gunshots.

We were stunned. Chambless stood shaking his head in regret. "Damned speed," he muttered. "You were right. We were talking to the speed all along, and it took over."

"What do you think we should do now?" Winthrop asked.

"Wait," I said. "That's all we can do. If he hasn't already shot her, he damn sure will if we John Wayne the place."

The next few seconds seemed to stretch out forever. Chambless hailed Graves time and again over the radio, all to no avail. Then he fell silent. Once again I became conscious of the mild breeze. Somewhere far away a crow cawed twice. I looked around. The woods and hills and fields seemed so completely familiar to me, the same sort of soft, kind landscape I'd known all my life. Yet at the same time they seemed strangely alien, like something from another country seen for the first time, made that way by the fear that a decent young woman lay needlessly dead inside the building in front of us.

"Try the radio again," I said to Chambless, my voice a near whisper.

He brought the walkie-talkie once more up to his mouth and was about to speak when it crackled and came alive. "This is Agent Styles. I've got control of the situation in here."

CHAPTER FORTY-SIX

Styles brought the two men out. Wilson had his hands hand-cuffed in front of him so he could drag the prostrate Graves through the doorway while she covered both with her sidearm. As soon as they were outside, we threw Wilson to the ground and got them both completely secured. The moment the cuffs were snapped on Graves, he came to life, his eyes wild. He started cursing and yammering at us, but no one paid any attention to him.

"Where's Sparks?" Winthrop asked.

"He saved my ass," Styles said. "He's still inside, badly wounded. Took two bullets. We need an ambulance."

"One's already on the scene," Winthrop said.

"Then for God's sake get them over here." She looked at me and motioned for me to follow her. "He's asking for you, Sheriff. You're the one he wants to see."

We found him propped up against the rear wall of the shed, a pair of bullet holes in his chest and a thin trickle of blood coming from the corner of his mouth. His eyes were still diamond bright, though, and his lips held a hint of a smile. I squatted down beside him while Agent Styles knelt on his other side. "Thank you," she said to him softly.

He winked at her and spoke, and when he did his voice was a near whisper. "Had to do it. You're too pretty to die so young."

"Hang on," I said. "The medics are on the way."

He shook his head a little and reached toward me. For a moment the gesture puzzled me until I realized he wanted to shake hands. When I took his hand his grip was surprisingly firm. "You like to fish, Sheriff?" he asked.

"Huh?" The question was so out of context that it surprised me.

"Do you fish?" he repeated.

"Some. I'm really more of a hunter. Quail, dove, deer."

"I loved quail hunting when I was a kid."

"You stick around and we'll do it," I said.

He laughed a little and then coughed, and when he did tiny bubbles of blood trickled out of his mouth. "You know a convicted felon isn't supposed to touch a gun."

"I bet Winthrop can get you some slack on that. Enough at least for us to have a day hunt at that plantation up near Carthage."

"That would be a fine day," he said, his voice now almost inaudible. "But . . ."

"Jasper—"

He cut me off with another shake of his head. I nodded in understanding and knelt there with his hand in mine until his grip relaxed and his eyes dulled and he was gone.

I led Agent Styles gently outside. She was shaking and pale. "You haven't ever seen anybody die before, have you?" I asked.

She shook her head.

"It's never pretty."

Just then the paramedics arrived, a male and a female, both in their late twenties. "Too late, folks," I said. "The man is gone."

"We need to confirm that," the man said. "For our records and liability purposes."

"Okay, but don't move the body. We'll need to get crime scene photos."

"How's Agent Cole?" Styles asked.

"He's conscious," Winthrop said. "They've taken him to the hospital in Nacogdoches for an X-ray and observation."

"He's lucky to be alive. That was one hell of a blow on the head he took."

"What happened?" he asked. "How did you wind up in there?"

She took a deep breath and began. "After we checked that trailer back in the woods and found it empty, we were headed back to the clearing. Graves and Wilson just came out of nowhere. Graves slammed Agent Cole in the back of the head with that shotgun, and after that he handed it to Wilson and took my sidearm. Then they started hustling me toward that shed. Sparks saw them and came along too, trying to talk them into giving up the whole time. Graves told him to back off and leave, but Sparks wouldn't pay any attention to him. When they dragged me into the shed he followed. Graves said he was going to demand a car and a head start or else they'd kill me. Sparks told him it would never wash, and that the Bureau wouldn't bargain with him. He told them that whatever trouble they were in it wasn't as bad as facing the needle if they killed me. He kept hammering that point in, and he must have gotten through to Wilson. But Graves was pumped, wild-eyed, crazy as hell.

"Not Sparks. He was calm as ice. All during the negotiations he had me behind him, with both of us backed into the corner. Graves told him to move several times, but he refused. Then out of nowhere Graves accused him of being an informant. When Sparks didn't deny it, Graves just lost it and and shot him twice. One bullet went all the way through Sparks and passed within a couple of inches of my ear. Sparks's legs gave way under him, and he just sort of sat down. That's when Graves said he was going to go ahead and kill me, too. Apparently that was enough for Wilson. He bashed Graves in the head with the butt of his shotgun and then he laid the shotgun on the floor in front of me and backed up with his hands in the air. That's when I brought them out, and you know the rest."

"You're lucky," I told her. "If Sparks hadn't been there that fool might have killed you on impulse instead." I took her arm. "Come on. I've got a bottle of whiskey in my department Suburban. You look like you could use a snort or two."

"But I'm on duty—" she began.

Winthrop leaned over and whispered to her, "Go have a drink. That's an order."

I got her seated in the front passenger seat and broke out the pint of V.O. I kept in the glove box. After three good belts a little color returned to her face.

"Feeling a bit better?" I asked.

She nodded.

"It happens to almost everybody. The shakes, I mean. I almost shook to pieces after that shooting scrape last night."

"I was so terrified."

"Of course you were," I said. "That's because you've got good sense and normal human reactions."

"But I don't think Sparks was a bit frightened."

"He wasn't a normal human being," I said.

She took one more sip from the bottle, then capped it and handed it back to me. "Then what was he?" she asked. "A hero who saved my life at the cost of his own?"

"Today he was, yes. I don't think there's any doubt about it."

"But forty years ago he was an armed robber and a hit man?"

"There's no doubt about that, either," I said with a nod. "As cold and remorseless as they come. Are you aware that he should have died in the Mississippi gas chamber back then? And that he deserved to?"

"Really? Why didn't he?"

"The 1972 Supreme Court moratorium on capital punishment came just before he was convicted. Then he claimed he had a religious conversion and became Catholic and—"

"I'm Catholic too," she said.

"Well, somebody was sure watching out for you today . . ." I let my voice taper off and left her to draw her own conclusion.

She shivered a little, then muttered softly, "There's a divinity that shapes our ends, rough hew them how we will . . ."

"I won't argue with that."

"So what was he? How would you describe him?"

I laughed a wry little laugh and shook my head. "I don't think the English language has a single word to sum up Jasper Sparks."

"Do you think his religion was sincere?"

"I think he wanted it to be. He told me once that he was tired of being dishonest with himself. Right here at the end, he made his life mean something. I think that's what he wanted more than anything, so I don't see his passing as especially tragic. As far as you're concerned, just think of him as your benefactor, and since Catholics believe in prayers for the dead you might consider—"

"Oh, I will," she said earnestly. "You can count on it."

We walked back to the center of the compound just as Carla and Eva rode up. Carla was on my big gray roping horse while Eva rode Sheila's dun gelding. Both women were booted and spurred and wore jeans and departmental blazers over regulation white uniform shirts. Both wore their side arms, and a pump riot gun protruded from each saddle scabbard. A lone miscreant plodded wearily along just ahead of them, firmly handcuffed and in leg restraints that gave him enough slack to walk normally but not enough to run.

"You should have seen this guy," Carla said. "We watched him for fifteen minutes before he flushed and made a break for the fence. He thought he was hidden in the bushes. When he finally did bolt, he came over that fence like a squirrel."

"Even better was the look on his face when we thundered out of those woods," Eva said. "He didn't like our arrival on stage."

"How did you get back in through the fence?" I asked.

"I came prepared and brought a pair of bolt cutters," Carla said. "We made him cut the hole for us. He didn't like that either."

Their captive was a small man with a bitter, monkeylike face and a short beard of coarse black hair. "What's your name, sport?" I asked.

"William E. Ridley the Fourth," he said in a quacky voice. "Of the Pennsylvania Ridleys. Not the Rhode Island Ridleys."

I couldn't help but be amused at his pomposity at such a moment. "You're the fourth, huh?"

"That's right," he quacked.

"If you're typical of the breed, one would have been enough," I said.

Layton Graves sat on the ground nearby, chained by the neck to a six-inch tree trunk and trussed up like a Christmas turkey. A nightstick had been inserted crosswise in his mouth and secured by a leather thong that went around the back of his head. Billy Don Smith stood guard over him. "What's the story here?" I asked.

"He won't walk," Billy Don said. "Hell, I don't know if he can walk. His heartbeat is up to about one fifty, and nothing he said made any sense. I didn't figure you wanted him to die on us, so I called for another ambulance to take him in to Nacogdoches to see if the doctors can get him calmed down."

"Good deal," I said. "What about the nightstick?"

He laughed. "Aw, he kept trying to bite everybody that got close to him, so I muzzled him."

Graves looked up at me without a shred of comprehension in his eyes, then his head turned away and darted first to one side, and then the other, and then up and down like a rodent in a cage. I think he was in full-blown amphetamine psychosis and had no idea where he was. I glanced back and forth between him and Ridley. A pair of bona fide Aryans: Monkey Man and Ferret Head. I had to laugh inwardly at the idea that a sullen little troll and a speed-addled halfwit were the cream of humanity.

I walked over to where Winthrop stood talking to O'Dyer. "Have you read that Ridley guy's file?" I asked, pointing toward Ridley.

He glanced at the man for a moment. "Sure."

"What's the story on him?"

"Nothing much to tell. He's the black sheep of an old Main Line family. A Dartmouth grad, if you can believe it. Among these guys he's more a hanger-on than a player."

"Seems like neo-Nazism attracts some unlikely followers," I said.

"Intel says it's the only way he could get laid. This movement does have its groupies, you know."

"No shit?"

He nodded.

"Somehow I wish you hadn't told me that."

A couple of minutes later Chambless came up to me and said, "Sheriff, could I have a moment of your time?"

"Sure," I said.

"Listen, I realize that I came on a little too strong this morning. I was mad about losing my drug case, and I want to—"

I cut him off, my voice friendly. "You did a fine job here today, so why don't we just let it go at that?"

He smiled and stuck out his hand. "If you say so."

After the crime scene photos were taken, I called Ott's Funeral Home in town and asked them to send the hearse out to pick up Sparks's body and take it to Nacogdoches for the mandatory autopsy. It was after dark when we finally got everybody finger-printed and booked and all the paperwork done. There was still the press to deal with. Leaving that to Winthrop, Liddy, and O'Dyer, I ducked out the back of the jail and headed for home. Once there I had a quick belt of Canadian, ate a corned beef sandwich, and fell into bed a little after nine. I'd been running too long on too much adrenaline and too little sleep. I wasn't a kid anymore, and I was utterly exhausted. A couple of hours later I awoke for a few moments when Carla slipped quietly into bed beside me.

"In case you're interested in my opinion," she said, "you did yourself a good turn when you hired Eva to replace Linda. She's a fine woman to work with."

"Now it's unanimous," I mumbled.

"How so?"

"Sheila and Maylene like her too, so I guess I get to keep her."

This bought me nothing more than a soft laugh as her warm body snuggled against mine and I drifted off once again.

CHAPTER FORTY-SEVEN

The next morning I awoke to the smells of frying bacon and fresh coffee. A rare thing for me. On the nights she stayed over, Carla usually was out of bed and gone at least an hour before I became conscious. That morning we had a leisurely breakfast like an old married couple, and I began to wonder if she was sending me a message.

At the jail I found a bus waiting to take the federal prisoners over to court in Tyler for their arraignments. They would be housed there in the federal tank of the Smith County Jail to await bail or trial, whichever came first. Winthrop was there even though the U.S. Marshal's office had sent deputies over to handle the transfer. "How did the search go?" I asked him.

"The haul was one hundred fourteen fully auto AK-forty-sevens, a total of about two pounds of marijuana scattered here and there in various trailers, and about a thousand caps of un-scripted speed, most of which was Desoxyn."

"Pharmaceutical methamphetamine," I said, grimacing. "Heavy stuff. No doubt that's what Graves was cruising on."

"We also found twelve handguns, some legal, some not legal since they were in the possession of convicted felons."

"Where were the rifles?"

"In a cellar under that tan metal building where they kept the printing press. The place has a concrete slab floor with a trapdoor to the cellar over in one corner. There were a bunch of heavy crates stacked on top of it."

"Any grenades or anything like that?"

He shook his head. "No. And only a hundred rounds of ammo per rifle. But we did find books containing plans for all sorts of booby traps and bombs, including truck bombs like McVeigh used. We're still sifting through all the paperwork we seized trying to determine if they had anything specific planned."

"Probably just recreational reading for these clowns."

"I was wrong about Ridley," he said. "He was more than a hanger-on. We found a bank bag from an Oklahoma City armored car robbery last month in his little travel trailer. Isn't that something? The guy is a college graduate and he didn't even have foresight enough to get rid of the damned thing."

"You'll find that kind of sloppiness time and again with these old criminals."

"Another fool had some currency bands from a Kerrville bank robbery that happened six months ago in the trunk of his car. It was a state bank, so Thornton's taking that one."

"No telling what you'll clear out of this bust once you put the pressure on these guys and they flip and start rolling over on each other. By the way, are you going over to Tyler with them?"

"I have to, but I should be back soon after lunch. What do you need?"

"See if you can get Chambless and O'Dyer out at the jail about three this afternoon. Maybe it would be polite to include Miss Dee too. Tell them I'll make it worth their while."

"Sure," he said. "What's up?"

"Liddy Snow and I have decided to try to help you on a little matter."

"Which is?"

I told him what I had in mind.

I arrived at the courthouse to learn that Judge MacGregor had appointed Dud Malone, the local state representative, to represent DeLoach until he could get his own counsel, should he so desire. DeLoach and Hahn were arraigned at ten that morning. Charged with capital murder, DeLoach was ineligible for bail. In Hahn's case it was denied. Carla came by on her way to deliver Hahn's signed confessions and the interview tapes to Liddy so she could begin building her case. We decided to go to an Italian place we both liked in Nacogdoches for a celebratory dinner that evening. After a quick kiss she went on her way to take care of her own affairs, which she'd let languish for two days. With a reluctant groan I applied myself to a stack of accumulated paperwork, and snacked on cheese and crackers for lunch. A little before three, I drove over to the north side of town to the new jail.

DeLoach was pale and limping, but I'd had the jailors snug him up in full restraints anyway. With a man like him it was foolish to take chances, especially since he had nothing to lose. Dud Malone, Winthrop, April Dee, and Liddy were all waiting in the interrogation room when Chambless and I brought him in.

"Don't tell me," DeLoach said after he sat down. "Let me guess. You want to make some kind of deal?"

Liddy opened her file folder and appraised the man with eyes that were distant in a face that was coldly impassive. "You're charged with two counts of capital murder," she said.

"So tell me something new . . ."

She gave him a tight little smile. "Okay, I will. Here's our offer:

We can take the death penalty out of the equation if you satisfy our federal friends on a few matters. I don't particularly like that, but as Sheriff Handel has taught me, there are times when you have to give a little to get a little."

This earned her nothing more than a shrug and a laconic, "Let's hear it."

"The essence of the matter is that once your good friend Mr. Hahn was apprised of the reality of his situation, he did what such people usually do in such circumstances. He began to cast frantically about for a way to save his own skin, which was ratting you out for both the Driggers killing and the Webern murder. The windup of the matter is that Hahn gets a vastly reduced sentence, and you get the needle."

"Maybe . . ."

"There's no maybe to it. I know my town and the kind of juries we get here."

"Then what do you want from me?"

"I'll get to that in a moment. First, let me tell you how much we know about your activities in the last couple of years. After that shootout in West Virginia, you went underground with the help of some East Coast drug smugglers you had contacts with. In return, they wanted you to kill Webern. You did, and you got enough out of the deal to pay Hahn a thousand to be your driver. Hahn is ready to testify to this. We also have as corroborating evidence a speeding ticket that Hahn got the very same day up in Henderson, along with a sworn statement by the issuing officer identifying you as Hahn's passenger.

"Hahn says his report on that trip is what got Professor Spencer interested in Caddo County as a possible place to relocate his base of operations. Exactly how tight you really were with Spencer is something I don't know since I'm pretty sure you considered him and his followers nothing more than a crew of marginally useful idiots even though you share their racist views. But that doesn't matter. Then Topper Smith and your now-defunct nephew, Dean Bean, got killed trying to rob the Royal Coffee Shop. No doubt they knew you were here and were trying to make contact with you for some addle-pated reason, whatever that may have been. Not that it matters. What does matter is that you killed Dual Driggers in revenge for your nephew's death, once again using the talkative Mr. Hahn for your wheel man."

Like that day I'd interviewed him in my office, nothing that she said touched DeLoach's eyes. "What do you want?" he asked.

"Plead out for two consecutive life sentences and give up your contacts in the drug ring. Specifically, who hired you to kill Webern and who it was that discovered him here in Sequoya. That, plus anything else you know."

He shook his head. "No. I want to walk and get witness protection. These drug people are big enough that it would be worth it to you."

"No damn way," Winthrop said. "Not on two murders. And that comes straight from the attorney general himself. After all the publicity, we're not about to buck the state of Texas on this. You'll never get a better deal than the one she's offering you."

DeLoach laughed ruefully and shook his head. "Can't do it."

"Why not flip and avoid the needle?" I asked. "What do you owe these people?"

He regarded me coldly for a moment before speaking. "If I did have something on these guys, and if I did rat them out, how long do you think I'd last in the penitentiary?"

"I don't see that you have much to lose," I said.

"That may or may not be true, but there's no point in turning a possibility into a certainty."

"We can make arrangements for you to serve your time in a secure federal institution," Winthrop said. "In isolation if necessary."

DeLoach laughed in his face. "Remember that high-level mafioso from Philadelphia that got whacked in the federal joint a few years ago? The story is that this same bunch you're talking about was behind the hit. If they can get to a guy like that, what chance would a nobody like me have?"

He had a point. And this was as close as he ever was to come to confessing or even admitting he knew what we were talking about.

"To tell the truth, I can't say your decision disappoints me," I said.

"Oh really? Is this going to be one of those dramatic moments like in the TV crime dramas where you tell me you'll be there watching the night they stick the needle in my arm?"

I shook my head. "Oh, hell no. I've spent enough of my time on you, and I don't aim to waste any more of it."

"Is that your final word?" Liddy asked. "Are you sure you don't want to think it over? Maybe consult with your lawyer?"

Malone spoke. "I've already told him to go for any deal that lets him slide on the death penalty. If he doesn't heed my advice there's nothing I can do."

"What's it going to be, Mr. DeLoach?" she asked.

"No."

"Fine with me," she said, snapping her briefcase shut. "First I'll try you for Dual Driggers and get the death penalty on that one. Next you'll go up for the Webern killing, though life may be the best I can do there unless I can convince the jury that it was murder for hire. Then to add insult to injury, I'll run you through for the Toby Parsons shooting, and that will add another fifty years or so on top of things."

"What?" Chambless asked. "He's the one who shot your deputy?"

I nodded. "Toby made a positive ID on him a couple of days ago. You see, the day Toby was attacked, he'd gone out the north end of the county on an unrelated matter. Eva, Don Thornton, and I were working the Driggers case while Toby was running the office and doing the scheduling and working a couple of theft cases of his own. On the way back to town he stopped at a little mom-and-pop store for a Coke. The proprietor told him that a guy who turned out to be Malloy had just left and had treated him to a vicious cussing because his gas pumps weren't working. Two miles down the road Toby pulled them over to give them a little lecture. For him it was just a routine stop. He had no reason to suspect the gray minivan, and that was my fault. I know I should have briefed him, but this isn't the LAPD and I don't have the time and the manpower to do everything I need to do. DeLoach was driving, and probably figured he couldn't run the risk of being arrested and fingerprinted. So what the hell? He'd killed at least three people already, so why not kill one more? Especially a black cop."

Liddy continued. "So if by some miracle we should miss the death penalty here in Texas, West Virginia will be waiting with their business on the murder of that state trooper. We may even be able to pin Crystal Henderson's murder on him if the ballistics on the gun you had in Houston match the one that came from her body."

"Who?" DeLoach asked.

"Your ex-girlfriend, numbnuts," I said. "The young lady who registered that gray minivan for you."

"Never heard of her," he said in a voice that wasn't meant to convince anybody of anything.

"What happened?" Liddy asked. "Did you catch her in bed with some black guy?"

DeLoach stiffened, and for just an instant there was a flicker of fire in his reptilian eyes. Then it subsided. "Like I said, I never heard of the woman."

"Even without her," Liddy said, "what it all adds up to is that you are never going to see another day as a free man."

"Do what you have to do," he said with a dismissive shrug.

And that was all. Liddy gave DeLoach one last cold smile and then strode briskly from the room. I motioned for the jailers to take the man back to his cell.

On the way to pick up Carla late that afternoon, I stopped by Sycamore Ridge Cemetery. Dual's children had already had his death date carved on the stone he now shared with his long-dead wife, and the groundsmen had removed the wilted and faded flowers and leveled the mound. In the spring they'd seed the cemetery with crimson clover, just as they did every year, and by fall his would just be one more seldom-visited grave among the hundreds whose dates stretch back into the town's earliest days.

A psychologist might say I was seeking closure, but I'm too old to waste my time looking for something that doesn't exist in this world. But there is consolation. DeLoach would get the death penalty. Of this I had no doubt. The average stay on Texas's death row these days is twelve years, and much of that time he'll have to spend looking over his shoulder because as long as he's alive he's a liability to the drug cartel since even some of the most hardened of criminals have been known to clear their slates in the death house. Back three decades ago you could buy a hit in the Texas prison system for a couple of cartons of cigarettes. Now smoking is no longer permitted, and I don't know what the going rate for a human life is. But he's a tough man, and I believe he'll make it through to the end. Lawyers hired by well-funded opponents of capital punishment will comb his courtroom transcripts backward and forward for errors. The case will go through numerous appeals. Despite the man's stoicism and apparent resignation, there'll be occasions when his hopes will rise and his spirits soar, only to be dashed back to earth as his motions and writs are denied time and again. Finally the day will come when he'll have his last meal—anything he wants "within reason" as the prison rules state. Then about sunset they'll come to take him to that grim little room with its observation windows and its table and tubes and all the cold, clinical paraphernalia with which the state of Texas exacts its final retribution. If I'm still around then, my consolation would come in knowing that I did my job. Yet I'll still be left to wonder why some people are willing to sell their lives so cheaply.

CHAPTER FORTY-EIGHT

The next afternoon I had a few personal errands to run, things that I'd pushed aside and left hanging in the heat of chase. I got all my business tended to by five, and was just getting into my pickup in front of the courthouse when my cell phone buzzed. It was Eva. "I tried to call you earlier," she said.

"Sorry about that. I left my phone in the seat of the truck all afternoon. I just now noticed it. What's up?"

"We're out at Dr. Spencer's house," she said. "He's dead."

"What happened?"

"Suicide. He shot himself."

"Who's working the scene with you?"

"Billy Don Smith."

"Did Spencer leave a note?" I asked.

"We haven't found one."

"Do you need me out there?"

"I don't see why we would. It's clear cut. CNN did a feature on the raid just before noon. His wife said he watched the whole thing, including a statement from Washington that seemed to implicate him in the bust. After that, he casually went over a few business matters with her, told her where various personal accounts were to be found, and so forth. Then he went in his study, locked the door, and put a thirty-eight in his mouth. She called us, and we had to break down the door when we got here."

"Did she think the raid was the reason he did it?"

"She said it was a combination of things. According to her he'd been periodically depressed for a couple of months. He had emphysema, you know. He was on oxygen at times and still he couldn't quit smoking. No doubt the raid had a lot to do with it, but he had other problems too. Seems tragic in a way. I mean for a man with all that education and—"

"Not really, Eva. When somebody with Spencer's intellect gets involved in such damned foolishness with such people and winds up shooting himself, it's not a tragedy. It's slapstick."

"I guess you're right," she said with a sigh. "I feel sorry for his wife, though. You know, she told me that he was the best husband a woman could have possibly wanted. A good provider, utterly devoted. She said she never doubted for a moment that he would have died to protect her. That makes me wonder . . ."

"About what?" I asked.

"I saw him as a monster. A complete monster. I mean, for God's sake, the man compared me to a cur dog. He meant it too. Yet she saw him as a human being she loved."

"Are you asking me who was right?"

"Yeah," she said.

"You both were."

The following Monday Winthrop came by the office in mid-afternoon to say good-bye. "It's been a pleasure," he told me.

"Well, I can't say that," I said. "Too many dead bodies. But you were a good man to work with."

"Thank you. So were you, and I must say you really took control of things when you left us in the dark about DeLoach being in Houston. The press conference afterward wasn't bad either."

"I did what I felt like I had to do. I know that you personally would have been opposed to giving DeLoach witness protection, but the powers-that-be might have wanted his drug contacts badly enough to . . ." I let my voice taper off.

He nodded. "I understand."

"Besides, you should be happy. You wanted to go ahead with the raid, and I forced the issue for you."

"I am," he said. "I do have a question to ask, though. The story is that DeLoach caught his girlfriend in bed with a black fellow, right?"

I nodded. "That's what one of the Harris County deputies who worked the case told me when we were in Houston."

"So the logical conclusion is that he snapped, and that's what initiated this whole odyssey. One minute the guy is just a working stiff and the next he's a stone killer. Do you buy that?"

"Not on your life."

"Neither do I," he said.

"Over the years I've handled at least a dozen incidents where some old boy found his woman in the sack with another man, and not a single one of those guys wound up working as a hit man. As far as DeLoach goes, we don't know what else he'd been doing while he was managing that boat place in Kemah. I would bet anything that he was a criminal and maybe even a killer before that assault business. It's just the first thing he got caught at."

"I don't suppose we'll ever know for sure what else he might have done."

"I've got a question too," I said. "How did they really find Webern down here?"

"You don't buy the story Hahn gave?"

"Do you?"

"I don't know," he said. "The Marshals Service did one of the most complete in-house investigations in its history and came up with nothing."

"The Marshals Service is an honorable outfit, and I trust their investigation. But maybe somebody should look outside the Marshals Service. The fact that Bierman's retired agent friend knew where Von Greim was is proof that someone outside the Marshals was privy to some of their inner workings. If some people in the Bureau knew, then there could have been others as well."

"I hadn't considered that, but you're right."

"It just ain't human nature for secrets to be all that secret," I said.

He nodded and rose from his chair with his hand extended. "Since this is question-and-answer time, I have one more."

"Fire away."

"How is it that you know so much about classical music?"

"Why? Does it seem out of character?"

"A little, yes."

"Innate musical talent. I was playing the piano by ear by the time I was six, and my mother saw to it that I got excellent private lessons. Then I got an academic scholarship to Rice University—"

"Rice?" He sounded surprised.

I nodded. "Then right before my last semester my dad died, and I had to come home and take over the family timber business and take care of my mother, who had MS. At the time we owned two sawmills and the local lumber yard. I sold the sawmills a few years later, but my sister and I still own half interest in the lumber yard."

"So you were majoring in what down at Rice? Music?"

"Classical piano."

"Do you still play?"

"I play a little every week just for myself, but when other people are around I try not to get near a keyboard unless I've had enough to drink that I don't care how bad I sound."

He smiled again and shook my hand. "You are an interesting

man, Sheriff. This case has been most interesting, as well. If you ever need anything—"

"I'll come calling. Count on it."

While I'd been out actually fighting crime, the paperwork had piled up and now lay stacked accusingly in my in-box. I applied myself diligently for a half hour or so, then pushed it all aside in disgust and yelled out to Maylene, "Close the door to my office and don't bother me for the next hour unless somebody steals the courthouse."

"We're in the courthouse, Bo," she hollered back. "So even a man as dense as you are ought to notice if it got swiped."

"We are? That must have slipped my mind."

I flipped through my rack of CDs, took one out, and slipped it into the portable stereo that sat on the credenza behind my chair. I'd just got myself tilted back with my feet on my desk when the first notes of the Schubert String Quintet came through the headphones. You should listen to it sometime. The adagio will tear your heart out.